H.J.

RAVE REVIEWS FOR VIRGINIA FARMER!

SPENCEWORTH BRIDE

SIXPENCE BRIDE

AN UNAVOIDABLE BANG

"Caira, the trip wire!" The warning in his voice barely registered before his arm circled her waist and he spun her around. A moment later, Caira's feet left the ground and Brian held her against the length of his muscular body. Their gazes met, and Caira watched the concern in his eyes change to awareness. The heat from their bodies mingled. Her breasts pushed against his chest as she breathed, inhaling the scent of his skin, pulling it deep within her. Anticipation hummed in her veins as she gazed at his lips, a mere breath away from hers.

Kiss me, she thought, lifting her gaze. She stared into his eyes, seeing the flecks of silver lighting the passion in their depths; felt the beat of his heart against her breast.

He loosened his hold on her, and she slid down his body until her feet touched the ground. Bringing his head down, his lips whispered across hers. Then, with a groan, he matched his mouth to hers.

A BLAST TO THE PAST

VIRGINIA FARMER

LOVE SPELL NEW YORK CITY

LOVE SPELL®

April 2004

Published by

Dorchester Publishing Co., Inc.
200 Madison Avenue
New York, NY 10016

ISBN 0-505-52572-0

Visit us on the web at www.dorchesterpub.com.

A Blast
to the
Past

Explosive Ordnance Disposal, EOD, is an intricate part of all branches of the military around the world. They work quietly and with steady hands to render bombs, bullets, mines, and other explosives harmless. It is to these unsung heroes that I dedicate this book. And especially my very own Master Blaster, Terry Farmer, who gave me the idea for Chief Petty Officer Brian Skelley's story.

Chapter One

Strathaven Training Area,
Scottish Highlands; 2004

"I hope we get to blow this one up."

The words rode the breeze to the hill where Chief Brian Skelley stood watching the men sweep the heather-covered field below, and he chuckled. He shared their sentiment—he loved a good blast too, one that shook the earth and rattled the windows. Of course, out here in the Highlands of Scotland the only windows that would rattle were those in the Land Rover parked a short distance away.

"Did the farmer give a description of it?"

Brian rolled his eyes at the clipped British words. He'd given the men the drill scenario not ten minutes ago, all but telling them what kind of ordnance they were looking for. Had Lawrence Shaw forgotten already? Or was he just trying to prod the others?

Lawrence constantly tossed out digs, always getting frustrated when the others failed to rise to the bait.

1

He had a strained relationship with the others and Brian shook his head, unable to understand its dynamic.

While the Scots had no trouble forming a team, Lawrence remained aloof, strutting around, trying to take the role of leader. The Scots ignored him, which only fueled Lawrence's animosity. It amazed Brian that one of the guys hadn't decked the Brit yet.

"Yeah. Ninety-six, sixty, ninety," one of the Scots on the team called out with a chuckle.

"Rather curvy bit of explosive, don't you think?" another shouted back.

"Those are a woman's measurements, you bloody idiot." Lawrence's voice held a note of irritation. The man's sense of humor resided somewhere in his boots, Brian decided, still watching the progress of the team.

"And a wonderful armful she'd be." Obviously, the first Scot wasn't taking the bait, for which Brian was grateful.

"Yeah, she'd be a real blast," another Scot said, tossing his opinion into the mix. The men all laughed again.

"Too bad you didn't find a nice Scottish lass to take home with you, Chief." One of the Scots offered with a shake of his head and a grin.

"I wasn't looking for one."

"Yeah," Lawrence chimed in. "She could carry your sea bag and be the first to salute you every morning."

Brian glared at the Brit. "Can the chatter, men. I don't want to be here all night." His voice carried down to the field and the men below. Knowing this was a training exercise and anything they found would be harmless dummy ordnance made it harder for him to do his job of maintaining the team's focus.

"That's right, the Chief has to get back to the Colonies," Lawrence half-sneered. "In two weeks he'll be an officer, too good to have a pint with the boys."

One of the Scots glanced up and pulled his hat lower on his forehead. Clearing his throat, he shouted, "Right, then. Best be at this."

The drill site was situated in a remote section of the Scottish Highlands, accessible by only two narrow roads. It was a trek getting up here, but worth it. A fresh breeze swirled around Brian as he watched the men settle down to work amid the heather blanketing the cordoned-off area.

He scanned the pine- and fern-covered hills beyond the field, his gaze locking on the tall, rocky mountain in the distance. He'd been told of the crumbling remains of a castle near its base. Of course, in the year he'd been in Scotland, he'd seen a couple of castle sites and had come to the conclusion that if you'd seen one, you'd seen them all.

Leaving the men to their drill, Brian stepped into the makeshift command post: a strung-up tarp. This would be his last assignment to this remote training area. He'd enjoyed his tour with the British Explosive Ordnance Disposal School, but in a few days he'd be home, stateside, and realizing his goal—receiving his commission as a Navy chief warrant officer. And his old man would be turning over in his grave.

Carl Skelley had been a hard-drinking mechanic with a quick temper, whom Brian had spent many evenings at the movies with his mother avoiding. It had been impossible to escape it all, though, and his mother had suffered quite a bit of physical abuse protecting him. And she hadn't been able to do much about the old man's constant verbal assault.

"You're a mama's boy. You'll never be a man. You'll never amount to anything," Brian's father would shout. Brian would tighten his spine and focus on a spot over the man's shoulder. Inside he'd shake, but he stubbornly fought against any show of weakness.

Carl's liver had finally given out when Brian was seventeen, leaving his wife with a mountain of debt and their angry teenage son.

Pushing such thoughts of the past aside, Brian dodged a stack of sandbags and several shovels, and grabbed a bottle from his pack. He took a long pull of lukewarm water, then stepped back out from the protection of the tarp to watch the men.

Black clouds moved to block the sunshine, and the once-blue sky turned dark and ugly. Fat raindrops fell, landing around Brian with audible plops. He tugged at his hat and hunched his shoulders. "Shitty Scottish weather," he grumbled.

A shout came from the field, and Brian peered out into the rain. *Guess they found one,* he thought, watching as the men gathered around one of their fellows. "Wonder which?" he mumbled to himself. He'd planted several different types of inert ordnance in the drill area.

After a brief discussion, the men headed back up the hill. Lawrence was left in the field. He would measure and sketch what they'd found before joining them all under the tarp.

Brian returned to the command post and took a seat on a folding chair, out of the way. From there he could observe the men, hear their conversation, but not hinder the exercise or influence their decisions. The rain thumped on the tarp overhead as the squad arrived. Brian leaned back in his chair, arms crossed over his chest, and watched them crowd together.

One of the men picked up the logbook, checked his watch, and started making notes. Another pulled out his ordnance identification guide and thumbed through it, looking for a picture to match what they'd found in the field.

A few minutes later, Lawrence came up the hill. Rain dripped from his camouflage jacket. Everyone gathered around him as he stepped under the tarp. Pulling a clipboard from inside his coat, he flipped the plastic protector back. The men all bent their heads, studying his drawing.

"It's forty centimeters long by thirteen in diameter. The cylinder is iron, the surface rough and pitted. The ends are capped with wax, and there are faint markings on the top. The bloody thing looks ancient."

Brian stood up. That wasn't what he'd placed in the field. He walked around and looked at Lawrence's drawing over the man's shoulder.

Nope, it wasn't his. That meant one of two things: Either the Brit couldn't draw for crap, or the device had been inadvertently left by another instructor.

Brian glanced out at the sky. The rain had let up some, was just a light mist now. Might just as well check out the bomb while the men tried to find a match in the identification guide.

Buttoning up his coat, he left the men behind.

He stood at the edge of the rim above the field, inhaling the rain-freshened air and frowning, sensing a tension around him. Glancing back at the men, he found them involved in a discussion, their low voices carried away by the breeze.

He turned back to the field, unable to shake the wariness that settled around him. Looking to the horizon, he spotted another bank of black clouds rolling closer. Must be the next round of rain that unsettled him, he decided. With a shrug, he headed to the drill site.

Half sliding, he tramped down the soggy ground of the hill. Training exercises such as this were conducted in restricted areas owned by the government, assuring the instructors full control of the activity, but sometimes training aids were left behind by other instructors.

Spotting the red flag marking the location of the suspect bomb, Brian felt a chill work its way up his back. He glanced around.

Something didn't feel right.

He scanned the area again but couldn't find the source of his unease. The sky darkened, and the wind picked up, rustling through the bushes and trees around the perimeter of the training ground.

Making his way to the fluttering red flag, Brian kept his gaze on the earth, pushing aside the tension knotting his shoulder muscles.

Dread weighed his steps, confusing him. Why the hell did he dread viewing this ordnance? He'd done so dozens of times. Hell, he'd never felt such a sense of foreboding while diving on mines during the Gulf War. Why now, during a drill?

He came to the flag and looked down at the ordnance nestled in the damp earth. He'd been in the

Highlands long enough to recognize Gaelic—all the road signs were in the old language, making some of the letters familiar—but he'd concentrated on spoken Gaelic at the Adult Learning Project, so he couldn't decipher the message.

Well, this wasn't in his training objectives, so he'd better let the men know they had to start the search over again.

He glanced up at the dark sky, and a raindrop landed on his chin. It was followed by another.

Damn, he thought. First this—he glanced down at the iron cylinder—and now the weather. It was going to make the drill a long, uncomfortable experience.

"No worries, Chief. I can handle it."

Brian snapped his gaze up from the ordnance to find Lawrence standing beside him. The Brit moved forward, and Brian grabbed his arm.

"No. This isn't part of the drill."

An eerie silence fell. The wind stopped blowing, the rain ceased. The hair stood up on the back of Brian's neck. Hell, he couldn't even hear the squad's voices. The stillness was deafening. Brian shook his head to clear the mysterious sensations edging into his mind.

Lawrence shrugged off his hold and knelt down beside the bomb. "I'll just remove it, then." He glanced over his shoulder with a wink. "It's just a training aid. Piece of cake."

Brian stepped forward. "No," he shouted, reaching out to stop him.

A second later, his body burned, his ears rang, and a flash of light blinded him. He met the ground face first.

Chapter Two

" 'Tis a wonder we didna meet up with the Wallace. Ye ken he's been spotted near Mackenzie land."

"Malcolm, ye're not going to start that again, are ye?" Callum asked. His friend was always talking about Wallace. " 'Tis rumor, nothing more."

"He's a canny mon, he is," Malcolm continued. " 'Tis said he's taken to wearing disguises so he'll not be recognized."

" 'Tis a fanciful tale ye weave." Callum shook his head. "Are ye longing for the entertainment of a *seanachaidh* so badly that ye'll take up the telling of stories yerself, then?"

They followed one of three passable trails leading into the Mackenzie valley. It wound through forests of tall pines, oaks, and rowan trees, and ferns carpeted the ground beneath them. Through a break in the foliage, Callum glimpsed the craggy mountains ringing the clan holdings.

"Ye ken one of the men in the village saw Wallace and a few of his men in these woods," Malcolm protested.

" 'Twas more like he *thought* he saw him." Callum shook his head. "The Wallace hasna been seen in months, and I'll wager 'tis the way he wants it just now, what with Longshanks proclaiming him a traitor and vowing to see him dead."

"Well you may say, but I've a feeling the mon is close by." Malcolm met his gaze, raising his gray-bearded chin in challenge. "Ye ken my feelings, Callum."

Callum snorted. "Yer feelings? Ach. *Now* ye're fey, are ye?" He shook his head. "Malcolm, I fear ye've tottered into your dotage."

Malcolm harrumphed. "Come along, Bridget." He pulled on her lead, and the horse whickered. "*You* ken I know from whence I speak, eh?"

Bridget snorted.

Bloody hell, Callum thought; *now Malcolm's even telling his stories to his horse.* He glanced at his own mount, and his heart warmed. Nessie was a beautiful, long-legged English horse, the deepest shade of brown with a white blaze on her neck and lower jaw. Her eyes matched her coat, and he could swear they smiled at him.

He and Malcolm had found the two horses one afternoon a year ago. They weren't the sturdy Highland ponies the men were used to riding. Nay, Nessie and Bridget's legs were longer and more delicate. Rather than risk injury to the mounts traversing the rugged Highland trails, he and Malcolm had taken to walking them in the forest a few times a week. Neither man had much use for the English, but English horses—well, that was a different matter altogether.

Callum reached back and rubbed Nessie's ear. Aye, 'twas a different matter entirely.

A boom made the horses sidestep. Their ears flattened against their heads, and the beasts started to rear up. Each man shortened the reins of his frightened animal and muttered soothing words.

Callum met his companion's startled gaze. " 'Twas strange," he said, frowning and looking up. "Nary a cloud in the sky."

"Came from there." Malcolm nodded to a spot ahead. "What think ye it was?"

" 'Twasn't thunder." Callum guessed. " 'Twas too short. Never heard thunder that didna roll around the sky."

"Do ye ken what it was, then?"

Callum shook his head. "Mayhap we'd best see."

Malcolm nodded.

As they climbed the hill before them, leading their mounts, Callum tensed. A tickle of dread inched up his back. The English were ever taunting the Scots, breaching the Mackenzie borders and harassing anyone they came across. This could be some new trick.

He and Malcolm reached the top of the hill, and Callum spotted a large hole in a glade below, a green mound beside it. Glancing at Malcolm, he tightened his hold on Nessie's lead; then, with a nod to his friend, he descended. Malcolm followed.

They stopped a distance away, scanning the area beyond the small clearing.

"That great hole wasna there when we left," Malcolm whispered, moving his hand to the hilt of his sword. "What could have made it?"

Callum shook his head, squinting at the green mound. "Ye ken what that is?"

"A pile of leaves?"

Cautiously, the men approached, Malcolm sliding his old weapon from its sheath. He and Callum stopped a few feet from the mound, dropping their horses' leads.

Malcolm nudged the pile with the toe of his boot. "Bloody hell, 'tis a mon," he whispered, stepping nearer Callum's side. "Do ye ken who he is?"

"Nay, I've never seen him before." Callum frowned. "Strange garments he's wearing."

"Never seen the likes of them."

Callum snorted, staring at the man. "Well, whoever did the weaving must have been deep into the whisky barrel." He met Malcolm's bright gaze.

"Do ye think it's the Wallace?" his friend asked.

Callum blinked. "What the bloody hell put that notion in yer wee brain, Malcolm? Ye're obsessed with the mon."

Malcolm straightened his shoulders, deeply offended and glaring. "Wallace *has* been seen nearby." Callum snorted. "Well, he could be Wallace."

"Malcolm," Callum growled.

"Well, then, who do *you* think he is?"

"English, probably." Callum looked around the area and frowned. "I dinna see tracks, neither animal nor human. How do ye suppose he got here?"

"English, ye say?" Malcolm asked. Clearly, this was a new idea to him. He narrowed his gaze at the man on the ground. Stepping closer, his sword at the ready, he nudged the stranger with the toe of his boot, then glanced at Callum.

"Dead," he said.

He kicked the man then, which elicited a groan.

Jumping back, Malcolm raised a staying arm to his friend. "Stand back, Callum. I'll skewer him, does he more than breathe."

Callum rolled his eyes. Shoving Malcolm aside, he said, "Put yer sword away, before ye hurt yerself." He hunkered down, rolled the unconscious stranger onto his back.

"Jesus, Mary, and Joseph," Malcolm muttered, crossing himself. "What's happened to him? Is he burned?"

Callum stared at the stranger's blackened face, covered with numerous little blisters. Reaching out a finger, he gently rubbed the forehead. "Not too badly. 'Tis mostly just soot." He glanced around again. "But where was the fire?"

The stranger's eyelids fluttered open. Confusion and pain clouded his eyes' blue depths.

"Who are ye?" Callum asked, his gaze locking with the man's. "What happened to ye?"

The stranger opened his mouth and emitted a croak. He blinked once, then his eyelids slid closed. His head lolled to the side.

"*Now* is he dead?" Malcolm asked, standing close by.

"Nay, ye old fool. He's unconscious."

"God's bones. What are we to do with him?"

"He's hurt. We must take him to Caira." Callum looked up. His companion's gaze was shocked, and

12

Malcolm said, "Take him to Kilbeinn? Are ye daft, mon?"

"Well, we canna leave him here."

"But we know nothing about him. What if he be English?"

"A moment ago you thought he was a Scot." Callum glanced from Malcolm to the man at his feet.

"*You* were the one who brought up the English!"

Callum sighed and said, "Aye. That's what I'm saying. He may be English. And if he is and we leave him here, dinna ye think his people will claim that we've harmed him?" Callum shook his head. "We dinna need to give them any more reason to harass us."

He glanced up at the sinking sun. " 'Twill be dark soon." He met Malcolm's gaze. "We canna leave him here." Pushing to his feet, he suggested, "let's pick him up."

" 'Tis too dangerous, Callum."

" 'Tis more dangerous to leave him. The mon opened his eyes and saw us. We must be certain he doesna accuse us of bringing him down."

"Nay." Malcolm shook his head. "I say we leave him here."

Callum took a deep breath. He didn't wish to stand around arguing with his friend in the dark. He arched a brow, swallowing the grin a new thought provoked. "And what if ye're right and he is the Wallace? Would ye chance that?"

Malcolm looked from the stranger to Callum, then back again. The light of hope appeared in his eyes. "Ach. Nay, I wouldna leave him, then." He frowned. "But how are we to get him to the castle?"

13

Callum looked past Malcolm and nodded.

"Nay." Callum's friend shook his head. "My Bridget will never carry such a burden."

"Then Nessie can."

"Ye'd ask such of her?"

" 'Tis necessary. I'll have a care that she doesna step wrong. 'Twill not harm her—she's strong and can carry the load." Callum walked over to his horse. "Ye willna mind, lass, will ye?" He rubbed her neck, and the beast nickered. Grabbing her bridle, Callum walked her closer.

Malcolm stood over the stranger, staring at him.

"Come, help me get him on her back," Callum called. He moved to the unconscious man's shoulders. "Ye take his feet, I'll take his arms."

Grumbling, Malcolm did as his companion asked. The two draped the stranger across Nessie's back, then they all turned toward home.

"See that the flock is moved to the high pastures. They'll be safe there from the English," Caira Mackenzie called, offering a reassuring smile to the old shepherd to whom she spoke.

"Aye, 'tis a distance, but I ken yer wisdom in moving them."

She nodded. "I'll send a few of the village boys to help you."

"My thanks, Caira."

She watched the aging Scot cross the bailey, a sack of food tied to his walking stick and his dog beside him.

The sheep were a valuable asset to her clan—the wool essential to the weaving of cloth and, in the win-ter, when the flock was culled, there would be meat to feed on.

She climbed the steps of Kilbeinn Castle and turned, searching the area beyond the gate for Callum and Malcolm. Relief smoothed her brow as she spotted the old Scots. She'd begun to worry for their safety as the evening shadows lengthened; it was unusual for them to be gone this long when they took their horses for a walk.

She shook her head. They treated those animals as pets, fawning over them and refusing to ride them. They claimed the long-legged English mounts were too delicate to be mounts across the rough terrain of the Highlands.

Frowning, she brought her hand up to block the setting sun from her eyes. She groaned, noting a dark shape draped over Callum's horse.

"What have they brought home this time?" she muttered. The pair never seemed to return without dragging some poor creature home for her to nurse. She knew what they were doing, trying to make her comfortable and confident, but it would never be enough; healing an animal was not the same as saving the life of a human.

She should have paid closer attention to her mother's teachings. As a young girl, she'd thought there was plenty of time to learn the healing arts from her. How wrong she had been. Now she had only her mother's journal to teach her, and animals were the only things fit for her to heal.

The years since her mother's death had been hard for Caira. Guilt was a demanding companion, and an unforgiving one, and now Callum and Malcolm would present her with yet another test of her paltry skills. It wasn't as if she didn't have enough to do without their constant contributions.

"Malcolm? Callum? What have you there?" she called, narrowing her eyes. "I told the two of you that I'd not be tending another of your creatures. Not after you brought Goose home."

A honking followed her words, and Goose waddled by, the bandage on his left wing still intact. Caira sighed.

Both men ducked their heads.

"Saints preserve us," Caira said aloud, descending the stairs and approaching the horse and its burden. With a gasp, she touched the blackened hand of the man slung over the animal's back.

" 'Tis a mon," Callum offered.

"I can see that." She glared at the old warrior, and he shuffled his feet. "Where did you find him?" She turned on Callum's counterpart and gave him a piercing look.

"In the forest." Malcolm reached a hand out to the passing Goose, and received a nip for his troubles. Rubbing the tender finger, he turned soulful brown eyes on Caira. " 'Tis the Wallace!"

Caira turned her gaze on Callum. "The Wallace?"

He shrugged. "Mayhap."

Caira narrowed her eyes. "Mayhap?"

The old warrior stepped closer and whispered, "We dinna know *who* he is, Caira—but if perchance he's English, we couldna leave him."

"English? You'd bring the enemy to our door? Are you mad?" She rubbed her temples, anger and fear thrumming through her veins. "You'd endanger the entire clan?"

"Think on it, lass." He met her angry glare. "Did we leave him, the English would lay the blame for his wounds on our backs."

She nodded, only too aware of that possibility. The English goal was to drive the Scots from their land, and they were doing it in any way possible.

Callum touched her arm. In a low voice he continued, "He need know nothing of the clan." He shrugged. "He may not even be English." Shaking his head, he suggested, "Like as not, he just wandered into our forest and got lost."

Caira nodded, not at all convinced.

Malcolm pulled the man in question from Callum's horse, staggering under his weight. "He's not a small mon."

Callum rushed to help. Settling the stranger's weight over his friend's shoulder, he stood aside as Malcolm mounted the stairs of the castle.

Falling into step, Caira fingered the strange material of the burnt man's garment and looked at Callum. "Getting lost does this to a person?" She nodded at the sleeve of the tunic where small holes and mud were sprinkled amid a strange design of varying shades of green.

The stranger's dark head bobbed with each of Malcolm's steps, and Caira noted that his wavy hair, cut short, exposed a thick neck. Pulling her fingers away from his sleeve, she grazed the man's large hand with hers. Warmth tingled up her arm at the contact and she frowned, wondering at her odd reaction.

17

"Well now, I dinna ken what happened," Callum was saying. "Mayhap after ye've tended to him, we can find out a bit more." He opened the large main door to the castle, allowing Malcolm to enter. His friend carried the stranger over to a bench along the wall of the great hall, then set him down and stepped away.

"Gitta?" Caira called. A woman of middle years appeared from the far side of the room. "Aye, Caira?" Her gaze took in the man Malcolm had deposited on the bench. "And who's this?"

Caira shrugged. "Will you fetch some water, clean rags, and my box, please?"

"Aye, lass." Gitta swung around and mounted the stairs to the solar. There Caira kept her box of medicinal herbs.

As she examined this new foundling Malcolm and Callum had brought home, Caira was struck by the strong line of his jaw, his high forehead, and the sardonic slant of the stubby remains of his brows. She frowned. How had his brows been singed? She smoothed his hair from his forehead, and the ends powdered between her fingers. Would she find ugly burns beneath the soot and dirt clinging to his skin?

Pray God, it was only burns she must tend, for she had a salve that would help. But what if his injuries were worse? Her hands started to shake, and a bead of perspiration slid down between her breasts.

Nay, I will not think on the worst. She focused on the man's features again. Clean of the dirt and soot, he would be handsome.

18

For shame, she chastised herself, lifting her gaze away. She knew nothing of this man. No doubt he was English. Her gaze slid back to his face. She'd never known an Englishman to be kind, handsome or no.

Her gaze moved to his clothing. Writing above a pouch sewn onto the material of his shirt caught her attention. "Skelley," she read. The English pronunciation tripped her tongue and panic raced through her blood. A sick feeling settled in her stomach.

This was the enemy, for a certainty. Logic urged her to order Malcolm and Callum to return the man whence they'd found him. But Callum was right. The English would accuse them of the deed regardless.

She glanced at the stranger's face. With his eyes closed, soot darkening his features, and his large body limp upon the bench, he looked so vulnerable . . . but even wolves needed time to lick their wounds.

Caira sighed. Her heart could not turn from one in need, whether he was friend or foe. No matter she doubted her healing skills, still she had to try.

Ignoring her negative thoughts, she continued to focus on the man's clothing and its label. *"Seana-chaidh,"* she read again, more comfortable with the Gaelic pronunciation. She nodded. "Storyteller." But why was it written on the man's garment?

On the other side of his tunic she read, "U-S. N-a-v-y." Unable to relate those letters to a Gaelic word, she set the question of the writing aside.

Noticing a row of buttons marching down his tunic, she extended a finger and lightly grazed them. Canting her head, she leaned closer. Its smooth surface felt like bone, but the button was a dark green. How was that possible? Looking closer, she noted tiny stitches, and using her fingernail she explored the space between the two rows.

"Ach. How clever!" The buttons held the material together over the man's chest. She'd never seen anything like it before. Buttons, yes. Her best undertunic had small bone buttons marching up the sleeves, with loops to push them through to hold the edges together, but never had she thought to stitch an opening in a garment's material.

The man's chest expanded then contracted, and his breath feathered over Caira's hand. She recoiled, her gaze going to his face. The heat of a blush climbed into her cheeks. She should be tending to the man's wounds, not ogling him and his strange garments.

"Caira, here are the items ye requested," Gitta said behind her.

Caira turned, and the woman stood at her elbow, medicinal box in one hand and a stack of rags balanced in the other. "And yer water." She nodded to a young lad holding a basin of water.

"My thanks." Placing the things on another bench nearby, Caira watched everyone move off. The two old men who'd found the stranger stood back a ways, but they were still close enough if she had need of them. She smiled at their protectiveness, then frowned. She would have no need of it in her own hall, did they not bring the stranger here.

Wetting a rag, she cleaned the soot from the burnt man's face and hands, willing her fingers to stop their trembling. She opened her box, taking out a jar of salve. The stranger's hands were littered with small blisters, reminding Caira of the ones she tended on the children who played in the forest. But those were itchy and red.

How had he gotten these?

"Callum?"

"Aye, Caira?"

"Was there a fire nearby when you found him?" She glanced from her patient to Callum.

"Nay." Callum took a step closer.

Malcolm cleared his throat.

"Yes, Malcolm?" Caira asked.

The old man took a step closer, moving next to his friend. "There were no tracks or footprints either, just a huge hole."

"A hole? What do you make of it?" Caira looked to Callum for an answer.

" 'Twas as if he dropped from the sky" was the old warrior's response.

Caira arched a brow, disappointment settling in her stomach. Callum was getting as fanciful as Malcolm. It was sad to watch those you love grow old, she thought, gently bandaging her patient's hands.

With a deep breath, she scooped some salve from the jar and gently smoothed it over the man's face. The warmth of his skin heated the pads of her fingers as she did. Never had the act of tending a wound felt so intimate. The urge to pull her hand away warred with the tantalizing electricity of the moment.

The stranger's eyelids fluttered, then opened, and Caira jerked her hand away, staring into pain-filled, sky-blue eyes. "Where do you hurt, sir?" she asked in Gaelic. She stayed her instinct to back away, wondering how and why the man unnerved her so.

His brow furrowed.

"Do you have other wounds?"

He squinted at her, his gaze locked on her mouth.

"Can you understand me?" She spoke slowly.

He lifted his panic-darkened gaze.

Caira tried again, this time in English. "Where do you hurt?"

His eyes widened, and he shook his head.

Dear God, he was deaf. Pain lanced her heart at his suffering. No matter whether he was English or Scot, he was a man—a very vulnerable man.

She patted his shoulder and smiled, then turned to her box of medicinals. "Gitta, would you fetch me a cup of warmed wine?"

"Aye," the woman agreed. She bustled off, and Caira looked back at her patient. He gazed around, confusion evident in his squinting eyes and thinning lips.

Gitta returned with the wine, and Caira took a pouch from her box, placed two pinches of the contents into the cup, and swirled the wine around.

"Callum, will you support him?" she asked. She turned back to the stranger. "Here now, drink this up. 'Twill ease the pain and make you sleep."

Callum stepped over, lifting the man enough to drink from the cup.

"He canna stay on the bench," she said. Callum gazed at her intently.

"Where will ye put him, then?" he asked.

"The tower room," she decided. There were but four sleeping chambers in the small keep: hers, her father's, the tower room and a small chamber above it used for storage.

Glancing at her patient, she saw his eyes close and he slept. Pray God she'd done the right thing and he wouldn't learn her secret.

Chapter Three

Brian forced his heavy eyelids open and gazed at the beamed ceiling above him. Where was he?

He shifted on the lumpy mattress, groaning as pain shot through his body. The sound of a thousand chirping crickets filled his ears, intensifying the pounding in his head. He reached up to rub his temple, but stopped his hand in midair to examine the bandage wrapped around it.

What had happened?

He closed his eyes, forcing himself to reach past the pain and think back. He'd been at the drill area with Lawrence, examining the training aid. . . .

Lawrence.

His chest tightened. Where was the Brit? Panic clawed up his throat, and he closed his eyes, clenching his fingers over the cloth that covered his hands.

What had happened in the field? Despite the pain thumping in his head, he concentrated harder. But no matter how hard he tried, the memories weren't there.

Instead, the image of a woman with amber eyes came to mind. Who was she?

Possibly a Catholic nun, he thought, as her image became clearer in his mind and he saw her face surrounded by the white headcovering she wore. He must be in a medical facility run by the Church.

He turned his head and followed the shaft of sunlight streaking the floor. A long narrow window, devoid of glass, was set in a thick stone wall, allowing a draft of cool air into the room. Glancing to his left, he saw a small table and a stool beside his bed.

Anxiety settled heavily on him; he had to find Lawrence and see how the man was doing. Pushing up on his elbows, he inhaled sharply as pain erupted in his head. He waited for it to lessen, then sat up.

He frowned, noticing coals glowing red in a grill on the floor by the foot of the bed. What the hell was a barbecue grill doing in the room? he wondered.

He brought his hand up to massage his head, but stopped when he saw the bandages again. Searching his mind, he tried to remember how he'd hurt his hands, but the time between Lawrence and the field and seeing the woman was blank.

The doctor would know, he realized, his panic inching away. He'd find out everything soon enough.

A more pressing need pushed his questions aside, but first he'd have to remove his bandages. His wounds couldn't be that bad; there wasn't any pain. Using his teeth, he untied the knot holding the material on his hand. With both bandages removed, Brian examined the damage. Small blisters covered the tops of his hands and wrists.

He frowned at the injuries, but still he couldn't remember how he'd gotten them. His headache remained a dull throbbing behind his eyes, clouding his memory.

He rose from the bed and padded across the room to an open doorway. Clad only in his skivvies and T-shirt, he shivered against the chill.

The room beyond the open door proved to be a small L-shape, with a wooden seat at the short end. It was little more than a port-o-john, but Brian's need was urgent and he gave the amenity no more thought.

Finished, he left the bathroom and glanced around for his clothes, but he didn't see them. Muted voices penetrated the low ringing in his ears, and he followed the sound to the only wooden door in the room.

Caira trudged up the stairs. She'd made this trip to the tower room several times since last evening, and each time found the stranger deep in sleep, her draft having done its work.

Malcolm and Callum had been assigned guard duty, with express orders to fetch her the moment the man awoke. She would see him gone from Mackenzie land the very moment he was able. The less time the Englishman spent here, the safer for everyone.

She reached the landing to find Malcolm and Callum standing before the door, arguing.

" 'Tis yer fault she's angry," Malcolm snapped, leaning toward Callum.

" 'Tis better she's angry with me than have the English beating at the gates."

"Enough," Caira growled. She glared at the two.

Nodding to the door they guarded, she asked, "Has he awakened?"

Both men shrugged.

"What have you been doing, then? 'Twas why I stationed you here, to watch him."

An exasperated sigh left her lips. Stepping between the pair, she pushed the door open, took several steps into the room, and met the surprised gaze of the stranger. With a gasp, she stepped back. She hadn't expected to find him awake and moving. Her heel came down on Malcolm's foot. The old man grunted, his hands coming up to her shoulders to steady her.

"How are y . . ."

Her words faded as her gaze skimmed his body, and heat flooded her cheeks. A dark green shirt clung lovingly to his sculpted chest. She swallowed and let her gaze drift down to the stark whiteness of the short drawers shamelessly hugging the muscles of his hips and thighs, muscles of which he had plenty.

Another wave of warmth washed over Caira as she took in his nicely formed, straight legs, their sprinkling of dark hair ending just above his ankles. She forced her gaze back up to the odd white garment and collided with . . .

Holy Mary, Mother of God.

She whipped her gaze back to the man's face, feeling the fire of her blush inch its way down her neck to her chest. His cool, blue questioning gaze met hers.

What ailed her? His garments might be strange, but beneath it all he was just a man.

She straightened her shoulders and, clearing her throat, she turned to Malcolm. "Will you get the man

27

his garments?" The calmness of her voice belied the trembling of her knees.

Her gaze devoured the man again. How could garments reveal that which they concealed? Never had she seen such before. Her fingers itched to travel the smooth hills and valleys of his chest, to feel the softness of the cloth covering him.

Ach, he's a braw man, she thought with appreciation.

Shocked by the path of her thoughts, she gave herself a mental shake. A stranger was in their midst, posing a threat to the safety of her clan. She should be escorting him from the keep, not ogling him.

It was not as if she were a sheltered young maiden. Nay, she'd seen a handsome man before. Had not her husband been pleasant to look upon? Verily, this stranger was no different from any other.

Why, then, was there a fluttering low in her stomach? She clenched her shaking hands together.

"What the hell?"

His strangely accented words drew Caira from her musings, and relief washed over her to find he'd donned his trews. He stood staring at the tunic he held in his hand.

He glanced at her. "What happened?"

He *was* English. His question confirmed it. Disappointment weighed her shoulders, surprising her. Without realizing it, she'd heartily hoped he would not be the enemy.

Just for the safety of the clan, she assured herself.

"Where's Sergeant Shaw?"

She gazed at him, bemused by his strange words. They were English, but his accent made them sound even more foreign. Mayhap it was due to his loss of hearing. Ofttimes, if a child lost his ability to hear early on, it would hamper his speech.

"How badly is he hurt?" he asked.

She sorted through his words. The heavy weight of dread settled low in her stomach, as their meaning became clear: There was another man. "I know not of whom you speak. You were the only one found."

"That can't be. We were together."

Caira shook her head. Dear God, there was another out there injured as well. Would Callum's dire predictions come true? Would the English come calling with swords drawn, ready to lay blame for injuries to their men?

"Did my men bring me here?" the stranger asked.

"Nay. Malcolm and Callum found you." Sweet Mary, whom had the old Scots brought to the castle? Just how many men did this stranger have with him? She inched back toward the door.

"Are the others still here?"

Caira frowned. "You can hear me?"

Could he hear her?

"Of course I can." The drone of crickets in Brian's ears had settled into a low, hollow hum. But even that couldn't be blamed for the difficulty he had understanding the nun's English. He turned to the two men beside the woman. "Are you Callum and Malcolm?"

Both men stepped forward.

"I'm Callum." The shorter of the two men pointed to himself. "That's Malcolm." He nodded to his friend.

Malcolm put his hand on the hilt of his sword and glared at Brian. "And who are ye?"

29

"Brian Skelley." He turned to the nun. "When can I see the doctor? I need to get hold of my command and let them know where I am and find out about Sergeant Shaw." He glanced around the room. "By the way, where am I? This *is* a medical facility, isn't it?"

" 'Tis Kilbeinn Castle, not a . . ."—the woman canted her head, her brow puckered in a frown— "medical facility."

Brian stared down at the small holes littering his shirtsleeve. Bringing his other hand up, he gingerly touched his face, feeling blisters on his cheeks and forehead. His fingers grazed the stubble of his eyebrows, and his gaze shot to the woman, then the old men.

"Holy shit!" He glanced at the nun, embarrassed. "Sorry, Sister." Though he couldn't remember much, he knew from the condition of his hands and face, and his singed eyebrows, that he'd been involved in an explosion.

On the heels of that thought came fears for Lawrence's condition. "There had to be another man." He looked at her.

" 'Twas no other." She met his gaze, anger and . . . was that fear darkening her gaze? "And if you think to blame us for what happened to you, you'll be thinking again."

Brian shook his head, holding up his hand. "I'm not blaming you for anything. I just want to know where— oh, forget it." He headed for the door. He'd find someone in charge. It was obvious these people had no idea what was going on.

Slipping into his shirt, he went down the stairs, followed by the others. He stopped short just two steps from the bottom, the woman and two men halting behind him.

His gaze traveled around the large room. Fires crackled in the twin fireplaces, one on either end of the room. Several rows of tables and benches were being dismantled and moved against the walls. On a raised platform stood another table, a woman busy removing the white cloth draped over it.

The door to his left opened and several men and women entered, dressed in an assortment of odd costumes. All the women wore headcovers similar to that of the nun behind him.

Yeah, this must be a convent, he thought, taking the last few stairs. He turned his head and addressed the woman who moved around him. "Where is the doctor, Sister . . . ?"

"She's not yer sister." The Scot named Malcolm glared at Brian, and he and Callum took up positions on either side of the nun.

"Caira, come away from the mon, he's addled," the other Scot said, and the three backed away from Brian.

"This isn't a medical clinic?" Brian frowned at her. "You're not a nun?"

The woman shook her head.

"But what about the bandages?"

"Caira is a healer," Malcolm spoke up, a note of pride in his voice.

The woman gave a choked groan and looked away.

"Well, I need to talk to the person in charge."

The woman took a step forward, her shoulders straight, her amber gaze chilly. "Then you'll be wanting to speak with me." She propped her hands on her hips. "But first I'll be knowing what brought you to Mackenzie land."

Brian narrowed his gaze. "I'm part of the personnel exchange program."

She gave him a puzzled glare.

"Civilians," he said, and sighed to himself. "I came over here, and one of the Brits went to the States. You know, like an exchange student." All three looked at him as if he'd stepped off another planet.

He ran his hand through his hair. Why wouldn't these people tell him about Lawrence? A chill snaked up his spine. Unless . . . "Is Sergeant Shaw dead?"

The three exchanged frightened glances, and Caira stepped back, her spine stiff, her gaze challenging. She said, "We've taken no one's life, though 'twould be our right, since you trespassed upon Mackenzie land." She turned to the two old men and added softly, "Take him to the English fort at Garethmuir, but have a care that they dinna see you."

An English fort? That would work, Brian thought, anxious to leave the confusion of this place. He had to find out what had happened. "Fine. Let's go, then." He glanced at Caira and smiled, holding out his hand. "Thanks for everything."

Peter, Lord Whitcomb, gazed out the window of Garethmuir Keep at the rare sunny day in the wilds of Scotland. Pray King Edward called him back home soon. He longed for the bustle of London and the sound of cultured English conversation. Scotland and its inhospitable occupants were not to his liking.

But, as peer of the realm, he was subject to the whims of the king.

"My lord?"

Peter turned from the window and met the nervous glance of a page. "Aye? What is it, boy?"

"A missive from the king, my lord." The rolled parchment trembled in the lad's outstretched hand.

Taking it from him, Peter said, "You may go." He waited until the boy disappeared around the screen separating his sleeping chamber from the hall of the keep before breaking the red wax seal.

Ironic, he thought, that just as he'd wished the king to send for him, he'd received a communiqué. He grinned as he unrolled the parchment. Mayhap he'd see the last of this foul land.

His grin faded as he scanned the missive. "Bloody hell!" The shout burst from his lips, and the parchment crinkled beneath his clenched fists. Taking a deep calming breath, he read the message from King Edward again:

> *My Lord Whitcomb,*
>
> *We have been informed that William Wallace has been spotted moving toward the eastern coast of Scotland. We believe he means to travel to France to solicit aid in his endeavors against the English crown.*
>
> *Do not be lax in your patrols. We are aware of the professed neutrality of the Mackenzies clan, but I would remind you to be alert. These Scots are not an honorable lot.*
>
> *I will see you returned to my court upon the capture of Wallace and his rebels.*
>
> *Edward, King of England,*
> *Scotland and Wales*

"Smythe!" Peter yelled for his second-in-command.

"Aye, my lord?"

Peter stopped his pacing and faced the soldier.

John Smythe straightened, puffing his chest out. "How may I be of service, my lord?"

"Take men out and check the Mackenzie borders. Wallace is on the move, and 'tis our duty to capture him and his rebels."

"Aye, my lord." Smythe turned to leave.

"And, Smythe?"

The soldier stopped. "Aye, my lord?"

"You are aware of the king's agreement with the Mackenzie laird?"

"Aye." He glanced at his master. "But . . . mayhap they harbor Wallace?"

"Exactly my thought. Do nothing rash, simply let our presence be known. We'll step up our patrols and mayhap catch them in any treasonous activities."

Smythe grinned. "Aye, my lord. I'll see to it."

Chapter Four

Brian stepped out into the morning sun, squinting against its bright rays. As he descended the stairs, the bark of a dog drew his attention. His progress across the dirt courtyard was halted by a large white goose. One of its wings bandaged, it waddled by, quacking loudly, followed by a black-and-brown, three-legged mutt.

"Ach, Three-legs, leave Goose alone." Malcolm stepped into the dog's path. The aptly named canine stopped, his tail wagging, his tongue lolling to the side.

The goose glanced back at the dog and changed direction, heading straight back for its nemesis.

Callum pushed past, brushing aside Malcolm, waving his arms and chasing the fowl off. "Get on with ye, or ye'll find yer way to the cook's pot, ye will."

With a loud, angry quack, the bird again changed directions to disappear around the corner of the building.

"What happened to his leg?" Brian asked. Malcolm

glanced up, narrowing his gaze, then the old Scot looked at the dog.

"Don't know. His leg was half gone when we found him in the forest. Must have been another animal." He shrugged. "We brought him back to Caira, and she fixed him up. Had to take the rest of his leg off, though." Rubbing the dog's head affectionately, Malcolm added, "Don't seem to slow him down none."

"Come on, Malcolm, let's get this done." Callum had returned, and he gave Three-legs a pat before setting off. Brian and Malcolm followed.

Brian glanced around. Several small outbuildings took up space in the open area around the castle. Clumps of grass sprouted here and there, defying the hard-packed earth. Looking back over his shoulder, he scanned the stone building.

They called this a castle? Hell, the entire place would fit inside some of the castles he'd seen. He shrugged, turning his gaze to the high thick wall ringing the buildings, and the gate opening where people came and went. He'd seen a couple other fortresses similar to this, managed by the Scottish Historic Society, but they were all clean and barren of life. From the obnoxious odor wafting on the breeze, people actually lived here. And needed to pump their septic system, he thought with disgust.

Glancing overhead, he frowned. He didn't see any power or phone lines. But then, he reminded himself, Scotland didn't spoil the scenery with power poles and lines running everywhere.

He scanned his surroundings. Nothing modern had invaded these ancient walls; not even fashion, he thought, watching the swing of Callum and Malcolm's faded brown kilts and the leather strips crisscrossing their calves, holding up what he thought were their socks.

Beyond the wall, Brian looked around for a car or truck. He saw nothing.

"Don't you have a vehicle?" he asked, stopping and staring around him.

"A what?" Malcolm looked at him in confusion, then shook his head. "Come on. We canna break our fast 'til we see ye back to yer fort."

Brian ran his hand through his hair. The military facility was some ten miles from the drill area, but where was this castle in relation?

He caught up with the Scots. "Where the hell am I?"

The old men exchanged glances, then Callum said, "Caira told ye. Kilbeinn Castle."

"Yeah, but where exactly *is* the castle?"

Both men fixed Brian with frowns, then looked pointedly back up at the large stone fortress.

Brian resisted the urge to roll his eyes. Snatching on to his patience, he asked, "Where is Kilbeinn in relation to the military base?"

"Base?" Malcolm echoed with a shake of his head. "Ye mean the fort?" He nudged Callum with his elbow. "He canna be English, he doesna speak the tongue well enough."

Brian let the comment slide, rather than waste time arguing. "Yeah, the fort."

" 'Tis south." Callum started walking again and took a narrow trail heading off to the left.

Getting his bearings, Brian followed. "And where did you find me?"

"To the west—and I'll be knowing why ye were on Mackenzie land." Callum glared at him. "And dinna give me that nonsense ye spouted to Caira."

Brian shook his head. "Listen, it's not important."

"Mayhap not to ye, but 'tis to me." Callum stopped at the edge of the woods.

This sure wasn't the Highland hospitality he'd been accustomed to, Brian thought, meeting the old man's belligerent stare. Why did they act so hostile toward him?

He looked west, south, and back to the castle behind him. And then it hit him.

Kilbeinn was the castle he'd been told about. "But . . ." He stared at the keep backed up against the mountain. "I was told it was nothing more than ruins now."

Callum barked. "Aye, thanks to ye and the rest of the Sassenach." He glared at Brian.

"Bloody English bastards, should kill the lot of ye," Malcolm muttered. "Ye think they'd miss him?" he asked his friend.

Callum shook his head. "Who's to know, but I wouldna want to chance it." They entered the forest beyond the castle, and the old Scot slowed his steps. He glanced from Brian to Malcolm. "Caira would have our heads, besides. She said to see him back to the fort, and 'tis what we'll do—though I'm thinking we'll just get him within sight of the place. Let him find his way after that. I'd not want to run into one of them English patrols."

Brian blinked, confused. What the hell were these

two talking about? Granted, he didn't understand everything they said, but he got the gist.

He frowned, letting his gaze travel from the top of Malcolm's matted, dirty gray hair to the matching scraggly beard. A dingy, long-sleeved shirt was tucked into a kilt, belted around the man's thick waist. A length of the material was tossed over his left shoulder. Brian had seen a lot of kilts in the time he'd been in Scotland, but nothing like these. Made of a dull brown wool, they reminded him of the costumes in *Braveheart*—except these weren't plaid.

Was it just a quirk of the two old Scots that they walked around looking like they'd just stepped off a movie set?

But no, the few men he'd seen in the castle were dressed the same. What the hell was going on?

A rhythmic thudding pulled Brian from his thoughts.

"Bloody hell," Malcolm mumbled.

"Just hold yer temper, will ye, Malcolm," Callum warned. A moment later, five men on horseback burst from the trees and surrounded them.

Damn, this just kept getting stranger and stranger, Brian thought as he looked up at the newly appeared men. "Well, I'll be damned," he whispered, his eyes rounded in surprise. "They're wearing chain mail."

No one answered.

"Well, well, well. What have we here?"

Brian jerked his gaze to the speaker. The man stared coldly at him, his eyes glinting and his thin lips curled in derision. Five swords scraped from their scabbards and were pointed at Brian and his guides. The armored men's mounts danced nervously, moving in close enough for Brian to feel their heated breath. The leader of the quintet moved the tip of his sword just inches from Callum's head.

"What's brought you out of your hovels, eh?"

Anger shot through Brian. Damned bullies. Picking on two old men, and from horseback? Bastards. One thing he wouldn't tolerate was a bully. As a kid, he'd put up with it from his father because he'd had no choice—he'd be damned if he'd tolerate it now as an adult. He didn't know what the problem was, but brutal intimidation wasn't going to happen in front of him.

He stepped in front of Callum and Malcolm. The five men just laughed.

"Do I scare you?" the leader taunted. "You'd do well to fear the sword of an English soldier." He glared at them, demanding, "What are you doing so far from home, eh?"

"Just returning one of yer own," Callum responded, a bit of challenge in his tone.

Brian's eyebrow shot up, and he glanced from Callum to Malcolm. "I'm not one of these bastards."

"What did he say?" The leader looked from Brian to Callum.

"Ye mean ye canna even understand yer own?" Callum shook his head. "He called ye a bastard."

"Bastard, you say?" The man brought his sword up to Brian's neck.

Malcolm muttered behind him: "I'm going to skewer the bastard, then slice him from gut to gullet."

It took Brian a second to make out what the Scot

40

said, because apparently it was a different dialect of Gaelic than he'd learned. But, "Don't do anything stupid," he responded in the same language. He was rewarded with a gasp from Malcolm.

"Where's Wallace?" the head Englishman demanded, his sword point pressing into Brian's skin.

Brian leaned back, knocked the tip away. "Wallace who?"

The Englishman's lips turned up in a sneer, and his gaze narrowed. "Who?" He gave a harsh laugh. "William Wallace, the thief of Scotland."

It was Brian's turn to laugh. These guys were nuts. "Hell, Wallace is long dead."

"Bah, you stupid fool, you don't know anything." The leader looked to his men. " 'Tis an example of the common Scot, stupid as a stump." His men laughed, and behind Brian, Malcolm began swearing.

The laughter died, and the Englishman glared at Brian, Malcolm, and Callum. "You'd best hie yourselves back to your sties. In the future, I would advise you not venture too far from them." With that, he and his men turned their mounts and galloped off.

Callum turned to Brian. "Ye speak Gaelic?" he asked. Before Brian could respond, Callum turned away. "Did ye hear him, Malcolm?"

"Aye. I was standing right next to him." Malcolm gave Brian a long, searching gaze. "Is Wallace truly dead?"

Brian shook his head. "Yeah, for nearly seven hundred years now."

"Are ye daft, mon?"

Brian looked from Callum's wide-eyed gaze to Malcolm's narrowed glare, then he smiled. "No. Wallace died early in the thirteen-hundreds. That would be about seven hundred years ago."

"Eh?" Callum's brow furrowed. "What year do ye think this is, mon?"

Brian stared at him. What kind of joke was this? "What year do *you* think it is?"

"I *know*—'tis the Year of Our Lord 1301."

Chapter Five

"Thirteen oh one?" Brian snorted. "You guys *are* nuts." He glanced around, looked up to the sun to get his bearings, then turned west and started walking.

"Where are *ye* going?"

Brian glanced over his shoulder at Malcolm's question. "Strathaven." He estimated the small town was closer than the base, and the less time he spent with these men, the better.

"Ye ever heard of such a place, Callum?"

Brian stopped, turned on the two men following him. "It's just east of Stonegrave." He glared at them both. "And I don't need company, either."

"Ach, I think we'll just come along anyway. Ye never know what's around the bend." Malcolm propped his hands on his hips and met Brian's gaze. In an aside to Callum, the old Scot added, "And mayhap we'll get to meet the Wallace."

Brian rolled his eyes. "I don't know this Wallace guy."

"Oh, aye." Malcolm winked. "That's right, he's dead, eh?"

Brian shook his head. "Yup. You're nuts," he muttered.

"Malcolm, I never heard of Strathaven," Callum said. "My stomach's grumbling. If ye have a mind to wander the woods, I'll leave ye to it. I'm for home."

"Well, go, then," the other Scot responded. "I'm going to meet up with Wallace."

"Yeah, sure." Brian looked between them. "Are you two part of some kind of a cult? Couldn't fit into normal society, so you moved out here to revert to simpler times?" Frustration snapped his patience. "You can tell me, I'm weird tolerant. I'm an American."

Both Scots turned, obviously surprised.

Brian went on: "Listen, just wake up and smell the twenty-first century long enough to help me get back to my people. Then you can get back to your game, and I'll no longer be a thistle up your kilts." He walked away.

"Do ye ken what he's blathering about?" he heard Callum say.

"Nay, but I willna let what may be one of Wallace's men wander the woods. Mayhap Strathaven is a secret hiding place for them."

"I hadna thought of that. Well, I canna let ye go alone—ye'll end up lost, and then Caira will slice the hide from my bones."

Brian kept walking. He felt sure that by taking a westerly direction, he'd come to one of Scotland's motorways or roads. From there, he'd make his way to Strathaven and call his command.

Since Lawrence hadn't been brought with him to the castle, the odds were that the Brit hadn't made it through the blast. Regret that he hadn't been able to stop the man ate at Brian, deafening him to the conversation behind him between the Scots.

He walked for about an hour, unease niggling his mind. Why did things seem so strange? And where the hell were the roads?

"Stonegrave's just beyond that hill," Callum offered, pointing to a slope about three miles ahead. "But there isna another village around it."

Brian stopped and looked at the hill, remembering the rise between Strathaven and Stonegrave and the cellular tower atop it. He gazed at the area around him.

"Where the hell is the tower?" he asked. He frowned. This couldn't be the right place. He turned to the old men. "Stonegrave is due west? Not northwest or southwest?"

Both men shook their heads. " 'Tis west, over that hill." Callum pointed. He added, "For one of Wallace's men, he's got no sense of direction." Though the words were mumbled for only Malcolm to hear, Brian heard them as well.

"Ach, he's just trying to throw ye off—make ye think he's not one of them." Malcolm grinned.

"Are you sure it's west?" Brian repeated. He ran his hand through his hair. "Strathaven should be right here." He glanced at the pair of old men. "It's been here since the sixteen-hundreds, damn it. A town doesn't just pick up and move."

Callum scratched his nose. "Well, if ye wait a few

hundred years, mayhap ye'll be able to find it again."
He rubbed his stomach. "I'm for home and a bit of
food. Ye coming, Malcolm?"

"We canna just leave him here."

"What are we supposed to do with the mon? He's
addled, I tell ye." He shook his head. "Thinks I dinna
know the year." Callum snorted, ambling back the way
they'd come.

"Well, I'll not leave him behind," Malcolm called.
" 'Tis sure he's had some kind of accident. What
would Wallace think if we abandoned one of his
men?"

Callum turned. "And would ye bring the English
down on us with him in our midst?"

"Ye think they'd not have taken him if they thought
he was one of Wallace's?"

"Aye, well, ye've a point, there."

"We're the only ones who knows he is," Malcolm
bragged, straightening his shoulders.

Brian listened absently to their conversation, a corner of his mind turning over the location of the town
and the drill area. "Can you show me exactly where
you found me?" he asked. Maybe that was the answer.
Hoping so, he caught up with Callum.

"Aye, 'tis just a wee bit out of the way," Callum
agreed.

As they set out, Malcolm walked beside Brian. "So,
will ye be telling us of Wallace, then?"

Brian rolled his eyes. "No." The man just didn't listen. "I'm telling you, I *don't know* Wallace."

"Ach, course ye do. At the very least; 'tis yer calling.
Ye're a storyteller, after all."

"Jesus, where'd that come from?"

Brian met Malcolm's baffled gaze, which darted to

Brian's right shirt pocket. He pointed. " 'Tis yer name . . . Skelley." He shook his head. "Ye dinna ken the meaning of yer own name?"

Brian decided to ignore the question and picked up his pace.

A while later, he stood on a rise overlooking a small valley dotted with pines and blanketed with ferns. Familiarity washed over him. As he followed the Scots down the incline, he had the distinct feeling he'd done it before. He scanned the area, but nothing familiar jumped out at him.

Shaking off the weird feeling, he stopped beside an indentation in the ground. The area around it was bare of growth.

"No." Brian shook his head. "This isn't the place."

"Aye, 'tis." Malcolm bobbed his head, motioning to the hole at their feet.

"No, the field was larger, cleared of all trees." Brian glanced around, his gaze locking on the hole at his feet. He knelt down and examined it, rubbing the pulverized dirt between his fingers. A grayish-black residue ringed the indentation.

"This was definitely caused by a blast," he muttered, squinting at the area just outside the indentation. But where *was* he?

There was no sign of the training site, no indication that there'd been an accident other than the indentation at his feet. If it had been a blast, and he didn't doubt it now, then both he and Lawrence should have been fragged . . . unless Lawrence took it all. But then there should be signs of blood, at least.

He walked around the area, noting the footprints and horse tracks.

47

"We found ye here." Callum motioned to a spot near the hole.

"Was there anyone else? Did you search for others?"

"Nay. Why should we?" Callum gave him a puzzled frown. "We werena looking fer ye. Just found ye there."

"Has it rained since you found me?"

"Not but a wee drizzle, hardly enough to dampen the ground."

Not enough to wash away any evidence, Brian decided.

"There was an odd rumble, like no thunder I ever heard before. 'Tis what brought us to ye," Malcolm said.

Callum adjusted his kilt. "Well, then, we'd best be getting home. As 'tis, we'll be begging Cook for a crust of bread and a swallow of ale."

Brian stepped over the crater, and the glint of something caught his eye. He moved dirt aside with the toe of his boot. Bringing his right hand up, he felt the empty spot above his left pocket.

"My crab." He knelt down and picked up the silver pin he hadn't realized he'd lost and examined it carefully, wiping off the dirt and turning it over.

Yup, it was his; the post on the right was bent.

"What have ye there?" Malcolm peered over Brian's shoulder. " 'Tis yer clan badge?"

"It's my Master crab." Brian rubbed it.

"Yer what?"

"My EOD badge." The metal warmed beneath his fingers.

48

Henry's mother had given it to him after Henry's funeral.

In high school, Henry had been the nerd and Brian the bad boy. They'd been paired up in chemistry class and become best friends. Henry had found the Master crab at an Army/Navy surplus store.

Brian could still hear his voice:

"Brian, they've got bomb experts in the Navy who wear these. Did you know that? They're deep-sea divers and parachutists, too! Someday, we're going to wear them," he'd sworn. He'd been so excited.

From the threshold of the castle door, Caira had watched Callum and Malcolm leave with Brian, a worried frown drawing her brows together. Was the man well enough to be leaving? And what had brought him here?

Bah, what did she care? He was gone, and so the rest need not concern her.

" 'Twas a braw mon."

With a startled jerk, Caira turned to face Gitta. " 'Twas a stranger and a threat to the clan."

"Ach, I think ye see what's not there, lass." The other woman arched a brow and then looped her arm with Caira's. "Ye did see that they broke their fast before they left?" she asked hopefully.

Caira moaned. "The stranger left in such a rush, there was no time."

"Well, then, he'll have a most unpleasant journey. Ye ken how Callum is without his food." Gitta shook her head and laughed.

Caira nodded, glancing out the opened door.

"Come along. We've much to do today and canna be moonin' after a braw lad, now can we?"

"I was not mooning over him, Gitta."

But the older woman only smiled, propelling Caira to the high table as the servants brought in the morning meal and the clan settled down to eat.

Later Caira sat in her solar, carding wool, a gentle breeze from the open window touching her face. She glanced out, and her movements stilled.

"Jesus, Mary, and Joseph."

Gitta looked up from her work. "What is it, Caira?"

"They brought him back." She dropped the wool in her lap. "When I told them to see him back to the fort."

Anger bubbled in her veins, accompanied by a cold fear as she rose from her seat. "I will speak with Callum and Malcolm. They will not get any food 'till they've returned him from whence he came."

"Now, Caira, mayhap there's a good reason."

She turned to the older woman. "There can be no good reason to bring the enemy among us." Striding to the door, Caira flung it open and marched down the stairs.

She stood on the last step as the men entered the hall. "Callum? Malcolm? Did I not tell ye to return him to the fort?"

Both men came to an abrupt halt, Callum avoiding her gaze and Malcolm looking quite pleased with himself. Caira's temper flared anew. "You'd keep an Englishman among us? What were you thinking? Or did you even bother to think what he could do to us?" She motioned to Skelley where he stood. "He could remove our heads from our shoulders whilst we sleep."

50

Malcolm glanced over his shoulder at the Englishman. "But, Caira—"

"Nay." She brought her hand up to stop his excuses. "You'll be taking him back this minute."

Skelley stepped forward. "I'm not the enemy, and I haven't taken anyone's head off in at least thirty years—and then it was the head of my next-door neighbor's Barbie doll."

Caira gasped. Though she understood the Gaelic words he spoke, they made no sense. Her gaze whipped from the man to Malcolm, who grinned hugely at her. "He's one of Wallace's soldiers, Caira," he said.

"Jesus." The man named Skelley seemed annoyed. "I've told him, I don't know how many times, I don't know the man. Hell, he's been dead for almost seven hundred years!"

Caira's eyes widened. The stranger continued to speak with an odd accent, his phrasing strange. Gaelic was not his native tongue, of that she was certain, and what he said about William Wallace made no sense.

Malcolm moved to Skelley's side. "Ach, Caira, he's just protecting William." The old Scot folded his arms across his chest. "Aye, he's one of Wallace's."

Caira turned her startled gaze on the stranger. "Is this true?"

"I've tried to tell this nu . . . er, Malcolm that I'm not, but he—"

"Ye should have seen him with the English," Malcolm spoke up.

"You met them?" Fear clogged Caira's throat. Sweet Mary, could it get any worse?

"Aye." Malcolm frowned. "I would have killed the lot of them, but the Skelley here turned them away, an' without even a weapon." He beamed at the object of his admiration. "He's loyal to Wallace. Willna tell me anything aboot the mon." He nodded. "Aye, loyal he is."

Skelley cast Malcolm a glare, then looked back at Caira. "Don't listen to him. I need to talk with you." He glanced at the men beside him. "Alone."

Caira drew in a breath of air.

Alone? She glanced around in a panic. Nay, she would not be alone with the man. But before she could respond, Malcolm said, "Callum and me will just hie ourselves to the kitchen. He's been a wee grumpy all morn."

She watched the two disappear through the door leading to the kitchens. Turning back to Skelley, she found that unease trickled down her spine as he met her gaze.

She didn't know what to think. Was he English or Scot? Was he a Wallace supporter or a spy? Either way, he was a threat to the clan. As the head of her people, she would never cower before him.

Turning from the stairs, she led the way to a pair of chairs arranged before the hearth. Sitting down, she motioned for the man to take the other seat.

Brian couldn't stop looking. The cloth covering Caira's head only served to emphasize her face. A beautiful face.

Her amber gaze regarded him warily. He glanced down to her lips—her very kissable lips. He swallowed

52

and pulled his gaze away, focusing on the slight dimple on her chin.

Damn, she's pretty.

She cleared her throat, and Brian blinked.

What the hell was wrong with him? It wasn't as if he hadn't seen an attractive woman before.

He met Caira's gaze, pulled his mind back to the problem at hand. "I have to get back to Strathaven as soon as possible."

"Strathaven?" Her brow wrinkled. "Where might that be?"

"Near Stonegrave." Brian watched her closely, hoping her response would be more helpful than that of the two old men.

"Strathaven? Near Stonegrave?" She shook her head. "Nay, there is no place by that name."

Brian held on to his patience. "Strathaven," he repeated. "A small town. The main street is pretty hilly, and at the bottom there's a tavern called the Royal Arms."

She gave him a blank look.

"It's the oldest building in the village. The plaque on the building said it was built in 1647?"

Caira's eyes widened, and her eyebrows rose. "Sixteen forty-seven?"

He nodded, and her mouth formed an O. Then she frowned. "Are you unwell?" Concern turned her amber eyes a dark brown. "Mayhap you rose from your bed too soon."

He brushed aside her concern. "No, I'm fine."

"But you think you've seen a tavern built in 1647?"

"I don't think—I know. I've been inside." What the

hell kind of game were these people playing? And how could he get them to stop?

The woman shook her head. " 'Twill be three hundred and forty-six years before 'tis built, then. Are you saying you've visited the future?" Amusement lit her eyes, and she smiled. " 'Tis a wondrous tale, though, Skelley. Fitting for a *seanachaidh*. You'll have to tell me the whole of it."

Chapter Six

Brian sat, dumbfounded. "You've got to be joking."

Caira shook her head. "Alas, I dinna have time to listen to your tale. Mayhap at dinner." She stood, and Brian came to his feet. Looking him in the eyes, she demanded, "Tell me: You're not English, are you?"

"No. But what would it matter?"

Caira gasped. "What would it matter?" Her voice rose. "Then you are not Scot either, or you'd know." Her gaze narrowed, and she propped her hands on her hips. "Just where do you come from, then? I canna place your accent. 'Tis not one I've heard before."

"The States." He stared at her when he got little reaction.

Her finely arched brows drew together. "The States? I've never heard of the place. Where is it?"

"Are you joking?"

"Joking?" She shook her head. "What does this word mean?"

"Oh, come on—"

"Are your people friend or foe to the Scots?" Her voice rose above his.

What the hell was Caira up to? Granted the remoteness of this place might make it hard to get the news, but to not know about the U.S.?

"Well?"

"Jesus, woman." Brian ran his hand over his face. "We're your damned friends."

Her skeptical gaze ate at his waning patience, ruffling the anger simmering beneath the surface. "Just what the hell is going on here, anyway? If this isn't a cult, are you involved in some kind of Renaissance festival?" He glanced around the hall, searching out answers.

"I know not of what you speak. You are at Kilbeinn Castle, and there is naught 'going on,' as you say." Her voice held a note of reciprocal anger, and she angled her chin a bit higher. Taking a deep breath, she continued, "But if you are friend to the Scots and not the English, you may stay until you're well enough to continue your travels." She narrowed her gaze. "But do not think to betray our hospitality." The icy timbre of her voice punctuated her words. " 'Twill not go well for you."

She started to turn away. "I'll find Malcolm and Callum and have them show you to a room."

"Wait." Brian held out his hand, noticing it shook. "Are you telling me this is the way you *live?*"

"And what is wrong with it?" Caira arched a brow. "Are you used to better?" Color rose in her cheeks. "If it doesna please you, then leave."

She turned and strode from the room, leaving Brian to stare after her.

What the hell was going on? He'd thought her intelligent. He shook his head and wandered to the door. Pulling it open, he stepped out into the late-morning air and gazed around.

No paved roads, no power, no running water met his eyes. He focused on the people coming and going in the courtyard. They all wore clothing from another time. Most of the women had their heads covered, and their long skirts brushed the ground as they walked. The few young men he saw wore clothing similar to Callum and Malcolm. Young girls, gathered around a well, helped one another draw buckets of water.

It hit him in the gut with the force of a punch: He wasn't in his own time. The Royal Arms hadn't been built yet; the town didn't even exist.

Malcolm and Caira claimed it was 1301 and there was nothing he could find to dispute them. He shook his head. How the hell had it happened? And why? Could he go home?

Caira entered the kitchens, tense with anger. Her gaze alighted on Callum and Malcolm eating at the worktable, talking with Cook, who kneaded the bread dough.

"Is it not enough that you bring every wounded, lost, or abandoned animal to the castle for me to practice my healing skills on? Are you two now taking in the daft as well?" She glared at Malcolm and Callum as they looked up from their food. "Just what are we to do with the man?"

"The clan hasna had a *seanachaidh* in a long while, Caira." Malcolm said; then he stuffed another piece of bread in his mouth.

She shot him a withering glare. "He's *daft,* Malcolm."

"What were we to do, then Caira?" Callum asked. When she met his earnest gaze, he explained, "We couldna just leave him." He put his cup of ale down. "What if he was a Wallace soldier? We couldna turn away from him."

"But he's not." She rolled her eyes.

"Aye, well, mayhap ye're right. But what else could we do at the time?"

Caira's shoulders slumped, the anger leeching from her.

Aye, what else could they have done? Both men had soft hearts, and, truth be known, so did she. In their places she would have done the same, no doubt.

The stranger they'd found seemed so confused, she thought. But was he truly daft? His deep-blue gaze was filled with intelligence, and he spoke two languages—hardly the accomplishment of a witless soul. His muscled body moved with confidence and power: the sign of a man in control. Her cheeks warmed at the memory of him standing in the tower room, clad only in his strange short garment.

She shook the disconcerting image from her head.

Nay, he was simply confused, not daft. Whatever accident had befallen him must be responsible.

"Mayhap you should take him to your cottage. Watch over him and keep him out of trouble," she suggested to Callum. Aye, that would be best. It was for the safety of the clan, and had naught to do with the way her heart beat a wee bit faster whenever he was near.

Both Callum and Malcolm looked up at her, startled. Their mouths opened and closed several times before the first man spoke. "Caira, we've no room for another. As 'tis, we trip o'er one another." He shook his head.

"Well, he canna stay here!" Frustration put an edge to her voice, but she refused to soften. "Though I dinna think he wishes us ill, I willna risk him learning the clan's secret. 'Twill only be a day or two until he's well enough to leave." She walked to the kitchen door and turned. "You'll see him moved to your cottage by the evening meal."

Without giving the men a chance to argue, she stepped from the kitchen door and headed to the inner bailey. There was laundry to be checked on.

"Caira?" Gitta appeared from around the corner of the keep, a frown knitting her brow. "Do ye ken what is wrong with that mon?" She nodded toward the gate.

Caira looked over and saw Brian talking with one of the villagers. Panic seized her.

"He's been asking one and all the date."

Caira blinked, the panic receding as the villager gave Skelley a pitying gaze, patted his arm and walked away. "The date?" She shook her head. " 'Tis his accident." She pulled her gaze from Brian and turned to Gitta. "He's still a bit confused. Time will make things clearer for him."

"Well, he's frightening everyone." The woman harrumphed and left Caira to stare at Brian, who approached another villager. Surely, Gitta overstated the situation.

But later, as she helped wring out a bed linen, yet

another person approached Caira seeking assurance that Brian wouldn't harm them, that he wasn't a threat. That he wasn't mad.

Frustrated at the constant interruptions, and by the true fear she saw in the woman's gaze, Caira dried her hands and went in search of the stranger.

He'd spent the last couple of hours questioning everyone, young and old, male and female, and they'd all said the same thing.

It was 1301.

Time travel was impossible, right? Brian pinched the bridge of his nose, an ache pulsing behind his eyes.

He looked around him.

Wrong. Time travel *was* possible.

But how? And why? How was he to get back?

He'd asked himself the same questions over and over.

There was no doubt in his mind that he had to get back. He didn't belong here; he had responsibilities in his own time. He had to let his mother know he was okay. There would be the investigation into the accident; he'd need to make a statement. And then there was his commissioning in two weeks.

Mulling the situation over for the last hour, he came to one conclusion: It was the blast that had brought him here, and it would take another to send him back.

Apprehension settled like a fist in his stomach. His military career, so far, had centered around not getting blown up. Now he had to purposely do it?

He shook his head. How the hell was he supposed to do that? He didn't have the chemicals to make modern-day explosives. Glancing down at his shirt, he brushed off the soot clinging to the material.

"Looks like it'll be black powder," he muttered to himself.

Yet there weren't any cannons on the walls, so he could assume black powder hadn't been introduced in England yet.

He knew it was made up of carbon, sulfur, and potassium nitrate, but where the hell was he going to find those? He couldn't just go to the local hardware store and buy the ingredients, he realized with a disgusted grunt.

He took a deep breath and exhaled. He'd have to make them.

He grinned, remembering the days he and Henry had worked on making black powder in chemistry class. When they'd finally got it right, the small explosion had sent a Bunsen burner through the lab window. Poor Henry had shook in his boots, worried the teacher would toss them out of class. But he needn't have worried; Brian's reputation as a problem preceded him. It was him the teacher automatically disciplined.

Detention and paying to replace both the window and the Bunsen burner had been worth the experience, though. Now more than ever. The Navy taught only the basic uses of black powder, not how to make it. So, if it hadn't been for Henry and their chemistry class, Brian would be out of luck about now.

Carbon was easy—the charcoal left over from fires would yield what he needed. Sulfur could be found at mineral springs or around areas of volcanic activity; he'd have to scout around for that. But the potassium nitrate would take some work. Making saltpeter was a smelly proposition, and without it, the black powder wouldn't work.

This wasn't going to be easy, he knew. But if making black powder were easy, anyone could do it. And they hadn't—at least not here, not yet.

Caira came striding up, pulling Brian's attention from the problem of explosives.

"*I* dinna believe you're daft, but I canna say the same for some in the clan. So I'll thank you to remember you're a guest and cease frightening them with your questions." She fixed him with a glare. "You'll be staying with Callum and Malcolm for the non. But I expect you'll be on your way in a day or so." She propped her hands on her hips, her chest heaving. Brian saw anger heating her cheeks and firing her eyes.

He stepped back. Words failed him. They thought he was nuts? Him? He started to respond, and she raised her chin. He swallowed his retort. No point trying to reason with a woman in the midst of a hissy fit, he realized. "Sure."

She harrumphed. "Since you're a storyteller—"

"I'm not a storyteller."

"Aye, ye are." She looked pointedly at his name written above the right pocket of his shirt. " 'Tis there, on your tunic."

"It's my name, not my vocation."

"Well, why are you called that if it's not what you do? I'll be expecting you to entertain us this eve. To earn your keep." Caira swung about, marching back the way she'd come, leaving Brian to stare after her. His gaze followed the swing of her skirt as she rounded a corner out of sight.

He grinned. Damn, she was cute when she was mad.

62

But his grin faded quickly when the full meaning of her words hit him. She expected him to come up with a story? Did she mean a story that started with "Once upon a time"? Hell, he didn't *know* any stories.

And also, she expected him to leave in a day or so? He needed more time than that just to make the black powder. It didn't matter to him where he stayed, except that there wasn't anyplace else to go.

Well, it looked like he had better come up with one hell of a story and hope it changed Caira's mind about how long he could stay.

As he headed to the stables, he thought, Damn, this is going from bad to worse.

Chapter Seven

Caira reached the laundry area and put her hand to her chest. Jesus, Mary, and Joseph. The man fair took her breath away. And she didn't understand it.

Why did a tingling start in her face and spiral down her body, leaving her short of air and feeling hot all over when she was in his presence?

She took up a stick and vigorously stirred the contents of the wash pot, slopping water over the edges, causing the fire beneath to sizzle and smoke.

Glancing up, she saw Gitta. She met the woman's worried gaze. "Ye've talked with him, then?" Gitta asked.

"Aye." Caira jabbed the contents of the pot with her stick.

"Did he not agree to quit frightening everyone?"

She frowned into the pot. "Aye." She pulled up a linen.

Gitta's brows relaxed. "Ah." She nodded. "Where is he from, then?"

"The States." Caira shook the linen off the stick and

it plopped back into the laundry pot. "Have you heard of such a place?"

"Nay, but I havena been far from Kilbeinn. There is much in this world I havena seen or heard."

" 'Tis unknown to me as well."

"Is that what has ye so upset?"

Caira looked up from the pot. "I didna press him for more. As laird of the clan, I should have. 'Tis my responsibility to protect the Mackenzies. I've allowed a stranger access to the clan, and I know naught of him."

"Dinna be so hard on yerself. Speak with him and dinna let him anger ye."

"Aye. 'Tis good advice." But worry still nibbled at her composure. With the English at the borders, it was hard to trust a stranger's words.

"Are ye thinkin' he's English?" Gitta interrupted her thoughts.

"I'm not completely convinced he isn't, despite his claims."

"Did ye not listen to what Callum and Malcolm said about their encounter? The soldiers didna know the stranger, and he stood up to them."

"Aye, but it could be a ruse."

Gitta fixed on her a narrow gaze. " 'Tis more to it than that, and well ye know it." She folded her arms over her bosom. "Ye find him attractive."

"Nay." Caira met the eyes of the older woman. "Well, mayhap. I'm not dead, you ken?" She looked away. "But I dinna have time for such things. I must think of the clan."

"And what of ye? Ye canna mean to live yer life alone, without a mate. Dinna let yer experience with yer husband taint yer view of all men." The woman put her arm around Caira's shoulder. "Ach, lass, ye've taken on a burden no woman should have to. And ye're doing a fine job, but I see how it wears on ye. Ye should look for a husband to help ye."

"I'm a widow but six months, and you think I should marry again?" Caira shook her head. "Have you forgotten how Jamie Munro and his clan didna honor their word with Da? The marriage was to join the power of the Mackenzies and the Munros, and our neutrality."

"Aye, I recall. But not all men are without honor, Caira. There are many who wouldna side with the enemy to fight against their own."

"I'll not risk it."

"So ye'll live only for the clan? Ye'll be content to sleep in that big bed alone, live and die in solitude?" Gitta pulled her arm away and frowned. "What of children? Will ye leave the clan without a Mackenzie heir, then?"

The weight of responsibility settled more firmly on Caira's shoulders. She would love to have children, but to have any she'd have to wed. And trust, once given and destroyed, was a hard thing to give again.

Caira glanced around. "And just where will I find a husband, eh? If you've noticed, there isna an abundance of eligible men about."

She met Gitta's gaze a long moment. A gasp escaped her as she read Gitta's response in the woman's eyes.

"He's a stranger. We know naught about him."

"Sometimes we know more than we think, lass."

Caira shook her head, pushing the idea away.

66

" 'Tis just that I worry for ye." Concern wrinkled Gitta's forehead.

"Is there something wrong? Have the people been complaining about me, then?" Panic crawled up Caira's spine. "Have they lost faith?" Not that Caira had any faith in herself, but she'd thought she'd kept her doubts hidden.

"Nay, lass." Gitta touched Caira's arm. "No one's complained, and all have faith in ye. Ye're the laird's daughter, after all." The woman gently squeezed. "But I can see the fatigue weighing your shoulders and the worry etching lines in yer face. 'Twould be good to share yer problems with a mon."

"But my last husband was one of our problems."

"Aye, but not all men are so dishonorable."

Gitta opened her mouth, but before she could utter the words Caira knew she would say, Caira thrust the laundry stick at her. "I'll be checking the stores, then."

Caira caught sight of Brian as he entered the hall and took his seat between Malcolm and Callum. Thoughts of him had followed her around all day, distracting her from her work. Gitta had flashed her a knowing grin the third time Caira had counted the candles.

"Ach, he willna leave yer mind, will he?" the older woman cackled gleefully.

"You find joy in this, Gitta? We know naught about him. I would urge caution."

"Ah, lass. Ye should view him with yer heart, not yer head."

But hadn't she done that with Jamie Munro? He had captured her young heart when first she set eyes on him. Like a young ram, Jamie is, her father had said: strutting around collecting his ewes. But Caira had refused to listen to his advice. And where had that left her and the clan?

Though she might shake her questions off, she could not dislodge the thoughts of Brian's body from her mind, and of a union, and her gaze fell frequently upon the man as they dined.

With the remains of the meal cleared away, Caira stood. The room quieted. She looked down from the raised table at the expectant faces of her clan.

There had been little to look forward to in the last few months, so rumors of the storyteller had flown to every man, woman, and child within and without the walls of Kilbeinn. Although they'd worried about his sanity, the man was a chance for something new and different. Excitement hummed in the hall.

"The Skelley will now entertain us with a story," Caira called. She looked at Brian, arching a brow, silently challenging him to decline. He glanced from her to the eager gazes of those around him.

He took a swallow from his cup, fighting a grimace of distaste. The ale was atrocious. He cleared his throat and pushed to his feet, sending a glare to Caira, who sat down, smiling serenely.

All day he'd wracked his brain, trying to remember a story, any story, to tell. His welcome here could ride on his success tonight. Though he couldn't be certain, he figured he had to re-enter his own time from where he'd left it, so he had to make sure he stayed around. He didn't want to get fired from his job as storyteller.

"Tell us of a braw knight in battle."

Brian glanced at the man making the request, whose

wife elbowed him and shot him a glare. She called out, "Nay, a romance."

Romance, he snorted. *God spare him from chick flicks.*

That's it, he thought: *a movie.* Mentally, he thumbed through his collection of DVDs. He loved movies and had an extensive library of both old and new ones.

His love of movies went back to his childhood, sitting beside his mother in the darkened theater, munching popcorn, praying the movie would go on forever. But they always ended and Brian and his mother would return to the reality of his abusive father.

Pushing aside the memories, he thought of his favorites. *Star Wars,* he discarded. How the hell would he explain it? He needed a tale—a tale of knights and daring deeds.

He grinned.

Dragonheart.

He cleared his throat and looked at Malcolm. "There once was a knight named Sir Bowen, charged with teaching King Freyne's son, Einon, swordsmanship and the knights Olde Code of Honour. The king was a cruel monarch, given to killing dragons and the peasants of his realm. So Bowen's job to guide the young Einon was a difficult one."

Brian scanned his silent audience. Yup, this was a good choice. He continued with the tale, telling of the king's death at the hands of angry peasants, and how Einon went to his father's aid only to have a young woman accidentally push him against a blade, mortally wounding Einon.

"Bowen found his charge barely alive, and at the Queen's order, followed her to a cave where he put the boy on an altar.

"A deep voice echoed in the chamber. 'What brings you here, daughter of the Celts?' the voice demanded."

The room erupted into cheers and it took Brian a minute to realize why. Celts . . . Scots. Damn, but that was a stroke of luck.

He nodded, holding out his hands to quiet the room.

" 'Heal my son,' she begged."

He looked out over the people sitting at the tables and told them how the dragon in the cave gave part of his heart in exchange for a pledge that the boy would honor the Olde Code.

He told them of the cruel misdeeds of young King Einon and the breaking of the pledge; that one of the peasants the king killed was the father of the young woman from the village.

"King Einon earned Kara's hatred and she vowed vengeance against him."

Chuckles skittered around the room and Brian stopped, frowning as goosebumps prickled his arms. Caira. Kara. Damned strange coincidence, he thought. And it *was* a coincidence. Until the moment he said the character's name, he hadn't thought of it.

He glanced at Malcolm and Callum, meeting both men's grins.

Oh shit, they thought he'd done it on purpose. Was that bad? He shook his head. Who knew?

" 'Twas the English side that made the boy bad," Malcolm offered in a loud voice.

Brian picked up the story where Sir Bowen turned from his charge and abandoned the Olde Code. He vowed to kill every dragon, until one day he came upon Draco, the last living dragon. The fight ended in a draw and the two forged a friendship.

Brian glanced at Caira. She looked right at him, and he could tell from her unblinking gaze that her mind was on something else. He wondered what she was thinking about.

Continuing with the story, he told how Bowen renewed his vow to follow the knights Olde Code and how Kara helped to convince the peasants to rebel.

"Draco fell into King Einon's clutches. The king had learned of his connection to the dragon and vowed to keep it safe for all time, for as long as Draco lived, so lived Einon."

In a quiet voice, Brian told his audience how Einon killed his own mother when she tried to kill Draco to save the peasants from her son's cruel reign.

Gasps sounded around him, and he finished the story.

"Draco begged Sir Bowen to end the cruelty, and so the knight sent a blade into Draco's heart and the king and dragon died.

There before all, the dragon began to glow a shimmering golden color. A moment later, the glistening cloud swirled around, lighting the sky with a million new stars forming the shape of a dragon."

Brian heard a sniffle beside him and glanced at Malcolm as the old Scot wiped his nose on the sleeve of his shirt.

It started with a few thumps and then the entire hall filled with the sounds of people beating their hands on the tables.

*   *   *

Caira jerked from her reverie and met Brian's gaze. He tilted his head and arched a brow.

She had tried to concentrate on the story, but time and again, her attention had been captured by the quirk of an eyebrow, the glint of strong white teeth in the arresting smile of the storyteller, or the devilment that crossed his face. Caira had lost herself in the deep resonance of Brian's voice, hearing not the words, only the soothing tone as it washed over her.

She smiled, canting her head, and acknowledged his success with a nod. Smiles swathed the faces of the clan as they left the hall. It was a wondrous sight, she thought, to see her people happy—at least for the non.

As Caira made her way to the stairs, she saw the Widow Turner loop her arm through Skelley's. Pressing her ample chest against his arm, the widow turned a seductive smile upon him, saying something as they walked toward the door.

Skelley extracted his arm from her grasp and stood aside to let her and several others precede him from the hall.

Would she find warmth and comfort this eve in the arms of the stranger?

Caira climbed the stairs. She understood the widow's loneliness. She'd lost those she loved, and often the weight of loneliness settled in her heart.

At the top of the stairs, she glanced over her shoulder at the closed door, seeing again the widow and Skelley.

Worry edged out another emotion Caira refused to acknowledge. Would the woman keep her wits about her and protect the clan? It would be best if Caira visited her and cautioned against trusting the stranger.

Gitta joined her in her room just as Caira readied herself for bed.

" 'Twas an entertaining story, eh?" Gitta fixed her with a measuring look.

"Aye." Caira turned from the woman's gaze and pulled off her wimple. Folding it, she set it aside and took a seat on a stool.

"Ye heard not a word of it, did ye?"

"Of course I did." Ducking her head to hide the blush heating her cheeks, she took off her shoes and stockings.

"Hah. Ye couldna take yer eyes from the mon, and ne'er before have I seen such a dreamy look upon a lass's face." She chuckled.

"Gitta." Caira brought her head up. "I did not."

"The Skelley is a gifted storyteller. 'Tis a shame ye didna hear the story of the Dragonheart." Gitta took Caira's stockings, then helped her remove her tunic. "What so captured yer attention, lass? What were ye thinking about?"

Unwilling to admit her thoughts, Caira replied, "I've much on my mind, and well you know it. Being a woman and leading the clan is a heavy responsibility, Gitta. I pray for the strength and wisdom to keep the clan safe from the English threat. If I drift off at a story, it doesna mean I—"

"Ach, ye're right, lass. I shouldna be haranguing ye, eh?"

And while she braided Caira's hair, Gitta told her the story she'd missed.

When Gitta left, Caira stood by her window, staring

out at the night sky. 'Twas a wonderful story Brian had told, but with such a sad ending. Hadn't she enough of sad endings? She frowned.

Why had he chosen a story about dishonor? Surely it wasn't coincidence that the heroine's name was similar to hers? Did he seek to curry favor? But why?

Fatigue pressed down on her shoulders. The day had been long, and she was tired.

But as she slid between the linens, Brian's image flared in her mind. When he'd first started his tale, she wondered if he truly was a storyteller, so hesitant and uncomfortable was he with being the center of attention. But then, as the story progressed, he seemed to relax. She couldn't take her gaze from him, mesmerized by the excitement glittering in his eyes and the warmth of his voice as the tale unfolded.

She gave herself a mental shake. What was she doing? With jerky movements, she smoothed the bed linens and harrumphed.

He was no different from any other man, she told herself.

Aye, his shoulders were broader than most. His blue eyes seemed to see everything, his smile a gift that brightened the room. She would admit that the quiet sense of power and competence emanating from him intrigued her.

What would it be like to be sheltered within the protection of his arms and share the clan's burdens with him?

"Nay," she whispered to the darkness. "He is not like any other."

Chapter Eight

"He's daft," the cooper proclaimed. The buckets dangling from his arm thudded together, catching Caira's attention as she walked toward the village.

"Who's daft?"

"The Skelley." The cooper shifted his wares to his other arm and fell into step beside her. "He asked for an old bucket."

"And that's daft?" She arched a brow. "You are the cooper, you ken?"

He shot Caira a withering gaze. "Aye, but then he put holes in the bottom of it."

Caira stopped and stared at the man. "Holes in the bottom?"

"Aye. Now I ask ye, what good is a bucket with holes?" He shook his head. "Daft, I tell ye."

"Did he say what he wanted it for?"

"Nay, just asked where he could find the blacksmith."

The cooper turned toward the castle and walked away, still muttering to himself.

What did Skelley's strange request mean?

She would stop by Malcolm and Callum's cottage; mayhap he'd spoken with them. Could this strangeness in Skelley be the result of his accident?

She adjusted the basket on her arm and quickened her pace, eager to complete her errands and speak with Malcolm and Callum.

The Widow Turner greeted Caira as she approached the woman's cottage.

"Ach, Caira, 'twas a fine story the Skelley told last eve. Will he be telling another tonight?" The widow waved Caira into her home.

"I know not, Mistress Turner." Caira stepped into the dim interior. A fire burned low in the center of the room. The widow's three young daughters looked up from their work and smiled at her.

"Good morn, lasses," Caira said.

They giggled and bobbed their heads, returning to their work of sorting wool.

"He's fine-looking, is he not?" The widow smiled, looking past Caira, a dreamy expression on her face. " 'Tis good to have such a mon among us."

Caira found herself bristling at the woman's interest in Brian, but stopped herself from commenting.

"But I wonder," the widow continued, "that he chose a name so similar to yers for its heroine." She gave Caira a sly smile.

"Excuse me?" The comment caught her off guard.

"Does he court yer favor, or does he have it already?" The widow gave Caira a shrewd look.

"Mistress Turner!" Caira gasped. "I've no time for such foolishness." She reached into her basket and withdrew a small cloth sack. "My concern is for the clan. I care naught for Skelley." The lie fell from her lips and resounded in the small cottage.

The widow cast Caira a knowing look.

Caira defended herself: "The man is a stranger. We know naught of him. You would do well—"

The widow laughed. "I saw how ye watched him."

"Nay." The single word burst from Caira's lips as heat inched up her neck to her cheeks. "I but warn you so that we guard the secret. We canna trust anyone outside the clan."

The widow's smile faded and she nodded. "Aye, ye've the right of it." She met Caira's gaze. "But he's a handsome mon, is he not? With the strength to lead a clan."

First Gitta, now the widow. Caira harrumphed. "Do you have a complaint, then?"

"Whist, Caira." The widow touched her arm. "Ye've done well, but ye ken it would be a mon leading the clan if there were one to do it."

Caira took a deep, calming breath and shrugged. Widow Turner was right. The Mackenzie male population was made up of mostly young boys and old men. There were a few young men, but they had not the experience or temperament to lead a clan. Most had left when Caira's father agreed to the neutrality pact with Longshanks.

It had broken her da's heart to watch the men leave, some taking their families with them; others leaving them in safety at Kilbeinn. But the deed had been done, and her father could not go back on his word. He should not have agreed to neutrality without first consulting his men. It was that more than anything that drove them away.

The snap of a log in the fire pit broke into Caira's thoughts, recalling her to her purpose.

Handing a sack of herbs to the widow, Caira instructed, "Three pinches brewed in hot water will ease the tightness in yer chest." Pray God she had not misunderstood the directions in her mother's journal for mixing the infusion.

The widow took the bag.

"Mind that you do it first thing of a morn."

"My thanks, Caira."

Caira nodded and left the cottage, making her way through the village, stopping here and there to speak with her people.

She reached Malcolm and Callum's home and rapped on the door. It swung open to reveal a rumpled Callum.

"Ach, Caira, what brings ye to the village this morn?" He ran his hand through his uncombed hair, making clumps stand on end atop his head.

"Did you not sleep well last night?" Caira frowned, noting the dark circles beneath his eyes.

"Nay. Malcolm's snores near brought the roof down." He stepped back to allow her entrance to his home. "Tonight I'll send him to the stables if he starts it again."

Caira glanced around the single-room dwelling. Two narrow beds were placed against the walls, a small table with two stools arranged in a corner.

"What is this?" She walked to the corner opposite the table and fingered the fishing net slung between two wooden poles.

" 'Tis the Skelley's new bed."

Caira pulled her hand back from the net and turned to meet Callum's gaze. "His bed?"

Callum nodded. "Aye. If ye've an extra blanket or two, he could use them. We've none to spare." She read the rebuke in his tired gaze.

Turning back to the strange bed, Caira hid her mounting shame with a nod. "But, Callum, it canna be comfortable."

"Ach, Skelley says 'tis. Malcolm is convinced 'tis what he wants, too. 'Twill give us more room, now that there's three of us sharing this small space. And a dog."

"A dog?"

"Aye. Three-legs has taken a liking to Skelley. Follows him everywhere and sleeps beneath his bed." He nodded to the space below the hanging net.

Guilt seeped into Caira's soul at the reproach in Callum's voice.

"You ken why he canna stay in the castle?" She gripped her basket, arranging the cloth covering the loaf of bread she'd brought for the old Scots. *"We canna risk the clan,"* she repeated. She met Callum's gaze.

"Aye, lass. Ye're right." He sighed.

"Where is he?" The words were out before Caira could stop them.

Callum grinned, and Caira prepared herself for his comment. But none came. He just gave her a knowing look that was more frustrating than if he'd said what he was thinking.

"He's about somewhere."

Panicked, Caira said, "You've let him wander where he will?"

"Caira, we canna follow him everywhere. He'll know we're hiding something then. 'Twouldn't do to get his suspicions up."

What Callum said made sense.

"Besides, the clan knows to keep their own counsel."

Caira nodded and pulled the bread wrapped in cloth from the basket. "Here's a loaf of bread for you."

" 'Tis good of ye to bring it, lass."

She left Callum then, and started back to the castle. Crossing the inner bailey, she saw Malcolm come out of the stables.

"He's daft," Malcolm said as he reached her side, and she knew before she asked whom Malcolm spoke of.

"Who?"

"The Skelley."

"What's he doing that makes you think so?"

"He taking the dirt and dung from the stable floor." He frowned and asked, "Why would a mon do that?"

Caira shook her head. "I've no idea, Malcolm. Did you ask him?"

"Aye." He rubbed his bewhiskered chin. "Said it was fer . . ." He frowned, scratching his head. "Pot-ass-um-night-rate." He glanced at her. "Do ye ken what that is?"

Caira shook her head.

"Ach, well, no matter. He devised a remarkable bed this morn. Have ye seen it?"

"Aye."

"He let me try it out—'tis quite comfortable." Malcolm nodded. "I'm going to see if I can find another net. I think I'd like a bed like that, too." He walked off, talking to himself.

As Malcolm left, Caira caught a glimpse of Brian. The man was turning the corner of the keep.

Now what is he up to, she wondered, following him.

She found him with a stick, poking around the smoldering ashes of the laundry fire, flicking out bits of charred wood.

"What is it you search for?" Caira asked. She stepped in and around the clumps of burned wood.

Brian looked up, then back down at his task. "Carbon." He muttered the word, then flicked out yet another piece.

"And what will you do with it?"

He stopped his poking and met her gaze. "Try to make black powder."

She canted her head. "And what does this 'black powder' do?"

"Hopefully, it will send me back where I belong."

She started to ask him where he belonged, and how powder could accomplish such a feat, when Brian let out a curse, leapt over the ashes, and swept her up in his arms. With a squeak of surprise, Caira wrapped her arms around his neck. "What are you doing?"

In the next moment, she was on the ground, away from the burned-out fire, and Brian was tossing dirt on her skirts.

"You were on fire," he said. His eyes were a stormy blue as he gazed down at her in concern. "Are you okay?"

"Aye." She breathed the word, her gaze locked with his, her heart thumping with fear. Or was it something other than fear, she wondered as his eyes cleared.

He stood up, offering her his hand. When he enfolded her hand in his, a shock of warmth shot up her arm. He helped her to her feet, his grip gentle but firm.

Up close, she could make out the small gray flecks in his sky-blue eyes. Heat pooled low in her belly, and with her free hand, she grabbed his forearm, fearful her legs would weaken and she'd collapse in a puddle at his feet.

One eyebrow inched higher, but he didn't release her hand. "Are you sure you feel okay?"

Flustered, Caira pulled her hand from his and brushed the dirt clinging to her tunic. "I am well. My thanks, Skelley."

Nodding, he reached up, plucked a twig from her wimple, then turned back to the fire pit.

Caira took a deep breath, willing her nerves to calm, her heart to slow to its normal rhythm. As she watched him, Brian picked up the charred remains he'd tossed from the pit and placed them in a nearby bucket.

She glanced down at her singed tunic, clenching her fists to prevent the shaking that threatened to rattle down to her knees. She sucked in much-needed air and gathered her thoughts. Strength returned to her legs and she straightened her shoulders.

She cleared her throat, and Skelley turned around.

"You said the powder would send you back where you belong." She brought her chin up a bit. "Where is that?"

Skelley ran his hand through his hair, leaving black smudges near his hairline.

"I belong in . . ." He shook his head.

"The States?" Caira offered.

"Yeah."

"In which direction is your home?"

"Southwest."

Caira thought a moment. "Ach, then you're from Ireland." She smiled, relieved to have established that. "I've never met an Irishman before. And your home is the States." She canted her head. "But what of this black powder? How will it take you home?"

A muscle flexed in his jaw and he narrowed his gaze on her. "Listen, I don't know. Hell, I don't even know if I can make the stuff, let alone if it will work." He looked beyond her. "But I need time to find out." He fixed her with his eyes again, frustration and anger darkening their color to that of storm clouds. "Think you could give me that?" His voice was tight, controlled.

Caira nodded and turned, leaving him to his work.

Skelley was Irish, and the Irish had sided with Scotland against the English. That eased her fears. And he would be returning home soon.

The last thought brought an unexpected pain to her heart, leaving her to wonder at her feelings for him.

Well, she would simply put him from her mind. There was much to be done, and mooning over Skelley was not only unproductive, it was foolish in the extreme.

Brian heaved a sigh of relief as he heard Caira's footsteps recede. He'd acted on instinct when he saw her skirt brush an ember he'd tossed from the dying fire. But the feel of her in his arms stayed long after he'd put her down.

She was taller than the other women around, and

her body fit well to his. And when he'd helped her up, it had taken all his willpower not to kiss her.

But her questions had effectively cooled his ardor. That he'd let her assume he was from Ireland wasn't far from the truth; he had a grandmother from Ireland. He'd only met her once, but she'd left a lasting impression, pinching his cheeks and telling his mother she should leave his father. Thank God for Granny O'Donnell, she saved him from trying to explain the truth to Caira. Hell, *he* was having trouble understanding all this himself.

With luck, he'd get himself back to his own time, soon.

And then he remembered the warmth of Caira in his arms and he struggled to remind himself to keep his distance. She was the sort of woman he avoided. He knew instinctively that there was something in her calling to him. He'd felt the emotional pull immediately.

And he knew that a relationship with Caira would include a deep, committed friendship.

He'd had one of those and knew the pain of its loss.

Henry had been a brother to him. He'd been devastated when Henry chose to end the relationship by taking his life. Brian had lived with the nightmares and gone through the stages of grief. And the result of the experience . . . Brian never allowed himself to get attached. He never got close to anyone, male or female.

His hands shook as he picked up his bucket and headed back to Callum and Malcolm's cottage. He wouldn't get involved with Caira or anyone else here in Kilbeinn. He had to focus on making the black powder, and in getting himself back to his own time. There was no room in his life for involvement—especially with Caira.

Lord Whitcomb tossed the reins of his mount to the stablemaster and strode to the keep.

He snorted. The dismal place could hardly be considered comfortable—mayhap to the barbaric Scots, but not to a cultured Englishman.

The king had sent missives off to several of his lords. A meeting had been called, and for the last two days, they had discussed the problem of capturing Wallace. It was an important move to combine with the forces of other lords. None wished to lose favor with His Majesty, so Wallace must be found.

But that was proving impossible. No one had seen him. They'd taken Scots in and questioned them, but it would seem the rebel leader had simply disappeared.

Whitcomb mounted the steps, pushed open the door, and entered the hall. His nose wrinkled at the odor rising from the foul rushes covering the floor.

"Have these bloody things removed and burned in the morn!" he shouted to the roomful of soldiers who were setting up tables for the evening meal. " 'Tis bad enough we have to live among the heathens, we need not emulate their slovenly ways."

Not waiting for a response, he went to the room behind the screens at the end of the hall.

Smythe stepped around the screen. "What news have you, my lord?"

"None." Whitcomb slumped in a chair, pouring himself a cup of ale. " 'Tis as though Wallace simply vanished."

"Bloody Scots. They know where he is, but will not speak."

"What news of Castle Kilbeinn?"

"We found two old men with another man."

"And?"

"Nothing more. Though the younger man said Wallace is dead."

"Aye?" Whitcomb felt hope surge in his breast.

Smythe shook his head. "Said he'd been dead for a long time." He laughed. "Stupid Scots. As if we would believe their foolish stories. I told them to hie themselves back to their homes and they did."

"Hmph." Whitcomb nodded, feeling his hope die. "I shall make a visit to Laird Mackenzie soon. Mayhap I can cull some information about Wallace from him, or convince the man to keep his people in his village. I do not wish to be forced to watch our backs as well as tracking down that bloody rebel." He left the room, his companion following. "These bloody Scots seem to think they are smarter than we English. But I'll show them."

Chapter Nine

Caira stood beside the old Scots' cottage, mesmerized by the tantalizing sight of Brian's back clad in that close-fitting garment. His muscles flexed and rippled in a sensual masculine dance as he poured hot water slowly into the bucket.

Ach, to be his shirt and cling so lovingly to him.

The unbidden thought slid into her mind, and her fingers tingled at the prospect. Pulling her gaze away, Caira retraced her steps through the village, but the enticing thought followed.

Over the past three days she'd watched as Brian went about his business with a determined purpose, keeping to himself, and spending most of his time at the cottage.

She sighed, rubbing her hands on her skirt as she approached the gates of Kilbeinn. How much longer would he be at Kilbeinn?

"Ach, there ye are, Caira."

Caira looked up. "Did you have need of me, Callum?"

87

"Not me, but Gitta's been searching fer ye. Cook and the brewer are arguing again."

Another sigh escaped Caira's lips. The weight of her responsibilities rested heavily on her shoulders. Not only did she carry the duties of the laird of the clan, but those of the lady.

"Ye should turn the household duties over to Gitta, lass."

"Gitta has enough to do. I willna add to her burden."

Callum placed his big hand on her shoulder. "Mayhap ye should find yerself a husband."

Caira snorted. "What? And who would you have me wed—you or Malcolm?"

Callum turned his shocked gaze on her, and she swallowed a chuckle. "Or would you have me wed the stable lad?" Her laughter faded, and she frowned. "Dinna fret over me, Callum."

"I canna help it, lass. All the worries will make ye old afore yer time." Callum shifted his feet. "Mayhap if ye had a husband to take the reins of the clan . . ."

"What, Callum?" Frustration lent a challenging edge to Caira's voice.

"Well, mayhap the Mackenzie men who left to join the rebellion would return."

She snorted indelicately. "Aye, and bring the destruction the rest of Scotland is suffering with them? They are considered outlaws now. Their return would spell our doom." Caira stopped in the middle of the road and stared at Callum. "My father risked all to protect this clan from the ravages of war. He'd seen enough of the hardships other clans suffered. He saw how the lairds wouldna ban together to fight against the English invasion, and he knew separate factions would be easily destroyed by Longshanks. 'Twould mean the end of Scotland, would mean the end of us Mackenzies." She shook her head. "And then what, Callum?"

The old man's shoulders slumped, and a worried frown puckered his forehead. "Ach, ye're right, Caira. But I would see you wed again just the same." He met her gaze. " 'Tis the way it should be."

Caira's anger melted away at his concern. "Well, if you can find a Scot who's neither too old nor too young, healthy, intelligent, not difficult to look upon, and strong enough to gain the clan's respect and lead them to peace, then bring him to me." She gave the old warrior a nod and then continued on to the castle.

There was not a Scot for leagues of Kilbeinn with such qualifications, though. She'd set an impossible task for Callum, and that was just as she wanted. She had no need of another husband. Leading the clan, while sometimes difficult, could be done by a woman. She was sure of it.

Yet it would seem the clan did not share her opinion.

Putting the problem from her mind, she focused her thoughts on how to bring peace between Cook and the brewer. That was trouble enough for the non.

She's gone, Brian thought as Caira's footsteps receded and his heart slowed. No matter where he went these last few days, he felt her gaze on his back. Awareness of her hummed through his body, and thoughts of her interrupted his work.

Setting his empty bucket aside, he checked to make

89

sure the water soaked through the muck he'd taken from the stables. A slow stream of foul-looking liquid drained out the holes in the bottom of the container and flowed into the catch bucket. The odor of wet hay, horse dung, and urine made his eyes water. He stood up, satisfied with his progress.

While Caira had been watching him these past few days, he'd also watched her. She usually came across as competent and decisive. But was he the only one who saw the uncertainty that occasionally crossed her face? The villagers and those in the castle relied on her for every decision. From the tired slump of her shoulders, he knew the responsibilities weighed heavily on her.

He'd seen the same reaction in women of his time. In order to prove themselves in a male-dominated environment, they tried to do it all without help from anyone.

Where were the men in her life? Hell, where were the men of the clan? He'd seen only a handful of boys, a few youngsters, and the geriatric.

Where was Caira's father? Out fighting?

He'd have to ask Callum about that.

No, he reminded himself; his only mission was to make the black powder and get himself back where he belonged—not to get involved with Caira or the Mackenzies.

Focusing on the task at hand, Brian checked the contents of the iron pot he'd placed over a small fire and added a few pieces of fuel. He sat on a stump and began grinding the charred wood he'd taken from the laundry fire.

The image of Caira, a ribbon of smoke spiraling up

from her skirt, popped into his mind. He'd reacted as he would in any emergency. The jolt of fear he'd felt was normal. And so was the way his heart pounded.

Yeah, right, buddy, a voice in his head laughed.

Damn it, don't go there. Concentrate on the mission.

Blocking out everything else, Brian focused on making the black powder. He'd acquired enough of the ingredients to do a few tests. But he knew it would take more than a few tries to get it right. There could be problems with the components he'd made, or he might get the ratio of sulfur to carbon to potassium nitrate wrong. This would be a process of mixing and making notes.

As he set the ground-up charcoal aside, he thought about what was going on in the twenty-first century. Surely, his other students had heard the blast. Brian wondered, not for the first time, what they'd thought when they couldn't find him—or at least pieces of him.

And then he thought of Lawrence. Was the Brit in a hospital somewhere in the twenty-first century? Or had the blast killed him?

Or, another possibility, was he, too, wandering around somewhere in medieval Scotland? Brian shook his head. There was no evidence Lawrence had traveled with him. He was certain of that. Wasn't he?

There was no way of knowing the truth until he got back to his own time.

Using a wooden spoon he'd taken from the castle kitchen, he measured out some of the ground charcoal into one bowl, the sulfur from another, and the saltpeter from the largest bowl.

Pulling a small notepad and pencil from the leg

pocket of his cammies, he wrote down the amounts he'd used and returned the pad and pencil to his pocket. After emptying the bowl of black powder onto a square of cloth, he tied the ends together and covered the other bowls. He returned them to the cottage, stashing them beneath the blanket in his hammock. Grabbing his shirt, he slipped it on, buttoning it as he opened the door of the cottage.

Poking his head out, he checked to make sure no one was around before stepping outside. He preferred not to run into any of the villagers. He'd received enough of their strange looks since he got here. What would they think if they caught him testing the powder?

And what if they wanted to use it against the English and it hadn't been introduced to England yet? His steps faltered.

Could one person actually change history?

"Shit." As if he didn't have enough to worry about. Well, he'd just have to make sure it stayed his secret.

Patting his shirt pocket, he felt the book of matches he'd taken from one of the soldiers before the drill. He shook his head. It didn't take a rocket scientist to know you shouldn't have any flame-producing devices around explosives. It surprised him how many students forgot that little piece of information.

He found a likely clearing far enough away from the village that, if the powder worked, no one but he would know.

As he got things ready, adrenaline surged through his blood. He hadn't made black powder since high school, and then he'd done it with the help of Henry. It had been his friend's intense curiosity that propelled the experiment. Any failures had only fueled Henry, making him more determined.

Too bad Henry wasn't here for this.

It would be a miracle if the first batch worked.

"Miracles seem to be in short supply these days," he muttered an hour later as a puny spiral of smoke floated up from the thin, shallow line of black powder he'd ignited.

"Back to the drawing board," he decided, stuffing the matches back into his pocket and shaking out the cloth, now empty of the first batch of powder.

This was going to be time-consuming, he realized. Just what he didn't have; a lot of time. For some undefinable reason, he felt the need to return quickly, afraid that the longer he stayed the more difficult it would be to get back to the twenty-first century.

It didn't make sense, but there it was. He returned to the cottage, checked on the contents of the bucket, and then grabbed the bowls from his hammock and returned to the woods.

It was going to take trial and error to get the right mixture. He just hoped he'd prepared the sulfur and saltpeter correctly.

Caira skirted a stand of trees, her gaze focused on the ground as she searched for herbs to replenish her stores. This was the only thing she'd paid attention to when her mother had tried to teach her the healing arts.

She loved wandering the woods. It had been easy to learn to recognize the different trees, flowers, and herbs growing wild. It wasn't so easy to remember which herbs did what and how to prepare them.

That lack of knowledge had cost Caira's mother her life. If only Caira had been the dutiful daughter and learned.

Movement to her left caught her attention. The pounding of her heart drove out the depressing thoughts, replacing them with fear.

Crouching behind a cluster of bushes, she held her breath, listening. Was it an animal she'd glimpsed, or something else?

Birds chirped overhead and a light breeze sighed through the boughs of the trees, rustling the leaves. No other sound reached her ears.

Cautiously, she leaned out, searching for more movement, and through the foliage she spied Brian. He was crouched down, his head bent. His garments blended so well with the surroundings, she had difficulty distinguishing him from the trees and bushes.

Relief eased her fear, and she pulled air into her lungs. She watched him a moment, then frowned.

What was he doing? She moved from her hiding place toward him.

"Have you lost something?" she asked, nearing him. She noticed several bowls set off to one side and a noxious odor floating in the air. He hunkered over a shallow hole with a black substance in the bottom.

He came to his feet in one fluid motion, spinning to face her and blocking her view.

"What are you doing here?"

His question took her aback. She met his direct gaze and arched her brow. "Have you forgotten this is Mackenzie land? And I am a Mackenzie."

She craned her neck to see what he tried to hide. He leveled a quelling gaze at her.

"I know where I am and who you are."

"Then I'll ask you the same question you asked of me." She gripped her basket of herbs a little tighter to calm the sudden shaking of her limbs. "What are *you* doing here?"

Turning from her, he didn't answer immediately. He stacked his bowls and picked them up; then, using his foot, he pushed dirt into the hole and tamped it down. "Trying to get home."

"Home?" She looked from the bowls in his arms to his eyes. "Surely you jest?" She nodded to his burden. "Those wee bowls will see you home?" She chuckled. "Would not a boat serve you better?"

A picture of him sailing off flashed in her mind, and a sudden, tightness wrapped around her heart.

'Tis best, she reminded herself.

"If only a boat *could* take me back," he muttered, starting down the path toward the village.

She followed. "Well, mayhap you need to ride to the coast, but after that, 'tis not so far."

He glanced over at her. "Oh, yes it is," he cut her off. "It's far." He turned his gaze back to the path. "Unbelievably far away. Like a few lifetimes."

Frowning, Caira touched his arm, and heat seared her fingers. "You ken that your words make no sense." Her voice quavered, and she snatched her hand back.

"Lady, nothing makes sense anymore." From his cool gaze, Caira was certain he hadn't reacted to their contact as she had.

Well, that was fine, she thought, switching her basket to her other hand. She stepped around a rock in the path, using the opportunity to put a little more distance between them.

When they reached Callum and Malcolm's cottage, he gave her a curt nod and disappeared inside, leaving her standing on the road and gazing at the closed door.

"Jesus, Mary, and Joseph," Caira mumbled. "That mon talked such nonsense." She was sorely tempted to bang on the door, demanding an explanation, but it would be dangerous to be so close to him . . . alone in the cottage with her desires.

Brian stood in the dim cottage, straining to hear any noise outside the door. He wasn't having much luck getting in the last word with Caira, and he didn't expect this time to be any different. He recalled a sign he'd seen in a sailor bar in San Diego: "Never argue with a woman: just dicker."

He chuckled. Seemed that bit of beer-joint wisdom transcended the ages.

After a long moment, he was rewarded with the light crunch of gravel, the sound receding until it was quiet again.

He let out his breath, surprised that he'd held it.

If Caira had barged into the cottage, he wasn't positive he could have kept his hands off her. The breeze had rippled the edges of the thing hiding her hair and he'd had a hell of a time controlling the urge to strip it off and find out exactly how long and what color her locks were.

He shook the image from his mind.

Maybe he should be using the saltpeter to curb his desires. He'd heard it acted as an anti-aphrodisiac. But then he remembered where it came from, and he decided he'd do better to just keep his distance from Caira.

One thing was sure:

She was more dangerous than black powder.

Chapter Ten

"So, Brian, what are ye making?" Malcolm hovered over his shoulder as he set the pot of liquid over the fire.

"Just keeping busy." Malcolm had dogged his steps all day, making it even harder to get the new black powder ready to test.

"Doin' what?" He was like an inquisitive kid, Brian thought as he stepped around the old man for the hundredth time.

"Experimenting." He glanced at Malcolm. "Know what I mean?"

"Oh, aye." The man nodded, gazing down at the pot over the fire and frowning. "Ye're experimenting."

Brian stifled a chuckle, turning his back so the man wouldn't see his grin. Malcolm didn't have a clue. The old Scot would die before admitting he didn't know what Brian was talking about.

"Well, then." Malcolm turned from the fire, wrinkling his nose at the noxious smell rising with the steam from the pot. "Tonight ye must tell us of Wallace."

Brian groaned. "Malcolm."

But the old Scot ignored the warning note in his voice and said, "Not that we didna enjoy the knight's tale of last eve. 'Twas a wondrous tale—how the squire took his knight's place and ended up being knighted himself by the Prince and then beating the Black Knight in the joust." Malcolm rubbed his whiskers. "But I'd rather hear of Wallace and his deeds. Ye ken, his story will be of more interest."

Brian just shook his head, sat down on a stump, and picked up the bowl of charcoal he'd been pulverizing with a smooth stone. Three-legs trotted up. Brian reached out to pat the dog's head, but the beast promptly stuck his nose in the bowl and then swiped his tongue across Brian's cheek.

"Three-legs, you need a girlfriend," he said. The critter wagged its tail and its tongue shot out again. Brian leaned away. "No kisses."

Bringing his arm up, Brian wiped his cheek on the sleeve of his shirt and coughed. Damn, he needed to wash his clothes—he sniffed—and his body.

"What are ye doing *there*?" Malcolm appeared before Brian, staring at the contents of his bowl.

"Listen, if I agree to tell a story about Wallace tonight, will you leave me in peace for the rest of the day?" About now, he'd agree to almost anything, even another story, if Malcolm would just go away. With the old Scot's constant yammering, he couldn't concentrate on preparing the next batch of black powder.

And with the failures of the past days, he really needed to focus on the job at hand.

Somehow he felt that time was progressing without him in the future, and that his chance of returning diminished as the day approached for his commissioning. There was no logic to the thought, but right now logic had nothing to do with anything. And he had only a week left.

"Oh, aye." Malcolm grinned. "Ye should tell of Wallace. Callum and I should be walking Nessie and Bridget this morn, anyway. 'Tis been a few days, and they need their exercise."

Brian glanced up as Malcolm walked away.

"Why don't you just *ride* them?" he asked. It had bothered him from the start.

Malcolm turned, a comical look of horror on his face. "Ye canna ride Nessie or Bridget. Have ye seen their legs? They're not like Highland ponies, ye ken? The hills of the Highlands would snap their wee, skinny legs in two—especially with the weight of a braw Scot on their backs." He shook his head. "Callum and me are real careful to guide them and keep them safe." He started to turn away, but stopped. "English mounts are used to carrying puny English soldiers, not braw Scots fighters."

Brian nodded, fighting off another grin until Malcolm left. Then he chuckled with all his might.

"The laird isna here at the moment." Caira pushed her fear aside, lest the English soldier see it in her eyes. "He's gone hunting." She raised her voice, praying that Malcolm and Callum would hear and remain in the stables until the English patrol left.

The man's eyebrows rose. "Hunting?"

She nodded.

"And wasn't he hunting the last time I was here?" Suspicion darkened the man's gaze, and Caira swallowed.

"Nay. He was helping one of the farmers."

"Where does he hunt?"

She gave him a withering glance. "Wherever the game is found, I would think. But since the English have over-hunted the woods, 'tis more difficult."

His eyebrows beetled in a frown. "Don't be impertinent, woman." He stepped closer to her, but Caira straightened her shoulders, refusing to give ground.

"Then dinna be asking silly questions." When his eyes narrowed, she bit the inside of her lip, cursing her sharp tongue.

"Then I guess I'll be returning later, won't I?"

Caira shrugged, controlling the shiver his greasy threat provoked.

"What is it you need to speak with him about? Mayhap I can save you the trip."

He laughed. "Oh, I don't mind the trip." He reached out a dirty hand and ran his index finger down the side of her cheek. She jerked away, glaring at him. He laughed again as he returned to his horse. Taking the reins from one of the men, he turned to her, raking her from wimple to hem with his eyes. "I'll return." He gazed up at the keep, and when he again focused on her, his eyes were cold and calculating. "And he'd best be here, or . . ." His threat hung in the air as he mounted and rode off through the gates.

Caira sagged against the wall of the keep. She rubbed at her cheek, bile burning its way up her throat. She blinked against the tears blurring her vision.

The laird had best be here. Hah! Do the bloody English think we should sit around awaiting their arrival?

Despair blended with her fear.

Dear God in heaven, what was she to do now? She was running out of excuses for her father's absence.

Did the English suspect the truth? Would he report his suspicions to the lord at Garethmuir?

Callum and Malcolm appeared at her side. "Do ye think he knows?" Callum asked, gazing from her to the gate.

"I know not." She followed Callum's gaze. "But I canna keep this up. And I dinna know what to do."

"Is there aught we *can* do?"

She turned and met the old Scot's gaze, filled with loving concern. Tears burned the back of her throat, despair curdled her stomach. She shook her head, not trusting her voice.

" 'Tis a good thing the Sassenach left when he did—I was about to relieve him of his head." Malcolm bristled, squinting toward the gate and the departed Englishman.

"With that rusty piece of metal ye call a sword?" Callum scoffed.

"Are ye saying I couldna do it, Callum? For if ye are, I wouldna mind demonstrating."

Caira held up a hand. "Please, Malcolm, you're a braw warrior, but lopping off the head of an English willna solve our problem."

"Aye, but 'twould be most satisfying."

Caira nodded distractedly. Stepping around the men, she entered the keep, worry eating at her insides.

"What are we to do?" Callum watched Caira disappear inside the castle. "Did ye see? The lass is near to tears with the worry."

"Aye."

Silence fell as they walked across the inner bailey, Caira's worry reflecting on the faces of all the people they passed.

"Do ye think we should tell Skelley?" Callum asked. He and Malcolm were headed back to their cottage. "Mayhap he could find a solution."

"Caira needs a husband, Callum," Malcolm said.

Callum stopped in the middle of the road. "Now, where did that thought come from?" He shook his head and started walking again. "Ask ye one thing and ye answer with a thought snatched out of the air."

"Ye mentioned asking fer Skelley's help."

"Aye," Callum cautiously replied. "But has one aught to do with the other?"

"So ye dinna think she should marry?"

"Aye, but—"

"Well, do ye not think Skelley would be a good laird?"

Callum frowned. "What makes ye think he would?" He gave his longtime friend a disgusted look. " 'Sides, Caira'd never marry him."

"Well, he's one of Wallace's men. That alone should speak well of him." Malcolm glanced around and edged closer to Callum. "And have ye not seen the looks they give each other?" He grinned. "I can hear

103

the sizzle and pop from the heat of 'em."

"What ye're seeing, Malcolm, isna attraction, but rather—"

"Ach, how can ye say that?" Malcolm interrupted. "Have ye not seen the way her cheeks turn all red. And she *watches* him."

Callum pulled on his earlobe, thinking over what his friend said. He'd seen the looks Malcolm was talking about, but they weren't exchanged looks. Nay— he shook his head—those were looks cast without each other's knowledge.

" 'Twould solve one of our problems," Malcolm suggested, intruding on Callum's musings.

"Which problem?"

"If Longshanks learns of the death of both the laird and Caira's husband, she'll already be wed. He willna be able to force an Englishman on her."

"Aye, but would Longshanks honor the old laird's agreement?"

"If not, then we fight."

"Malcolm, look around ye, mon. Do ye see a fighting force within the walls of Kilbeinn? They've all gone. We couldna hope to win."

"Have ye forgotten? Skelley is a warrior of Wallace. He could call upon the mon to help us."

Callum shook his head. "Ye're daft, if ye think the Wallace has time to aid us. He's a price on his head, and he has battles of his own he's likely planning."

"So, what? Ye think we should just sit back and let the bloody Sassenach take our land?"

"Nay, Malcolm." Callum lowered his voice. "But ye put too much faith in the stranger. What if he doesna want to wed Caira? Or aid the clan against the English?" He met Malcolm's gaze. "What if he's *allied* with the English? What if he's not one of Wallace's men? We've still not seen any proof."

"Ye're a fool, Callum. Did ye not see how he stood up to those soldiers days ago? Did ye see the look in his eyes? He was angry. I saw the way he took note of those men. Cool as a loch he was. Aye, he's the stuff to lead our clan and marry our Caira."

Callum watched Malcolm enter their cottage. He walked around the back, deep in thought.

Malcolm had a point, he realized, his gaze scanning the woods behind his home. There was something he'd not thought of: Longshanks being able to force an unmarried Caira to wed one of his kind.

Which would mean the end of the clan.

Three-legs raced off through the woods, and Callum watched him go. Mayhap Malcolm wasna so daft.

Skelley wasn't easily angered, and Callum liked his quiet confidence. The clan had mostly accepted him, enjoying his stories the other night. But would they accept his leadership? Bloody hell, would Skelley want it?

"Three-legs, stay." Brian flattened his palm in front of the dog's face. The animal was more curious than either of the old Scots, and he was afraid the dog would get hurt nosing around the black powder.

Three-legs plopped his butt down and thumped his tail on the ground, a cloud of dust swishing in the air behind him.

Brian stepped over to the thin line of black powder in the center of the path, crouched down, struck a match, and dropped it. It sparked and then sizzled, and a thin trail of smoke followed the path of the burning powder.

"We're close, buddy, damned close." He grinned at the dog, whose tail swished wildly back and forth, his pink tongue hanging out the side of his mouth. He rubbed Three-legs's head.

"Are ye a Scot?"

Brian jerked around. "Damn it, Callum. You shouldn't sneak up on a man like that."

He bent down and gathered up his supplies. He was so close. Another couple attempts and he felt certain he'd have the mixture just right. But he couldn't very well continue with the old man hovering over his shoulder.

"Well?"

Three-legs barked and brushed by. The bowls wobbled in Brian's grasp, and the top one teetered and fell. He swore, then put them down and lifted the upturned one. Sulfur had spilled over the edges of the cloth that covered the bowl, but luckily a good deal of it was on top of the material. Carefully, he lifted the corners of the cloth and poured it back into the bowl.

"What have ye there?"

Brian stacked the bowls and stood up, cradling them against his chest. "Nothing." He finally responded to Callum's question.

"Mayhap ye should put yer powders into bags."

"I would if I had some."

"I could find ye bags if ye need 'em."

Brian glanced at Callum, reading the calculating look in the older man's gaze.

"Yeah, and what would it cost me?"

"Just the answer to a question."

106

"Right." It couldn't be that simple, he thought. "What's the question?"

"Are ye Scot?"

Brian narrowed his gaze. "Partly." What was Callum up to?

"What do ye mean, partly?"

"I think there's some Irish as well." Hell, he had no idea of his exact heritage, except the Scot on his father's side and the Irish on his mother's.

"Irish?" Callum tugged on his ear, a frown drawing lines on his forehead. "Ye'll do, then," he stated with a nod.

"Do for what?"

"What?" Callum looked up.

"I'll do for what?"

"Ach, umm . . . Ye'll just do." The old man started walking off. "I'll get ye the bags. How many do ye need?"

Brian caught up with him. "Four."

"Aye, then."

An uneasy feeling crept over Brian as he walked beside the silent Callum. The old Scot was planning something, but Brian had no idea what. Or why it was important whether he was Scottish or not.

"So, have ye family?"

Callum's question came out of the blue, catching Brian off guard.

"Not much of one."

"What's that mean?"

"I don't have any brothers or sisters. My father's dead, my mother's alive." He met Callum's steady gaze.

"Ye dinna have a close relationship with yer mum?"

Brian snorted. "No." He'd been close to her as a child, but when his father died, she'd distanced herself from him. Brian always thought it was because of their physical resemblance. His father had been a bully, verbally abusing his mother and him whenever he was home. He'd spent most of his free time at the bar, though, which had afforded some relief. Brian couldn't understand why his mother hadn't shared his relief when his father died. Of course, he couldn't understand why she'd put up with his treatment in the first place.

He shrugged. With him in the Navy and moving around so much, the most he'd been able to do was call her occasionally. That didn't make for a close relationship with anyone.

"Ye've no other family?" Callum asked.

Brian glanced at him, putting thoughts of his mother aside. "No. Why?"

"Just wondering." Callum nodded to Three-legs, bouncing ahead of them with his odd tripod gait. "Never seen Three-legs so happy." He glanced at Brian. "Ye call him something different sometimes, eh? I've heard ye."

"Tripod." The dog heard his alternate name and came racing back to Brian, his tail swishing side to side.

"Aye. Tripod. What does it mean?"

Brian reached down and patted the dog, who then ran ahead. "Three legs."

Callum nodded.

Tripod reached the cottage and plopped down beside the door, his head resting on his front paw.

"No wife or bairns?"

"What?"

Callum stopped beside the cottage. "No wife or babes?"

Brian shook his head.

"Well, then, that's good." The old man grinned and ambled off toward the castle. "I'll bring ye them sacks."

Brian stared after him, wondering just what those sacks were going to cost him. He had a feeling it'd be more than he'd bargained for.

Chapter Eleven

"The bloody Sassenach rode into Kilbeinn as if he owned it."

"He touched her cheek, and 'twas all I could do not to run the bastard through with my sword."

Brian's step slowed as he made his way across the great hall, catching snatches of conversation. Tension hung in the air, and several people glanced at him with wary eyes.

"Do ye think he knows—" The speaker broke off as Brian passed by to take his seat for the meal.

"Not yet, but Caira canna keep it a secret much longer."

Brian heard the whispered reply and wondered, *What secret?*

Scanning the room, his gaze fell on Caira, who descended the stairs. He watched her glide down the steps, her body taut, her face a mask of control.

What the hell was going on?

"Ach, there ye are." Malcolm looked up at Brian's arrival.

"Yeah, here I am." Brian sat down, his gaze locked on Caira. He started to ask Malcolm what was going on, but clamped his jaw shut.

No, he reminded himself, he wasn't going to get involved.

Tripod nudged his leg, and he reached down and scratched the dog's ear.

He still had work to do on the black powder. And he had to figure out how to blow himself back to the present without killing himself. He was too close to getting back where he belonged—no way would he get involved in these people's lives. He'd be leaving soon . . . he hoped.

The meal followed the same pattern as usual. At the end, with the tables cleared, Malcolm stood, calling for everyone's attention.

"The Skelley will tell of William Wallace this eve!" he called out.

"What the—"

"Ye agreed," Malcolm challenged.

Brian scanned the hall, every face turned to him expectantly. He'd forgotten about their conversation. He stood up, took a swallow of ale, cleared his throat, and thought back to the opening scenes of *Braveheart*.

"William Wallace was the youngest of two sons," he began. Silence filled the hall as he continued with the story.

"Is he a braw, handsome mon?" one of the women called out.

"Well, yeah. I guess so." Hell, trust a woman to want to know that.

"Can ye tell us what he looks like, then?"

Brian scratched his temple. "Well, he's shorter than

I am, with dark hair." What else was there to say, he wondered as he met the gaze of one of the women. "The lasses all think he's good-looking. . . ."

He got a good reaction. Clearing his throat, Brian decided to trust *Braveheart* completely. What could it hurt? He continued with the story.

Gasps filled the room when he came to the killing of William's wife.

"Bloody bastards!" One Scot stood up, his face twisted with hatred. He met Brian's gaze. "Tell me Wallace avenged her death."

Brian nodded, and the man sat down.

"Wallace killed the man just as his wife had been killed. He tied the English lord to a post and slit his throat." A roar of approval rolled through the clan.

"And that's how Wallace was drawn into the Scots' fight for freedom."

Hands slapped the tabletops. Glancing down, Brian met Malcolm's approving gaze.

"I knew ye was one of his men." The old man beamed up at him.

"Malcolm, I keep telling you—I don't know Wallace, and I'm sure as hell not one of his men."

Malcolm straightened on his bench. "I admire ye fer protecting him this way."

Callum spoke up as Malcolm and Brian joined him and the villagers leaving the feast. "We'll be needing to muck Nessie and Bridget's stalls in the morn. Best we get some sleep."

Malcolm waved cheerily and followed the others out. Several of the men came up to thank Brian for the story.

"Ye'll be telling us more of Wallace tomorrow eve,

aye?" one man asked as another slapped Brian on the back. "Wallace is a braw warrior for Scotland, and we're honored to have one of his amongst us."

"But I'm not—"

"Ach, Malcolm said as how ye couldna admit to it— that ye're protecting the mon. 'Tis an honorable thing ye do Skelley."

As the men left, Brian looked up in time to see Caira. She was climbing the stairs. At the top, she glanced at him and their gazes caught. Her lips tilted in a smile, and she nodded before disappearing around the corner.

Had his story lifted her mood? Did she believe the nonsense about Wallace and him? For reasons he didn't want to know, it was important she knew the truth—at least about that.

He helped to dismantle the tables and move the benches against the wall for those who would sleep in the hall, then turned and headed for the cottage with Tripod as company.

"Well, buddy, we'd better get a move on if we want to get home before dark."

Home.

What the hell was he thinking? He wasn't home. He shook his head, trying to remember that. He had one goal and one goal only: to return to his own time.

With Malcolm and Callum busy in the morning, he would have a few uninterrupted hours to experiment, and hopefully make his first attempt to leave this place.

He picked up a stick and threw it. Tripod loped after it, and a pinprick of pain hit Brian's heart as the dog returned and dropped a rock in front of him. He tried to convince himself that he felt nothing for these people, but his conscience laughed.

"Keep your eye on the mission," he reminded himself aloud.

But Caira's worried face came to mind, and Brian wondered what kind of secret she guarded.

He reached down and patted Tripod's head as they walked on. "Yup, Tripod, time for me to get the hell out of here. It's none of my business what's going on. My job is to get back where I belong."

He heard Malcolm and Callum talking as he neared their cottage.

"Well, we have to do something. If the Sassenach finds out the laird is dead, he'll bring his bloody soldiers to Kilbeinn and murder us all."

"And if Longshanks learns that Caira is a widow, he'll likely marry her to one of his nobles."

Brian pushed open the door, and the men turned with a start. Brian simply nodded and went to his hammock.

" 'Twas a fine tale ye told tonight," Callum said. "Seems ye're a good storyteller."

"Were ye with Wallace when he killed the mon responsible for his wife's death?" Malcolm asked.

Brian took off his shirt and boots and stretched out on his hammock. Sighing, he said, "No, I wasn't with Wallace. I've never been with the man. I don't know him." He closed his eyes.

"He still says he isna one of Wallace's men." Brian opened one eye to see Callum glaring at Malcolm.

"Well, what did ye expect? He'll not put Wallace or himself at risk," Malcolm whispered.

The old men settled in their beds and the room went quiet.

So that's why Caira was so nervous, Brian realized as the old men's conversation played in his mind. With her father dead and the English breathing down her neck, she was in a hell of a predicament. And the English could prey upon that kind of situation.

He remembered the English patrol he and the two Scots had met that first day, and his stomach knotted. Cruelty was evident in the tightness of the sergeant's mouth and cold glare of his gaze. And then there was the more obvious proof of their evil: the physical intimidation of two old men by five young ones.

Over the last few days, Brian had wondered where all the Mackenzie men were—shouldn't there be soldiers manning the castle? There were some villagers, but they didn't seem trained to fight. What would happen to the Mackenzies if the English decided to attack? And what was keeping the English from it?

It had to have something to do with Caira's father. Had he been feared by the English? Or was it something— He caught himself in midthought.

Why the hell was he worried about it? He shifted in his bed. It wasn't as if he could do anything.

Yet his conscience nagged him to at least try.

No, he countered; he was leaving. He wouldn't let himself get drawn into these Mackenzies' problems. It was none of his business.

He rose with the sun.

"Tripod, you have to stay here." He tied the dog to a tree behind the cottage, a bowl of water placed within reach.

115

Tripod whined.

"You're safer here," Brian said. The dog sat, giving him a look that showed he felt betrayed.

His damned conscience prodded him. Reaching inside his pocket, Brian withdrew a chunk of bread and gave it to the beast.

Then, gathering up his supplies and checking his pocket for matches, he set off.

While working on the black powder, Brian had thought over what he needed to do. Early on, he'd come to the conclusion that if a blast had sent him back in time, it would take another to send him forward. Following that line of reasoning, he figured he'd need to be in the same place, too.

He reached the spot where Callum and Malcolm had found him. Sitting down on a nearby boulder, Brian consulted his notes from the day before and measured out the black-powder ingredients into the bowl.

He stepped away from the rock. Dragging the heel of his boot in the ground, he made an indentation. He poured some powder into it, then tossed a lit match into the powder. This time he got a little more smoke.

The book of matches wasn't going to last forever, he realized as he went back to his bags of ingredients. Gathering up kindling, he started a small fire he ringed with rocks. That would help.

As the day wore on, his frustration level rose, and doubts crowded out everything else. What if he'd prepared the saltpeter wrong? What if the sulfur wasn't pure enough?

What if, what if?

And how much of an explosion did he need to create if his black powder did work?

Gritting his teeth, he fought to hold on to what remained of his patience as he wrote down the ratios of the newest batch he'd tested.

"So what's yer plan, Malcolm?" Callum settled Bridget in her stall. "We canna *order* Skelley to wed Caira."

"Shh." Malcolm glanced around the stable. "They just need a wee nudge in the right direction," he whispered over the back of his horse.

"And how are we to 'nudge' them?"

"I'm not sure, but we'll come up with something."

The two men left the stable and found Caira bent over a large pot outside the kitchen.

Malcolm and Callum both looked at each other and wrinkled their noses. "Soap," they said in unison, and turned away before Caira spotted them.

Once out of sight, Malcolm heaved a sigh of relief. " 'Tis woman's work, soapmaking. 'Twould be nice if Caira understood that."

Callum agreed. "Near broke my back the last time. Ye managed to get away before she saw ye, so it was me who had to do the stirring."

"Let's hie ourselves home and try to figure out how to bring Caira and Skelley together. There's a pitcher of ale waiting fer us."

As they reached their cottage, they heard a pitiful whining. They followed the sound around to the side of their home.

"Do ye ken why Tripod is tied up?" Malcolm glanced from the dog, curled up beneath the tree, peering at them with his sad brown eyes, to Callum.

"Mayhap Brian's tired of being bothered by him?"

"But where'd he get off to?"

"Who's to say." Callum untied the dog and went back to the front of the cottage. He opened the door, and Tripod rushed in. Callum followed, going to the shelf on the wall and taking down two mugs.

Malcolm followed. "Mayhap we should find Skelley."

Callum glanced up from pouring ale into a cup.

"We could send him to help Caira with the soap."

Callum grinned. "Do ye think he'd stoop to woman's work?" He chuckled, picturing Brian, paddle in hand, stirring the pot of fat and ash and arguing with Caira.

Malcolm raised his brows, a grin splitting his lips. " 'Twould be worth the effort. And 'twould bring the two close together—ye ken?"

Downing his ale, Callum wiped his mouth. He nodded. "Where do ye think he's gone?"

"Where did ye find him yesterday?"

Callum led the way, and they set out down a path through the woods.

When they didn't find him at the first location, Callum turned them in another direction. After wandering for a while, they heard a loud pop. Glancing at each other, they nodded and headed in the direction of the noise.

They spotted Brian where they'd first found him.

Callum motioned for Malcolm to hide behind an outcropping of rock.

"What do ye think he's doing?" Malcolm asked, his voice low.

Callum shrugged. "We'll just watch a moment, and when he's finished, we'll call out to him. He doesna like to be surprised."

They watched as Brian tied a cloth package to the limb of a tree. Taking a twig from the small fire a short distance beyond, he set the package afire. He stood as still as a rock, a few paces away, and a moment later the bundle let off a loud pop. A cloud of smoke and soot puffed into the air.

"Yeah, just call me MacBoom!" Brian shouted to the trees. With a grin, he trotted back to a set of supplies next to a boulder.

"Do ye ken what he's doing?" Malcolm whispered, ducking down behind the rocks and scratching his head.

"Nay. 'Tis magic, ye think?"

Malcolm's eyes widened, and both men again looked out from their hiding places.

"Mayhap we should get a wee bit closer." Malcolm pointed to a stand of trees to their right. "There, behind those," he whispered.

Callum nodded and checked Brian's position, then they moved to the safety of the copse.

Brian hung another cloth package from the tree limb, and set fire to the tied end as they watched, edging a bit closer to it as he did.

A loud clap of noise erupted, making both Malcolm and Callum duck behind their cover. The crack of wood followed, and when they looked out again, the limb where the package had been came crashing down, the scrap of cloth tied to it fluttering in the breeze.

Brian jumped out of the way, but a branch grazed

his cheek and blood appeared. It streaked down his face.

"Hooyah!" he shouted.

Malcolm and Callum glanced around the area.

"Who's Hooyah?" Callum asked Malcolm.

His friend shrugged. "No doubt one of Wallace's men." He touched Callum's sleeve. "Do ye think the mon is nearby?"

Callum rolled his eyes. "We'd best see to Skelley."

Malcolm and Callum rushed from the trees, skidding to a halt beside Brian. The man stood there, looking down at the broken limb and wiping the blood from his face.

"Ye're hurt again," Callum pronounced, squinting at the scratch on Skelley's cheek.

Skelley glanced at Callum, frowned, and swore.

"It didn't work, but almost . . . maybe."

"And ye're covered in . . ." Malcolm ran a finger over the sleeve of Brian's tunic. "Soot."

Skelley just shook his head.

"Who is Hooyah?" Malcolm asked after a moment.

"What?" Brian shouted, frowning at the old Scot.

"Hooyah!" Malcolm shouted back.

"Yeah!" Brian raised a clenched fist. "Hooyah!" And he grinned at Malcolm.

"He's deaf again," Malcolm yelled to Callum.

"Ye dinna need to yell, Malcolm. *I* still got my hearing."

"Oh, aye. Sorry."

"What do ye think he's trying to do out here?" Callum asked, looking at the limb and the collection of bags beside a large rock.

Malcolm sniffed the air. "Dinna ken, but he's a penchant for foul-smelling things," he muttered in a low voice. He moved to Brian's side, sniffing again. "His clothes reek." He wrinkled his nose. "And he could do with . . ." He trailed off.

Callum looked from Brian to Malcolm, noting the glimmer in his friend's eyes. "What have ye in mind, Malcolm?"

"We must get him back so Caira can tend his wound, eh?" He waggled his eyebrows.

Callum stared at his friend in bemusement for a moment, then caught Malcolm's meaning and grinned. "Ach, ye're right about that. Could putrefy and then he'd die," He shouted for Skelley's benefit.

"We'll just have a tub sent up fer him, while we're about it."

Skelley rubbed his ears and looked from the fallen limb to the two Scots. "What? Did you say something?" he shouted.

Both men shook their heads and helped him gather up his things and put out the fire. Then they escorted him to the castle.

"Well, Smythe, what did you learn?"

"Naught, Lord Whitcomb. The Mackenzie was out hunting."

Whitcomb poured a cup of ale from the pitcher on the table before him. "Oh?"

"Aye, my lord, but I did notice that there be few men in the keep." Smythe shifted, eyeing the ale.

"No doubt they were out with their laird." He shot Smythe a glare. There was a reason some men were leaders and some followers, and Smythe was an excellent example.

"Don't see why we don't just attack. 'Twould take only a few men to take the keep."

"Because, you dolt, the king has an agreement of neutrality with the laird. We simply can't march in there without just cause."

"They're Scots. 'Tis just cause enough."

"Nay." Whitcomb sighed. He longed to return to his home. He shared Smythe's feelings, but he wouldn't risk his title and lands. While the king could, and often did, go back on his word when dealing with the Scots, he frowned upon his nobles doing so without his express permission.

"Unless we can prove the Mackenzies have taken up arms against the Crown or have harbored Wallace, we can do nothing." Peter picked up his cup and stood. "Speaking of that devil, Wallace must be getting help from the locals. No man can simply disappear without aid. Rumors have it he's in the area. I care not about the Mackenzies, I want Wallace." For it was that rebel's capture or death that would see him returned to the civilized world.

Whitcomb drank from his cup, dreaming of London, then fixed Smythe with a stare. "Send patrols out tomorrow. Work from the Mackenzie borders outward. Find Wallace."

Chapter Twelve

The dull ringing in his ears irritated Brian. He should have plugged them before setting off the blast. Gradually, his hearing would return, but until then he'd have to put up with straining to hear the voices of the two men walking beside him.

They entered the castle, and the old Scots ushered him upstairs to the room he'd occupied when he'd first arrived. A few minutes later, servants brought in a large wooden tub. A young girl entered behind them, a stack of linens in her arms. Setting the linens on a table, she took the top one and lined the tub with it.

A group of boys arrived carrying buckets of hot water. They filled the tub, leaving a few buckets behind for Brian to rinse with.

Stripping off his clothes, Brian climbed into the bath. The water was lukewarm but felt great, even if he did have to draw his knees up near his chin to fit. Cupping water in his hands, he rubbed some of the soot from his face, grimacing when the cut on his cheek began to sting. He wet his hair the same way and stood. Using the contents of a bowl left on the table beside the tub, he soaped his body and hair.

A cool draft skimmed over his wet skin as he dumped a bucket of clean water over his head. Blinking the water from his eyes, he turned and met Caira's surprised gaze.

Caira swallowed, and Brian watched the muscles in her throat contract. Her gaze traveled over his body, leaving behind a trail of heat. His body swelled to attention at the blatant desire sparking in her eyes . . . a desire he shared.

Her mouth moved, but she spoke so quietly, he couldn't hear her for the buzzing in his ears.

Their gazes met and held. She moistened her lips, and Brian's mouth went dry as he followed the path of her tongue with his eyes, imagining his mouth covering hers, his tongue tracing her lips before dipping in to taste her breath.

Her eyes widened as if she read his thoughts, and her chest rose as she sucked in air.

"Caira?" Her name rumbled from his throat. She blinked. "The door?"

The door?

"Sweet Jesus, Mary, and Joseph," Caira mumbled. "Did you not hear my knock?" Her gaze drank in every visible inch of his bared form. Molten desire pooled at the core of her womanhood as she clenched her hands in her skirt to stem the tide of desire sweeping through her.

Dazed, she turned to do his bidding, the image of his naked body blocking out the sight of the wooden door.

It was a very fine body.

She shut the door, but remained facing it until her cheeks cooled and her heart settled into a more normal beat. Closing her eyes, she fought for control of her wayward desires, lest he see the effect he had on her.

She choked back a laugh.

Her reaction was impossible for him to miss, she realized. She'd fair burst into flames before his very eyes.

Turning, she faced Brian, who climbed from the tub, a dry linen wrapped around his waist. Her hungry gaze followed the path of crisp dark hair sprinkling his chest to the edge of the cloth. The evidence of his manhood drew her attention where it bulged beneath.

Heat sizzled through her body, gathering between her thighs. Her breath came in short puffs. Caira stepped toward him, her hand outstretched. Catching herself, she stopped, her gaze sliding up his body to his face.

A smoldering fire brightened his blue eyes, one brow arched questioningly and the corners of his mouth lifted slightly. He was not unaffected, she thought with a smile of feminine satisfaction.

It was a moment before she noticed the scratch on his cheek. "You've been hurt." She frowned.

Well, of course he'd been hurt; it was what Malcolm had told her and the reason she'd rushed to his room. But the two Scots had failed to mention Brian was bathing.

She'd forgotten the wound upon sight of him in the wooden tub.

"It's just a scratch." He brought his hand up to touch it.

"You can hear me, then?" Callum had said that Brian could not.

"I'm fine. Just a dull buzzing in my ears."

"Sit there." She motioned to the bed. "I'll fetch my case. I've a salve—'twill keep any wound from putrefying."

"You mean that box?" He nodded, and Caira glanced over her shoulder.

"Aye," she said. Malcolm and Callum had sent it up with the bath, she realized. Fetching the case, she returned to Brian. Now she just had to overcome her shaking limbs to attend to his wound.

Brian's skin warmed beneath Caira's touch as she examined the gash on his cheek. He inhaled her unique womanly scent mixed with sunshine, and allowed himself a moment to bask in her concern.

"Where did you learn so much about medicine?" he asked, to divert his mind from her nearness and the effect she had on him.

"Medicine? Nay, I know no 'medicine.' "

"Yes, you do." The salve she applied cooled his heated skin. "You made this ointment, didn't you?"

She frowned, glancing at the jar in her hand. "Aye." Her mouth tightened, and she glanced away. "Your tale of Wallace was quite . . . convincing."

Brian nodded. Why had she changed the subject? Why was she reluctant to talk about her medical knowledge?

"Are you truly one of Wallace's rebels?"

He allowed her the line of questioning only because of the sadness he glimpsed in her eyes before she looked away.

"No. I'm not. I've said it many times." He ran his hand through his hair. "I wish to God Malcolm would believe me and quit telling everyone I am. He's got the entire castle thinking I know Wallace personally."

" 'Tis glad I am that you do not."

Brian raised his eyebrows. "So, you believe me?"

"You speak the truth, do you not?"

"Yeah, but I've been speaking the truth since I got here and no one will believe me."

Caira sighed. " 'Tis hard for them." She glanced toward the window. "There is little enough hope for this clan to hold on to. Mayhap the idea of a strong warrior in their midst gives them that."

"But it's not right to lie to them."

"You've told them the truth. 'Tis up to them to choose to believe you or not." She smiled, and Brian's heart thumped against his chest.

"So, why are you glad I'm not a Wallace follower?"

"The English search for such rebels and will see them drawn and quartered."

Brian remembered the ending of *Braveheart*, and he swallowed. "Hell of a way to die."

"Aye."

Silence hung in the air, and Brian searched for a new subject. "You've got a big job, taking care of the clan."

"Aye."

"You're handling it well."

"And how would you ken that?" Caira met his gaze.

"The buildings are all well maintained, the people aren't starving and everyone seems happy." Brian smiled. "I'd say that proves it."

Caira shrugged.

"You just need to learn to delegate so you don't wear yourself out."

Her mouth tightened and her gaze filled with anger. "Wear myself out? I'm not a weakling."

Brian caught her hand when she started to move away. "It's not a sign of weakness, Caira, but rather strong leadership."

He turned his hand over and laced his fingers with hers. The contact of their palms and the meeting of their gazes whipped up a storm of desire that crashed over him, bringing an aching fullness to his groin.

He leaned toward her. Their mouths touched, and Brian pulled her into his arms. She slid onto his lap, her bottom pressing intimately against him.

The feel of her so close, the heat of her through the towel against his erection sent a shock of excitement through him, and he traced her lips with his tongue, seeking entrance to her mouth with a kiss.

Caira opened for Brian, welcoming the intimate invasion. Her blood sang in her veins, setting off rippling waves of heat. She wrapped her arms around his shoulders, drinking in the feel of his skin.

Their tongues touched and she was lost—lost to the passion washing over her, surrendering to the security she found in Brian's embrace.

Emotions she'd never experienced blossomed within her heart. Surprised at the depth of her response, Caira pulled away and met Brian's stunned gaze.

For an awkward moment they sat frozen, and she searched for something to say.

Then, confused by the feelings flashing through her

and not wanting them yet, Caira moved off Brian's lap. Her legs shook beneath her. She stumbled to the door and rushed down the hall.

Caira slowed her steps only when she reached the stairs, and then she took a deep, calming breath. What was wrong with her? Did she not have enough to deal with? This man would leave Kilbeinn and take her heart, did she not guard it better.

Callum and Malcolm stood at the bottom of the stairs.

"Well, how is he?" Malcolm asked, a glint of mischief in his eyes.

"Fine." Caira brushed her skirts, forcing a casualness into her voice. " 'Tis but a scratch and not the mortal wound you implied." She leveled a stern glare at Malcolm and Callum each in turn. "I've tended it."

"But dinna ye think 'tis best if ye sit with him a spell?" Malcolm nudged Callum with his elbow.

"Aye," Callum chimed in, and Caira narrowed her gaze at them.

"What are you two up to, then?"

"Not a thing. We just thought Skelley should get the very best care." Malcolm shrugged. " 'Tis all."

Caira shook her head, stepping around them to meet Gitta's knowing gaze.

Brian pulled air into his lungs, willing his body temperature down, as well as another part of his anatomy. Damn, he couldn't remember ever reacting to a woman like this before. He reached for his pants and froze. What the hell was wrong with him? He had no business kissing Caira.

He stepped into his pants and was just pulling on

his shirt when the door to his room opened. Gitta walked in.

Looking him over carefully, she stared a moment at his cheek before surveying the rest of him. She pinned him with a glare.

"Do ye hurt the lass, I'll be using Malcolm's rusty sword to geld ye. Ye ken what I'm saying?"

Brian swallowed, believing every word the fierce, older woman said.

"I dinna ken what happened in here, but I'll not have Caira upset. There's enough fer her to worry over without ye adding to it."

Brian nodded, feeling like a grammar school kid facing the principal.

"Yer garments need washing." She *tsk*ed as she touched the sleeve of his shirt, her fingertips coming away black with soot. "I'll bring ye something else to wear."

"That's not necessary—"

"I said"—she narrowed her gaze on him—"that I'll bring ye something else." And she stomped from the room.

Brian ran a hand through his hair. Clean clothes were all well and good, he thought, but there was no way he'd wear one of those damned kilts. No, he'd never wear a skirt.

He left the room, closing the door quietly behind him. At the top of the stairs, he peered around the corner and found only a few people in the hall. He didn't see either Caira or Gitta, so he quickly descended the stairs and left the castle behind.

On the way back to the cottage, Brian pondered why

the last blast had failed to send him back where he belonged.

He couldn't imagine getting any closer. He found Tripod and the beast gave him a sad, beseeching look.

"Sorry, buddy, but those blasts would have scared the hell out of you—if they didn't kill you."

His supply of black powder was low. He'd have to make more, but first he had to replenish the ingredients.

He spent the rest of the day pulverizing charcoal and collecting the volcanic rock he'd found a short distance from the village. But it was damned hard to keep his mind on what he was doing when the smell of sunshine brought thoughts of Caira and the kiss they'd shared.

Chapter Thirteen

Caira stepped out the kitchen door and into the morning sunshine. Brian and the kiss they'd shared had invaded her dreams last eve. She woke in the middle of the night, clutching her bolster, her heated lips pressed against it as remembered passion thrummed through her body.

It was just a kiss, she reminded herself.

Aye—she smiled—*but what a kiss.*

She'd slept little after that, and woke later than usual. But the beautiful morn chased away any lingering fatigue or guilt. Smiling, she pulled in a deep breath of cool, clean air. It was a wonderful morn to tend the garden. No doubt Malcolm would be awaiting her. That was one job he seemed to favor above others, complaining only mildly at the chore.

As she made her way to the gardens, she recalled Brian's praise, and a surge of confidence washed over her.

Mayhap he was right: she should delegate some of

her tasks to others. But would the clan think her leadership weak?

She frowned, her steps slowing. And why should they? Her father certainly never concerned himself with household matters. 'Twas woman's work, he'd claimed, leaving them to Caira to manage.

He hadn't done all that Caira did, and the clan revered him as Laird of the Mackenzies.

But what would her people think when she assigned tasks to others that she normally performed?

Mayhap if she started small, with tasks in the keep . . .

Aye, it was a good plan. Later she would review the work and choose those best suited for the chores.

She rounded the corner and came to a halt, spotting a familiar wide back bent over a row of turnips. Her heart lurched in her chest, and her knees began to tremble.

What was he doing?

A twig snapped beneath her foot, and Brian turned. "Morning." His smile played havoc with Caira's pulse. This was the first time they'd met since the kiss. Not during dinner or any other moment. Had that kiss played as often in his mind as hers, plagued him even when he slept?

"Good morn," she said, wiping her damp palms on her skirt. "Where is Malcolm?"

Brian sat back on his heels. "The old cuss wouldn't listen to me, and he insisted on sleeping in my hammock last night." He shook his head, and a lock of hair fell over his forehead. "I tried to tell him it was a young man's bed."

"Ach, well, 'twas the wrong thing to say to him."
Caira chuckled. "Malcolm willna believe he isna a man
in his prime."

"Yeah, well, I think he believes it now. Anyway,
since he could barely get out of bed, he sent me to do
his chores." He bent back over the garden. "But you're
going to have to tell me which are weeds."

" 'Tis good of you."

"Good has nothing to do with it. It was easier than
refusing." He pointed to a plant. "This a weed?"

Caira nodded, a smile lifting her lips.

"This way I don't have to listen to him complain."

"Aye, poor Callum."

Brian looked at her, and his deep-throated chuckle
sent a shiver of delight up her spine.

Caira pointed out the weeds to Brian, then started
working at the opposite end. They worked in silence
for a while.

"Caira?"

She glanced up.

"About yesterday."

"Aye?" Her breath caught in her throat. Gazing into
his eyes, she wondered at the concern darkening their
blue depths.

"I'm sorry. I shouldn't have kissed you." The words
tumbled from his lips all at once.

"Why?" she asked before she could think not to.

He looked away, yanked a stubborn weed from the
soil, and tossed it into the growing pile. "Well . . . I'll
be leaving soon, and . . ."

Caira's heart contracted. " 'Twas only a kiss," she
said, her voice low. Would that it could be more, she
thought, watching as his mouth twisted into a frown.
She longed to feel those lips on hers again.

134

"Yeah, right. True. It was only a kiss." He seemed relieved.

Her vanity shattered, Caira stood up. Clutching a weed in her hand, anger and pain roaring through her veins, she hissed, "And do you go about the country-side kissing one and all?" She propped her hands on her hips, unmindful of the dirt clinging to the weed and soiling her gown. "Have you bestowed your kisses on Widow Turner?"

Meeting Brian's round-eyed gaze, she gasped, real-izing what she'd said. Rage boiled up inside her—at herself, at him—and she flung the weed she held at Brian's head and ran for the kitchens, choking back tears of embarrassment, fear, and anger as she went.

The weed hit him square in the face. Spitting out the dirt that flew from the roots, Brian stared after Caira.

"Damn it." *I screwed that up,* he thought.

He should have just kept his mouth shut. He pried another weed from the ground. Somehow he'd have to smooth things over with Caira.

"Damn." He hadn't meant to hurt her. He just didn't want to lead her on. He would be gone soon. He was only trying to do the right thing.

He finished Malcolm's chore and gathered up the piles of weeds.

"Ye ken what I told ye yesterday?" a harsh voice called over his shoulder.

"Gitta?" He turned and found the older woman, a sword clenched between her hands. He swallowed. Her gaze scorched him across the garden.

"Ach, she willna let anyone see her cry, but I've known her all her life and I can tell when she's in pain." The woman brought the sword up, the muscles in her skinny arms quivering, her hands shaking with its weight, and the tip wavered.

"Whoa." Brian held up his hands. "Just a minute, Gitta. I was trying *not* to hurt her."

She snorted. "I bid ye leave. Dinna darken this keep with yerself again, else ye'll feel the bite of this blade."

He fought the urge to laugh at the comical sight. The old woman and her sword were hardly a threat. But her concern for Caira was genuine, and he wouldn't treat her with anything less than the respect she deserved.

"Fine." He backed away and left the garden.

As he walked, he wondered how the hell he had gotten himself into such a mess. Gitta had actually done him a favor, he realized, heading back to the cottage. He needed to get himself back to his time—and pronto, before he managed to get himself anymore involved with Caira and her people.

Caira. Guilt soured his stomach as he remembered the emotions playing across her face. She was a good woman with more responsibilities than was fair. He admired her strength and devotion. How was he to know their kiss would affect her so much?

Or him? And it had. So much so, that he'd tried to dismiss it with hurtful words. But he'd never meant to hurt her—he was trying to save her the pain of attachment. He'd soon be gone, and where would that leave her?

"Well, then, the weeding done?" Malcolm asked. He stood at the door, a grin splitting his bearded face. Tripod squeezed out between him and the door frame, and came over to nudge Brian.

"Yeah, it's done." Brian narrowed his gaze at the crafty old man and absently rubbed the dog's head. "You seem to have recovered from your stiffness."

"Ach, I'm not as old as ye think." Malcolm straightened his shoulders.

"Just what the hell are you up to, Malcolm?"

The old man's gaze widened, innocence personified. But Brian wasn't buying it. He shook his head.

"Don't try that innocent routine with me. I know you're up to something. And it has something to do with me and the garden."

"Nay. Truly, Brian." The old Scot put his hands up. "I couldna bend over this morn. Ye spoke true when ye said the hammock wasna good for everyone."

Not mollified, but unwilling to waste any more time, Brian moved past Malcolm and went to the corner of the cottage where his black powder supplies were stacked.

He had work to do.

Caira strode out the front door and came to a startled halt.

"Where is the Mackenzie?"

"And just who are you?" Caira propped her hands on her hips and eyed the stranger who'd spoken.

"Lord Whitcomb." The man looked down upon her from atop his mount, his cold gaze raking over her.

Caira's knees trembled. This was the English lord in charge of the soldiers patrolling the borders of Mackenzie land.

"And you are?" he asked.

"Caira Mackenzie."

"Is your father here?" The English lord cocked an eyebrow. "Or is he hunting again?"

Caira glanced around at the mounted soldiers. "He's abed with a fever."

The man swung down from his horse. "Well, I'll just look in on him, shall I?"

She caught his arm as he started to brush by her. He looked down his long, thin nose at her hand, then lifted his gaze to her, but she stood her ground.

" 'Tis a fearful sickness," she gasped. He hesitated, so she added, " 'Twould be a shame were you to catch it and pass it on to your men."

His gaze narrowed. "How long has he been sick?"

"He returned from the hunt shaking with chills."

"Nevertheless, I'll speak to him."

He pushed by her and headed to the stairs.

Sweet Mary, they were doomed. When the man discovered her da's room empty, he would know she had lied. She searched for plausible excuses for her lie, anything to keep the man from guessing the truth.

She followed him up the stairs, the black cloud of dread settling over her.

"Where is the master's chamber?"

She nodded to the door down the hall, clenching her hands together to still their shaking. Frantically, she searched for something to say when he would find her father's room empty. But her mind kept racing in circles. Panic clawed its way up her throat.

He swept past, and she held her breath as he opened the door and stopped.

"Can ye not see the laird is sick?"

She heard Gitta's indignant voice and rushed to the

chamber, ready to put herself between the dear old woman and any harm the man might inflict.

"I will have a word with the Mackenzie," Lord Whitcomb said.

Caira skidded to a stop just behind the Englishman.

"Come in, come in. Surely ye will not sicken, ye being hardy English and all."

Caira's stomach knotted at Gitta's taunting. Did she have no care for her life?

Lord Whitcomb hung back and Caira looked at the bed, noting a grayish hand clutching the covers and a portion of a pale face peering out at the visitor.

From the pile of blankets on the bed came a croaky male voice. "What is it Gitta? Who's there?"

Caira flashed the older woman a questioning glance, but Gitta turned to her patient.

"Whist, dinna concern yerself. 'Tis but a Sassenach."

Caira didn't recognize the squinty eyes or the rough voice of the man speaking Gaelic from the mound of blankets.

"What's he saying?"

Lord Whitcomb looked to Caira for an answer, but the patient croaked out, "Tell me that isna an Englishmon in me own home. Canna a mon have peace when he's fevered?" Then came a dry, hacking cough, and the English lord stepped back and turned his pale face to Caira.

"I'll just return when he's feeling better," he said.

Shooting Gitta another confused glance, Caira followed Whitcomb downstairs.

She had just returned from watching the soldiers

depart when Caira found Gitta coming down the stairs. "Who's up there?" she asked.

Gitta grinned. "Skelley."

"But how . . ." Confusion tied her tongue. "He didna sound himself." She frowned. "He sounded like . . . an old Scot."

Gitta nodded. " 'Tis a good thing, too."

Caira was shocked. This was not what she would have expected from him. Until their kiss, he'd kept to himself, leading her to believe he cared for naught else but his own affairs. And after this morn, she'd been convinced of it.

Caira shook her head. So, what was he up to now? It was impossible to figure the man out.

"Skelley was in the stable collecting muck when the Sassenach arrived. He heard what the lord said and came to the kitchens demanding I show him to the laird's room." Gitta grinned. "He'd a plan, he did. So I took him up and he donned the laird's sleeping cap and into the bed he went."

Her grin faded. "And I'd said to him such . . ." She trailed off. "He'll be needing water to wash with, and some of yer salve fer his face."

"I'll tend to it, Gitta." Relief washed through Caira at the resolution to the near disaster, followed by nervousness at the thought of tending to Brian. She still could not believe she'd mentioned the widow to him earlier. Nor could she believe the sharp pang of jealousy thoughts of Brian and the woman had spurred.

A short time later, Caira climbed the stairs carrying a pitcher of water. Stopping in her room to get the salve, she continued to the laird's chambers.

Skelley sat on the side of the bed, pulling on his boots.

" 'Tis hard for you to keep your face clean, I'm thinking," she called out as she entered. She tried to make her voice light, hoping he would not bring up their last meeting.

He glanced up and grinned. Caira's heartbeat quickened in response, but then her gaze landed on the wound on his cheek. She frowned.

"You should wash that . . ." She squinted at his gray face and quirked a brow. "Ash?"

He nodded.

"Aye, that ash from your face, and I'll put some salve on your cheek."

She placed the water beside a bowl on the table and stepped away, her gaze moving to Brian as he stood.

Sweet Mary. She swallowed a gasp as her eyes locked on his bare chest, reminding her of another time when he'd worn even less, his skin slick with water; all hard, lean muscle beneath. And she recalled the warmth of his lips on hers and the taste of his tongue.

He was a braw man, of a certainty, she thought—but it was his quiet confidence and faith in her that had her longing to share her worries with him. She closed her eyes. To lay a bit of her burdens upon his broad shoulders; to share the long, lonely evenings with him—would that she could do it.

What was she thinking? Her eyes snapped open. What weakness overcame her? She didn't need a man to lean on . . . did she? It mattered not. He'd made it clear that she meant nothing to him. He might help her here and there, but—

The splash of water interrupted her thoughts, and she cleared her throat and turned around.

"I thank you for what you did," she said. Her thoughts had wandered so far afield, she'd nearly forgotten her manners.

Using the drying linen from the table, he wiped his face and hands and met her gaze. "You know I won't be here much longer. I'll be going home soon."

Caira schooled her features into a calm she didn't feel.

She didn't want to think about it now. There would be time enough for that in the long hours of the night.

"How long do you think you can stall the English?"

Caira shrugged, unwilling to face that problem either.

"If you'll sit . . ." She glanced around the room, noting the absence of a stool.

"How about here?" He walked over and sat on the bed.

Taking the top off the jar, she went to him. She stood beside him and dipped her finger into the container, recalling another time she'd done the same. Gently, she smoothed the salve on the scratch, noting a faint bruise around the edges.

"Does it pain ye?"

As Caira touched him, Brian met her gaze and brought his hand up over hers. "No." The single word came out as a whisper, their contact robbing him of breath.

He let his gaze wander over her face, marveling at the smoothness of her skin, the clearness of her eyes. He wanted to know what lay beneath her wimple and the long heavy gown she wore. He wanted to experience her passion, draw it out and wrap himself in her.

He shouldn't kiss her again, but he knew he would. He should leave, now. But he knew he wouldn't.

Just one more kiss, he promised himself. What could it hurt? He brought her hand down from his face and stood up, gently pulling her to him. Her eyes widened, but she didn't pull back. Wrapping his other arm around her, he lightly brushed her lips with his.

He kissed first one corner of her mouth and then the other, inhaling the fresh smell of sunshine that seemed to cling to her.

She stiffened in his arms and he knew he should back off.

But he couldn't.

When he covered her mouth with his, she moaned and all thought left Brian, replaced by an intense need to feel. He parted her lips with his tongue, pulling their bodies closer together, feeling the pillows of her breasts as they met the solid wall of his chest. He tasted the sweetness of her lips and released her hand, wrapping his arm around her shoulders. Her delicateness awakened his protective instincts. He wanted to keep her safe—safe from the English, safe from the harshness of her world.

He gently pulled back.

"Ach, Brian—"

"I'm so . . ." He looked into her eyes and couldn't apologize for kissing her, not again. He knew she expected his apology by the pain that flashed across her face. In all honesty, he wasn't sorry; he'd do it again given the chance.

"Look, I'm sorry I jumped into the middle of things," he amended. "It might have been better if

Whitcomb had found out about your father—"

"Nay, Skelley," she cut him off. "I'm most grateful for your aid." Then she shoved the top back on the jar and fled the room.

Caira rushed down the stairs, seeking solitude to deal with the emotions warring within her. She left the keep, and as she passed the outer gate, her steps slowed as guilt caught up with her.

Never had she enjoyed her husband's kisses. She blamed it on the lack of love between them. But she'd certainly found pleasure in Brian's arms, and she didn't love him.

She touched her lips. She could still feel the firm warmth of his mouth against hers. The way his arms enveloped her, making her feel safe and utterly feminine.

She brought her hand down and frowned at her thoughts, realizing for the first time that dealing with the responsibilities of the clan had left her with no time or energy for feminine pursuits. No longer did she have time to gossip with the women of the village. And of an eve, she was too tired to even play her lute. And what of love?

Weariness clung to her like soaked garments.

Chapter Fourteen

He had to get back to his own time before he did something *really* stupid, Brian thought as he slowly poured hot water over the dirt and droppings he'd gotten from the floor of the stables. What had possessed him to masquerade as Caira's father? The ruse couldn't go on forever; at some point the English would find out about the man's death. He might have bought Caira more time, but time wouldn't do her much good.

Before he was tempted to act on impulse again, he was going to have to get himself back to his own time. He had to avoid Caira, close himself off from the people of the castle, and concentrate on making his powder.

He'd set his plan in action last night and dined on a meal cooked by Malcolm. The old Scot's culinary experiment was far from edible, but he hadn't wanted to hurt the old man's feelings so he'd eaten the food. It was a wonder he wasn't dead this morning. He woke with a stomachache like he'd never had before.

Tripod started barking, circling around, and his tail slapped Brian in the face.

"Tripod, sit." The dog plopped down, tail thumping the ground, but he still barked.

"There ye are, Skelley."

Brian looked over his shoulder at one of the men from the village. To the dog's credit, Tripod didn't move, but his tail pounded the ground faster, raising a cloud of dust, and he started whining for attention. Brian reached out and rubbed the canine's ear, and Tripod quieted.

"We missed ye at table last eve. The clan wanted to thank ye."

Brian nodded, turning back to his work. Several men and women had stopped by this morning to thank him.

"What ye did yesterday was the mark of a good mon. Ye saved the clan, ye did." He slapped Brian on the back. "Ye're a hero now."

Brian didn't want to be a hero, for Christ's sake. He just wanted to go home before he got any more involved.

"Ye ken, we thought ye were English when ye first got here." The man laughed. "Then we thought ye was daft—what with yer bucket with holes, boiling rocks, and yer taking the muck from the stables. But we'll allow ye yer peculiarities fer coming to Caira's and our aid."

Brian poured the last of the water over the contents of the bucket, and turned to face his visitor.

"Yeah, well, it won't be happening again. The clan can't expect to keep something like the death of their laird a secret forever. I just postponed the inevitable."

The villager shrugged. "Mayhap with the time ye gave us, we'll come up with an answer."

Brian wasn't optimistic. "You can't raise the dead."

"Still, there has to be an answer. We just need time to find it." And then the man sauntered off.

Brian shook his head and went back to work. As he sat on a stump grinding the sulfur to a fine powder, Tripod lifted his head and then raced off. Brian grinned, watching the ungainly gait of the dog.

"Crazy mutt," he called. "No doubt you'll come back with another swollen nose or a thorn in your paw."

Delegating wasn't as easy as it sounded, Caira thought as she left the keep behind. If she stayed a moment longer, she would have taken over the task of candle-making. Resisting the urge to hover over the workers, offering advice made delegating difficult.

Since the morning was clear, Caira had assigned herself the task of gathering wild mint—both for her herb box and to use beneath the rushes. She wore her oldest, faded brown tunic and a frayed wimple for the task. A deep basket hung from the crook of her arm, bouncing against her hip as she moved through the heather-blanketed clearing to the shadowed coolness of the woods beyond.

Birds trilled in the boughs above her and a gentle breeze sang through the trees. She inhaled the fresh loamy scents of the woods, enjoying the sounds and sights of nature.

As she searched for the mint, the cool breeze came down from the treetops and flirted with the delicate petals of the wildflowers. A gust swirled around her, touching her face and playing with the ends of her wimple.

She bent and plucked a few of the flowers. The muted thud of horses brought her head up, and a scream rose in her throat. Three mounted men rode toward her. English?

Dropping the flowers and her basket, she lifted her skirts and began to run. Shouts filled the quiet of the forest and Caira ran harder, dodging saplings had prickly holly bushes.

She glanced over her shoulder. They were closer. Her lungs burned, her legs stung where the bushes had scratched her.

She redoubled her efforts. A horse snorted behind her, the jangle of harness loud in her ears. From the corner of her eye she caught a glimpse of the animal and then it turned toward her, hitting her and knocking her to the ground.

Before she could catch her breath, she was yanked to her feet. Held tightly about the waist by one of the men, she faced the other two astride their mounts.

"Well, what have we here, eh?" one of the men said, grinning at her, exposing the rotted stubs of his teeth. "A Scottish whore, is it?" The one holding her laughed and squeezed her breast. Caira clenched her jaw against her pain and fear.

"Who wants her first?" he asked.

"We're to find the rebel. There's plenty of willing wenches at the fort." the third man said, cutting a glare to the man beside him.

Relief washed over Caira.

He turned to her. "Where's Wallace?"

Caira shook her head.

He climbed down from his mount and came to stand in front of her. "I'll ask you once more: Where is Wallace?"

Again she shook her head.

His hand shot out, connecting with her cheek. Her head snapped to the side.

"He's here somewhere. Now, where the bloody hell is he?" He hit her again. Her ears rang and her jaw throbbed.

She shook her head. "I dinna know."

"Liar." Again his hand shot out and she flinched. The man behind her turned loose of her and stepped back as his companion grabbed her arm, wrenching it. Caira cried out in pain, trying to twist out of his grasp. Her tunic ripped and slid off her shoulder.

"Where's Wallace's camp? Who's helping him?"

"I've not seem him. I dinna know." Tears blurred her vision and the man hit her again and her knees buckled. He let her fall. Her head slammed against a rock. She turned her head away from the pain, and the warmth of her own blood flowed down the side of her face.

"Bloody bitch." He delivered a stunning kick to her ribs and she screamed in pain, curling into a protective ball. Her breath whoosh out with the next kick and she lost consciousness.

A few hours later, Tripod came back. He stood a few yards away from Brian and barked, then trotted off toward the woods and returned. Dancing around Brian's legs, the dog barked again and headed back to the woods.

The second time the dog returned, he nearly tripped

Brian as he threaded through his legs, jumping up to gain Brian's attention.

"What, Tripod? What do you want?"

The canine barked and trotted to the woods, looking back several times.

Brian sighed. "Okay, fine. Show me what you found." Probably a dead squirrel or something, he thought as he went after the beast.

He followed the dog through the woods, across a clearing, and to the edge of another wooded area. He found Tripod sitting beside a rock, whining. As Brian got nearer, a chill ran up his spine.

Beside the rock, Brian recognized Caira's rust-colored gown, and he broke into a run.

He skidded to a stop when he reached Caira's crumpled form.

"Caira?" He knelt down beside her, fear congealing in the pit of his stomach.

She lay facedown, unmoving on the forest floor. Dirt and leaves marred her once-pristine wimple. The torn shoulder of her gown exposed creamy white skin.

"Caira?" he called again. Pushing back panic, he grasped her wrist and checked for a pulse. Relief washed over him when he felt a faint but steady beat.

"Caira?" His heart constricted when she failed to respond. "Caira?" Panic edged into his voice, and he swallowed against its climbing up his throat. Had she fallen? Been attacked by an animal?

He knelt beside her, his hand hovering over her limp form.

Flashes of red held him immobile as a scene from his past filled his mind.

"Henry." His friend's name escaped his mouth on a groan. Henry had called to tell him the Navy had rejected his application. Brian had heard the devastation in his friend's voice. He had gone over to tell him he wouldn't be joining up, either—not without his buddy.

Henry's parents were at work, so Brian let himself in.

"Hey, Henry?" Brian called out, climbing the stairs. The eerie stillness of the house set his nerves on edge, and his steps slowed. "Henry, you here?"

Silence.

Henry's bedroom door was cracked open, and the smell of gunpowder and a strange metallic scent had reached Brian. But he ignored it and shoved the door open.

He stood there, trying to grasp the scene in the room, his hand clenching the doorknob. A dull roar filled his head, and tears burned his eyes as his best friend came into focus.

Like a rag doll tossed on the floor, Henry lay on his stomach. A pool of blood soaked the carpet beneath his head. His skin was a sickening shade of gray.

Without conscious thought, he moved closer and turned Henry over. His friend stared sightlessly out of a stiff, unnatural face. There was a hole, ringed in black at his temple. A gun lay beside him.

"Oh, God." Brian swallowed against the bile rising in his throat as past and present merged. "No!" The word originated deep within his chest and burst from his lips.

His hands shook as he gently rolled Caira onto her

back. Blood oozed from her lip, a bruise darkened one cheek and one side of the cloth covering her head was soaked with her blood.

He had to get her back to the keep. He focused on that, and with his heart pounding in his chest, he gathered Caira in his arms and stood up. A pained whimper escaped her swollen lips, twisting like a knife in his chest.

"I'm sorry, baby," he said.

With a quick glance around the area, he noted footprints as well as marks of horses near where he'd found her.

The only ones with mounts in the area were the Mackenzies, right? And why would they hurt their own leader? But then the image of the English soldiers he and the old Scots had encountered flashed through Brian's mind.

"Bastards." He glanced down at the woman in his arms, and his blood simmered.

He strode from the forest with Tripod at his heels, and headed to the keep. Forcing his anger back, he focused on not jarring the woman in his arms.

But as Kilbeinn came into view, his anger bubbled up.

"Caira?" Callum called. The old Scot stood just outside his cottage as Brian made his way toward the keep. "What happened?"

"I don't know. I found her in the forest." Brian's words came out in a tight growl.

The old man fell into step beside him, his gaze traveling over Caira. "Ye ken who did this, eh?"

Brian met his tearful gaze. "The damned English.

152

There were hoofprints and footprints all around the area."

"Bloody Sassenach. I'll see them all dead!"

"Let's keep this between the two of us, okay? Our first concern is Caira, then we'll take care of the bastards responsible."

"Aye."

Men and women came out of their cottages and followed Brian and Callum as they traveled through the village, and that halted the two men's conversation.

Word of Caira reached the castle before Brian, and Gitta stood at the door of the keep, a worried frown on her face. Her gaze traveled to Caira's wound and she gasped, moving quickly down the steps and to Brian's side.

"Ach, me poor lass." Her hand hovered over Caira's brow. "What happened to her, Skelley?"

"I don't know."

Gitta cast him a measured looked and then nodded, moving ahead of him to lead the way into the keep and up the stairs.

Brian gently laid Caira on her bed. The movement elicited a moan from her, but still she didn't open her eyes.

"Ach, there's so much blood on her wimple." Gitta turned her anxious gaze on Brian.

"Head wounds always bleed more than others," he responded. He didn't know for whose benefit.

She removed Caira's headcovering, and Brian sucked in a breath when the lump on her temple was exposed. A deep gash oozed fresh blood.

With his help, Gitta gently removed Caira's tunic.

Despite their care, she whimpered when Brian touched her torso to shift her on the bed.

"Damn." He glanced up at Gitta. "I think she's got a couple cracked ribs." He hoped they were only cracked. Gently, he ran his hands over her ribcage. The tension eased from his shoulders when he didn't detect any deformities.

"Do ye ken what to do?" Gitta twisted her hands together and frowned.

Brian pinned her with a glare. "You mean, you don't know anything about—"

"Healing?" She shook her head. " 'Tis Caira's calling, not mine."

"Shit." He rubbed his face. "We're going to have to bind her ribs, but we'll have to wait until she comes to." He hated the thought of the pain it would cause her, but he didn't want to jostle her unconscious body and risk injuring her more.

A young woman entered carrying a pitcher of water and cloths draped over her arm.

Brian took the pitcher, pouring some into a bowl on the table. Taking the rags from the girl, he dipped one in the bowl and started gently cleansing the blood from Caira's lip and then her temple.

"Caira?" He smoothed the auburn hair from her brow, noting its beautiful color. He felt physical pain seeing her injured like this. "Can you hear me, babe? Come on, wake up. I need you to help me." He rubbed her uninjured cheek. "Come on, honey, open your eyes."

She lay still and unresponsive. Brian clenched his jaw against the fear and frustration threatening his patience.

Reaching down, he took her hand in his and started rubbing it briskly. "Come on, baby. Wake up." He repeated the litany over and over until Caira's eyelids finally fluttered open. Her pain-filled gaze met his.

He grinned. "What's this, napping in the middle of the day?"

"Brian." She smiled weakly, then gasped as she shifted on the bed.

"It's okay. You've got a couple cracked ribs, I think. We'll need to bind them so you'll feel better." At least he hoped she would. He wasn't a medic. All he had was a little first aid training, thanks to the Navy.

She touched his hand, and he followed her gaze to the people crowding into her room.

"Okay, everyone. Caira is fine, she just needs to rest for a while. Out."

The room emptied except for Callum and Gitta.

"What happened, lass?" the old Scot asked. "Was it the English?"

"Callum, let's wait on that," Brian said. "She's been through enough for now." He turned to Gitta. "Can you get me a few long strips of cloth?"

"Aye, Skelley." She turned to Callum. "Come along, there's naught ye can do here."

Callum looked from Caira to Brian and back to Caira.

"Go," Caira said softly.

They left. Brian turned to Caira, his gaze captured by the thick rope of red-brown hair draped over her shoulder. He scanned her face, and had to grind his teeth against the anger filling him at any who might harm this tender, sensitive woman.

"How bad do you hurt?"

155

"I've an ache in my head." She took a shallow breath. "And it hurts to breathe."

"Once we get your ribs bound, that pain should ease."

"I've an herb in my box 'twill help the pain in my head, too."

Brain located her case of medical supplies. Bringing it to the bedside, he opened it. Inside were clay jars with wooden stoppers and small cloth sacks tied with different-colored, frayed ribbons.

" 'Tis the one with the saffron ribbon."

"Saffron?"

"Yellow." She gave him a pained smile.

He found the right sack and took it out.

"Two pinches in wine."

He nodded.

The door opened, and Gitta came in with the cloth strips Brian had asked for.

"Gitta, I need a glass of wine for Caira," he added.

"Aye." The woman went to the door and mumbled orders to someone in the hall. " 'Twill be here in a trice."

Brian and Gitta helped Caira sit up. With a sheet over her lap, they pulled up the white gown Gitta called an undertunic to expose Caira's ribs. Brian steeled himself against the ugly bruises contrasting so starkly with her pale skin. He began wrapping the strip of cloth around her. Glancing at her face, he caught her biting her bottom lip against the pain his actions brought.

"I'm sorry." He glanced up at her and she tried to smile. "Almost finished." He tied off the last of the bindings.

Gitta settled her back down while Brian answered the knock at the door, returning with a cup of wine. He added two pinches of the ground herb she'd indicated to the drink, then raised Caira enough for her to imbibe the wine and helped her back down.

"My thanks, Brian," she said.

"How are your ribs now?"

"They will mend."

He nodded. "You'll be up and around in no time. You just need to rest."

As Caira's eyes closed, Gitta left, taking the basin of water and the bloodied clothes with her.

Brian sat on the hard stool beside the bed, thoughts rolling through his mind like waves on the beach. Evening shadows crept into the room. Servants entered and fed the embers in the fireplace. Before leaving, they placed several candles around the bed, chasing away the gloom into the corners of the room.

The light from the candles flickered over the bruise on Caira's cheek.

What made men think they ever had the right to strike a woman? What drove them to do it? He didn't understand . . . hadn't understood as either a kid or an adult. An old rage built inside him, one he hadn't felt since before his father died. He longed to get his hands on those responsible for Caira's injuries and administer a few of his own to them.

She whimpered, and he looked over to find her asleep. He reached out and took her hand. Lacing his fingers in hers, he was amazed at the delicateness of her hands juxtaposed with the calluses on her palms. She worked so hard and worried so much over everyone.

157

It was one hell of a job, he thought, being responsible for so many people; to have everyone turning to you for answers. At least in the military there was a chain of command that spread out the responsibilities.

How did she do it? And so well? And what did it cost her?

Something in his heart turned over as he watched Caira sleep. The urge to ease her burdens, protect her from the English and the demands of her clan, built inside him.

He gazed out the open window. She needed help . . . *his* help.

He straightened his shoulders and pulled air deep into his lungs.

He couldn't abandon her. He'd stay until things were calmer.

But how long would that be? When in the hell had the Scots won their freedom? He didn't know the history that well. There was something at the end of *Braveheart* explaining what happened after Wallace's death, but damned if he could remember it.

Of course, what did it really matter? He was here for the duration.

It probably wouldn't make a difference if he returned to the present later than sooner. The worst that would happen was that he'd have to wait for his promotion and he'd lose a choice assignment.

When compared to Caira's problems, career worries seemed insignificant.

Chapter Fifteen

"So, have you word of Wallace?" Peter, Lord Whitcomb, glanced at the soldier walking beside him.

"Nay. A patrol found a village woman in the woods and questioned her. She refused to tell them anything." Smythe met Peter's gaze. "Though they were quite persuasive, I'm told."

"Is she still alive?"

He shrugged. "Probably not. Benson tends to have a rather heavy hand."

"They should have brought her to me. I'm sure I could have convinced her to part with the information we seek."

Smythe's gaze bounced away from Whitcomb's. "Well, my lord, They didn't think—"

"Bloody hell, Smythe. The men were under your command. You should have been with them. Don't want dead bodies lying about." He forced the angry words out through clenched teeth. " 'Twill only make the Scots harder to deal with."

Smythe's face reddened, and the man pulled the

door to the hall open. The smell of cooked cabbage rose to greet them.

"These people eat like pigs," Smythe mumbled.

"Because they are," Whitcomb agreed, looking around the hall and spotting a woman scurrying toward the kitchens.

"You there," he shouted.

She jerked to a halt and slowly turned to face him.

"How many times must I tell you? Don't cook your muck in my kitchen. It stinks." He hated his duty here, he thought again. The people were rebellious, uncivilized, and didn't know their place. He hadn't any of the comforts he deserved as a loyal vassal of King Edward.

The woman fled without responding.

"Damned impertinent people," Whitcomb muttered.

Together, he and his minion sat down at the table. Whitcomb looked at Smythe. "I would wager my best mount that the laird of the Mackenzies knows where Wallace is. I'm sure that neutrality pact was a ruse." He poured a cup of ale from the pitcher on the table. "Pray the bastard doesn't die before I can question him."

Caira opened her eyes. Pain lanced through her body, piercing her chest and renewing the ache in her temple.

She must have gasped, for in the next moment, Brian's face was before hers. His jaw was hidden by a thickening dark beard, and his hair stood out here and there as though he'd only just risen from bed. Fatigue drew lines in his forehead.

Of their own accord, her fingers reached up to smooth away the lines, but he captured them before she made contact. The warmth and strength of his hand enveloping hers sent a warm tide rolling through her veins, easing the pain.

"How long have I slept?" She met his worried gaze.

"Just a day." He gave her hand a gentle squeeze. "How are you feeling? Do you need more of the herb?"

"I'm better," she lied. "But a bit more of the herb wouldna go amiss."

He fixed her with a shrewd gaze. "You don't fool me for a second." Then he smiled and the lines in his forehead smoothed, but she saw the worry in the depth of his eyes.

He moved off, and Caira listened to the sounds of him preparing the draft that would still the thumping pain in her head.

She carefully shifted her position and found that if she didn't take deep breaths, her chest didn't pain her much.

"Here you go." Brian helped her rise and held the cup while she drank. She settled back against the bolsters and watched him move about the room, returning the cup to the table and pulling up the stool.

"Do you feel well enough to tell me what happened?"

Caira sighed, and the events of the previous day flashed in her mind.

She nodded. "I didna realize I'd traveled so far afield looking for flowers and herbs to freshen the rushes. The English were upon me before I could scream."

Brian took her hand, his thumb gently tracing a slow circle over her knuckles.

"I ran, but they were upon me quickly. One of the horses knocked me to the ground." Her voice cracked. She paused a moment, fighting against the fear of her memories. "When I couldna give them the information they sought, one of the soldiers slid from his mount and began hitting me, wrenching my arm and tearing my gown." Brian's thumb stilled.

"When I fell, he delivered several kicks to my sides until my head hit something hard and I lost consciousness." Brian's hand tensed over hers, and a muscle worked in his cheek.

"Was it the Englishman who came to see your father the other day?"

"Nay. 'Twas his underling."

Brian nodded.

"Up until yesterday, the English were content to simply taunt us. Never have they physically harmed anyone."

"Something must be in the works." Brian's thumb started circling her knuckles again, and he gazed at the wall behind her. "What were they asking you?"

"The whereabouts of Wallace." She shook her head. "I dinna understand why they aren't honoring the neutrality of the clan."

His eyebrow climbed his forehead, and he looked at her inquisitively. "Wallace must be giving the English fits by now." He canted his head and frowned. "What exactly was your 'neutrality agreement'? Can the English just come on Mackenzie land like they have been?"

162

"I dinna think so. 'Twas an agreement between my father and the king. The Mackenzies willna join in the rebellion or raise arms against the English. For this, the English willna attack our clan or take our land."

"Seems they're not holding up their end of the bargain. Maybe you should send a message to the king."

"Nay. If I send a missive, the king will know my father is dead and send his soldiers to take control of our land." She worried her lower lip. "Do you think Lord Whitcomb suspects my father is dead? Is that why he's become bolder?"

Brian shrugged.

"I canna appeal to King Edward." She glanced away. "I have no warriors to deal with the English threat—even were that an option, which 'tis not—because of the agreement my father made."

Like a dog chasing its tail, Caira's worries circled uselessly in her mind.

"Would that I could find a way to discourage the English without breaching the agreement." She glanced up at Brian and watched the deep concern dissolve from his face. It was replaced by a cocky grin.

"There just might be a way." He patted her hand and rose. "Don't worry about it. Just rest."

Brian met Malcolm in the great hall.

"How is Caira? Did she tell ye what happened?" the Scot asked.

"She's better, but she still needs to rest. Her ribs will take a little while to heal."

"Did she tell ye who did this to her?"

"Yes."

Malcolm followed Brian to a table and poured cups of ale for them both. "Well?" He pushed one toward Brian.

As he repeated the story Caira had told him, Brian's anger doubled. He couldn't and wouldn't ignore the situation any longer. Even if he didn't believe in the historical wrongdoing of the English, this matter was simple: Bullies were putting these Scots in danger, and it had to stop.

So much for not getting involved.

"The bloody bastards dinna have any honor," Malcolm said. " 'Twas agreed between the laird and Longshanks we would be left in peace. Ye can see their word means little to them." The Scot took a swallow of his ale. "Will ye be telling Wallace of this? Do ye think he'll bring his men and run the bastards off?"

Brian shook his head. "Malcolm, where are all the Mackenzie men?" He'd wondered before, but had shied away from getting involved. Not now, though.

" 'Twas the agreement that sent the few who'd not been killed in other battles off—they went to fight along with other clans." Malcolm moved his cup around. "The men werena happy with our laird's decision. They didna feel 'twas honorable to abandon their countrymen."

"I see."

"The laird only did what he thought would save the clan. Many have lost not only their land, but their lives. The Scottish nobles were too busy protecting their holdings in England and Scotland to worry over the fate of their people. 'If there is to be a Scotland, there must be Scots,' the laird said." Malcolm fixed

Brian with a steady gaze. "So, will ye be appealing to Wallace?"

Brian ran a hand through his hair and shook his head. "I've told you before, Malcolm: I'm not one of his men."

"But what of Hooyah? I ken ye know him."

"Hooyah?" Brian laughed. "Malcolm, hooyah isn't a person."

"Aye, he is. Ye were shouting for him in the forest."

Brian laughed harder. "No. Hooyah is a word." He met Malcolm's affronted glare, and swallowed back another round of laughter. "You use it when something goes really right. You shout, 'hooyah.' "

"Oh, aye. 'Tis what ye said." He gave Brian a broad wink. "But still we dinna have any warriors to defend us, other than the farmers. We need more men."

Brian decided to ignore Malcolm's comments. Finishing his ale, he started developing a plan.

"What the hell are you doing?"

The next morning, Brian walked into the room, surprising Caira as she settled her tunic on her shoulders and fought the dizziness the pain brought on.

"You should be in bed," he continued.

She smiled at him. "I've much that needs doing. I canna be abed any longer."

"But your ribs—"

" 'Twill hurt whether I'm up or down." She pulled her braid over her shoulder and started unplaiting her hair. Taking a comb from a table, she carefully pulled it through her locks. Raising her arms above her head to don her tunic sent white-hot pain through her chest.

She decided to be more careful, especially with Brian in the room watching her so closely.

"I thank you for the care you gave me," she said, focusing on the snarls at the ends of her hair. " 'Twould seem you impressed Gitta so, she's put away the sword she was keeping handy." She glanced at him and smiled.

"Well, that's a relief," he said. He grinned.

Slowly, she brought her comb up, biting back a groan of pain. Meeting his narrowed gaze, she stopped her hands and her breath caught in her throat.

"Damn it. You should be in bed," he muttered. Striding toward her, he demanded, "Give me that." He took the comb from her slack fingers and began working it gently through her hair.

The intimacy of the act sent a tremor through Caira's legs. Each long, sensuous stroke of the brush threatened to bring her to her knees. And then he stopped, and she heard his breath whistle through his lips.

He slowly turned her to face him and stared deep into her eyes. Her body shook and her knees rattled. Bringing her hands up, she held on to his waist.

"Caira." Her name came from his lips on a husky sigh. She gently pulled him to her. He gently wrapped his arms around her, and she drank in his comforting strength and soothing warmth.

He touched his lips to her temple and the embers of passion flared at the junction of her legs.

She turned her face to his and accepted his lips in a soft but searing kiss that wiped all thought from her mind and filled her with frantic need.

He tunneled his fingers through her hair and groaned. Caira opened her mouth to accept his questing tongue. Shimmering heat flooded her veins when he flicked his against hers, coaxing her to join him in a sensuous dance of love.

Mindlessly, he pulled Caira closer, desire ricocheting through his body as her feminine curves pressed intimately against him. His fingers tangled in the silk of her hair.

He wanted more.

He moved his hands down her back. Beneath the layers of heavy material, he felt the indentation of her waist and the flare of her hips. He pulled her against his hardness, knowing it wouldn't relieve the ache, but only make it worse.

He needed more. Oh, how he needed more.

Someone coughed, and the sound penetrated the haze of passion in Brian's head. He glanced over his shoulder, Caira still wrapped in his arms.

Caira gasped and stepped away. With the loss of her warmth, Brian's body cooled quickly and he glared at the two old Scotsmen.

His entire body aching for Caira, he looked at her. "Did I hurt you?" he whispered.

She shook her head, a blush coloring her cheeks. She turned her back and held herself completely still.

Glaring at the two grinning Scotsmen, Brian took two long strides to them. "I need to talk to both of you." He grabbed the arm of each and headed for the door.

Callum shook off Brian's hold. "There's something I need to discuss with Caira. I'll join ye shortly."

"Callum." The warning was heavy in Brian's voice, but the old Scot ignored it.

Caira turned. "Go, Brian. I'll speak with Callum."

The door closed and Caira took a deep breath, allowing her shoulders to relax. Her heart still hammered madly in her chest, her entire body humming with unsatisfied passion.

Never had she reacted to a kiss with such intensity.

"Is the floor scorched, then?"

Her gaze shot to Callum, who focused on her.

"Callum!" she gasped, her cheeks warming.

"He's a fine, caring mon, Caira—though he tries to hide it."

She frowned at him then turned her back, clasping her hands together to still their trembling.

"Ye could do worse, ye ken?"

"Callum," she repeated. She spun, grimacing when sharp pain shot through her chest.

"Did ye not tell me if I could find ye a Scot that wasna too young, nor too old, pleasant to look upon, and one able to lead the clan, ye'd wed with him?" Callum propped his hands on his waist. "Well, Skelley meets yer demands and more."

"But, but . . ." She spluttered, a hot blush climbing up her chest to her cheeks.

"Calm, yerself, lass." He put his hands up. "Ye've done a fine job—but whether ye'll admit it or not, ye need a mon to share the burden." He arched his brows. "And 'twould seem ye both share an interest in the other."

"Callum, 'tis none of your co—"

NAME:_____

ADDRESS:_____

_____

_____

TELEPHONE:_____

E-MAIL:_____

_____ I want to pay by credit card.

__ Visa   __ MasterCard   __ Discover

Account Number:_____

Expiration date:_____

SIGNATURE:_____

Send this form, along with $2.00 shipping and handling for your FREE books, to:

Love Spell Romance Book Club
20 Academy Street
Norwalk, CT 06850-4032

Or fax (must include credit card information!) to: 610.995.9274. *You can also sign up on the Web at* www.dorchesterpub.com.

Offer open to residents of the U.S. and Canada only. Canadian residents, please call 1.800.481.9191 for pricing information.

If under 18, a parent or guardian must sign. Terms, prices and conditions subject to change. Subscription subject to acceptance. Dorchester Publishing reserves the right to reject any order or cancel any subscription.

"Just think on it, Caira. 'Tis all I ask." And then he left.

She stared at the closed door.

Think on it, he said. She glanced down at the floor, fully expecting to see the wood singed where she and Brian had stood.

Could she think of aught else?

Chapter Sixteen

"Ach, the stench."

Caira looked up from her needlework as Gitta marched into her solar. "I know," she said with a sigh. "The women have been complaining these two days past."

"And well they should. The air is so heavy with stink, I can taste it on my tongue." Gitta made a face and plopped down on a stool. "What are the men doing?"

Caira shrugged, blew out a breath, and set her work aside. "I'll see if aught can be done about it."

She found Brian just outside the walls of the castle.

"Brian?" she called, stepping around a pile of charred wood. So absorbed were the men in their different tasks, they didn't look up as she passed.

Brian finally finished his conversation.

"What is it you're doing here?" Caira called.

Brian mumbled one last thing to the man with whom he spoke, then nodded to the keep. The Scot hustled off, and Brian made his way over to Caira's side.

"Did you need something?"

"Aye. An end to the foul smell coming from your fires."

"Wish I could help you there, but it's the only way to make the powder."

"What powder?"

A loud pop behind her made her jump. Caira turned, and a black puff of smoke rode the light breeze toward her.

Brian rushed to the side of one of his workers. "Damn it, be careful with that." He and the man started talking, and Caira was forgotten as several others gathered around, clamoring for Brian's attention.

Caira waited a moment, then realized she would get no explanation.

She spotted Malcolm bent over an iron pot. Mayhap he could tell her about the powder.

"Malcolm?" she called.

He glanced up from his work and smiled. "Aye, lass?"

She moved to stand across the small fire from him. "What kind of powder do you make?"

"Black." He ducked his head, focusing on pouring water over yellow crystals at the bottom of an iron pot.

"What does it do?" She recalled Brian mentioning the powder before.

He shrugged. "Things."

"Malcolm." Frustration deepened her voice. Why were the men being so secretive? An air of excitement

171

had filled the hall last eve, and the men in Brian's group had all been suspiciously quiet.

The old Scot put his bucket of water down and stood up. "Ach, Caira, dinna fash yerself over this. 'Tis mon's work."

Her eyes widened, then narrowed. "Mon's work, is it?"

"Aye." He bobbed his head. "Mon's work."

"I see." She clamped down on her rising indignation. Clearly, the old Scot could not answer her question, but he would never admit it.

But mayhap she could gather enough information that she could figure it out herself. She smiled. "What is it you're doing, then?"

"Well, now." He puffed his chest out. "I'm purifying sulfur." He pointed to his iron pot. "Not the most pleasant of tasks, but better than that one." He nodded toward a man pouring hot water over the contents of a bucket.

" 'Tis muck from the stable floor he has. When the hot water is poured over it, the smell near brings a mon to his knees."

"Why? What is the purpose?"

"Saltpeter." Malcolm said the word with an officious nod, but Caira could tell by the vague look on his face that he had no idea what saltpeter was.

Yet neither did she. It would take questioning Brian if she wanted answers to her questions.

Recalling her purpose, she asked, "Well, can you not move your work farther from the castle? The stench is making its way to the hall."

The breeze shifted, and the smell from Malcolm's pot hit him in the face. His eyes watered. "I'd have to hie myself to England to keep *this* odor from Kilbeinn."

"Can you not convince him to stay abed?" Caira pleaded with Brian as Callum started down the steps of the keep. His knee was bandaged, and he was holding his back and leaning heavily on Malcolm.

"I'm not a child to be coddled," the old Scot grumbled, carefully descending the stairs. "If Malcolm wouldna argue over every wee thing, I would have been paying attention to where I walked. 'Tis not the first time the bird's been underfoot, ye ken? But if I trip over Goose again, he'll go in my stew pot." He spoke in a raised voice, casting the offending fowl an aggrieved glare where it sat contentedly on a clump of grass.

Caira looked to Brian for support.

"I'll make sure he takes it easy," he said.

His oddly phrased assurance eased her fears. Yet she would rather Callum have remained where she could watch over him. It wasn't that she didn't trust Brian; she simply knew men and their pride.

She touched Brian's arm to get his attention and felt the familiar leap of her heart when he turned his blue gaze on her.

"This powder that you're making, what will you do with it?" She'd not seen him since yesterday, and this was the first opportunity she had to gain the answers to the questions plaguing her.

"Protect the borders of Mackenzie land."

"With powder?" She chuckled. " 'Tis highly unlikely that the English will give it any consideration."

Brian grinned. "Oh, I think they will." He patted her

hand and ran over to Callum as the older man reached the bottom of the steps.

"He stinks," Gitta said, sniffing pointedly at Brian. "Smells just like the bloody smoke coming from his fires. His garments could use a good washing. Tried to convince him of that when he last bathed, but he'd have nothing of it. I left some of yer father's garments in the chest in the tower room."

Caira chuckled. "Well, if the mon desna want his clothing washed, we canna make him."

Gitta's brows arched. "Is that so?"

"Gitta," Caira warned.

"I've a mind to get the smell of his powder from the keep. Follows him around like that bloody three-legged dog of his."

"And just how do you think to accomplish this?"

The woman grinned, her eyes lighting with mischief. "With a wee bit of help from ye, I think I can see it done."

"What's to be done next?" Malcolm asked as Brian walked with the two Scots toward their cottage.

"I'll need you to show me the areas where the English most often enter Mackenzie land."

"I'll be coming along, just to make sure Malcolm desna get ye both lost," Callum called, hobbling between them.

"Callum, there's something more important I need you to do."

The man gave Brian a suspicious look. "And what might that be?"

"I'll show you when we get to the cottage."

A few minutes later, Brian held a length of thin

174

twine one of the men had made for him, and a deep pot with black powder in the bottom.

"I need you to add enough water to make a thick soup, then put this twine in it. Make sure it's completely immersed."

" 'Tis woman's work," Callum harrumphed. "A thick soup?" He shook his head. "Why the bloody hell do ye need to soak the twine?"

"To make a fuse."

"What's a fuse?"

"Ach, Callum, can ye not just do what Skelley asks?" Malcolm asked.

"I'll not be led around by the—"

"Callum," Brian interrupted. "I'm going to create an early warning system so we'll know when the English are coming. It may very well scare them enough that they'll leave the Mackenzies alone, too."

"Scare them, ye say?"

Brian nodded.

Reaching out, Callum took the twine and pot. "Why did ye not say so?" He grinned.

Brian added one final detail: "Tomorrow, you'll need to take the twine out and stretch it to dry."

Leaving Callum to make the fuse, he then followed Malcolm around the vulnerable areas of the perimeter of Mackenzie land.

"The English fort is over there." Malcolm pointed to the east. "Most times, the *Sassenach* come from that direction."

Brian nodded interestedly, but said nothing.

"What about the wildlife?" Brian looked around. Rabbits and small rodents wouldn't pose a problem, but sheep or deer could spoil his plans.

" 'Tisn't any. The bloody English have hunted them all."

"What about the sheep?"

"Caira had them moved to the upper pastures, well out of reach of the bastards—else they'd kill them too."

As they walked, Malcolm pointed out the boundaries of clan property. Brian made notes in his pad as to the terrain and ideas for the defenses needed.

"So what have ye in mind?" Malcolm finally asked.

Brian slipped his notebook into his pocket and looked around for the most vulnerable Mackenzie land. "Oh, just a little welcoming for the English."

"Ye're going to welcome them?" Malcolm's face mottled, and he glared at Brian.

"Oh yeah, it'll be a welcome like they've never gotten before." He chuckled. "It'll scare the shit out of them."

Malcolm's anger drained away, and he grinned. "Ach, ye're a rare one, ye are, Skelley. What will ye do, then?"

"We're going to set booby traps."

"What the bloody hell is a booby trap?"

"A surprise for the English, Malcolm. We'll make a few of them. You'll see—they'll be a blast."

"Are ye sure 'tis safe?"

"Yeah, I'm sure. But if you see me running, catch up," he warned. He chuckled at Malcolm's open-mouthed shock.

Brian started back to the castle. He had some thinking to do, and quite a bit of preparation.

He worked through the day, and by later that afternoon, dirty and tired, he was pleased with his progress. Heading back to the castle in search of more cloth and twine, he stopped to check on Callum and the fuse. Caira stepped out of the cottage, the old man close behind her.

"Now you must promise not to do too much, Callum."

"Ach, lass, dinna fret over me."

Caira glanced over her shoulder and smiled. Brian returned it. Reluctantly, he looked away from her to the Scotsman. "How are you feeling, Callum?"

"I'm fine." Callum ground the words out. "Will ye cease with the coddling? I'm not so old that a puny bird could do more than give me a few wee bruises."

Brian chuckled as the man disappeared inside his cottage. The door closed with a thud.

"I fear he doesna appreciate my concern, either." Caira said. Turning, she started for the castle.

Brian fell into step beside her. "Oh, he appreciates it, all right. He just doesn't want to show it." When she canted her head, he explained, "It's a guy thing."

"A guy thing?" Caira frowned.

"Yeah." He scratched his forehead. "You know: a *manly* thing."

"Ah." She nodded, smiling.

"Do you have any more cloth to spare?"

"Aye. What are you doing with it all?"

Under ordinary circumstances, Brian wouldn't have thought twice about explaining, but he didn't want to have to answer her questions about how he knew what he knew—questions the men hadn't asked. The men were content with the idea of protecting the clan from the English. He knew they didn't understand what he was doing, but they'd be damned if they'd admit it.

"Malcolm said 'twas for the protection of the clan," Caira prompted when Brian failed to respond.

"Yeah, well, I hope it will. But, Caira, you'll have to figure out something. You can't keep the situation here at Kilbeinn a secret forever."

Her sigh reached into his heart. "Do you have an answer, then? I confess I've thought of naught else, but I canna see a solution."

"Can't you just tell the king that you'll honor the agreement he reached with your father? That seems easy enough."

"He wouldna believe a woman could control the Mackenzie warriors." A rueful chuckle tumbled from her lips and she clenched her hands together. "Ah, to have that worry." She met Brian's gaze. "Actually, I am certain that by now Lord Whitcomb has informed the king of Kilbeinn's lack of guards. We will be like fresh meat dangled before a boar."

"Is there any way to get the men to return?"

" 'Twould put us in more danger were they to come back, even if they could be found. They have fought on the side of Scotland. 'Twould be yet another reason for Longshanks to invade."

They walked along in silence while Brian turned the problem over in his mind.

"You canna seem to keep your face clean," Caira said softly beside him.

Pushing the problem aside, he focused on her. "Yeah." He grinned and rubbed his forehead.

" 'Tis worse now." She giggled. "Your face is near as black as your hands. You'll need a bath if you hope to get clean."

They entered the castle together. "I'll get you the

cloth you need." She nodded to Gitta as the woman crossed the hall. "And send a tub upstairs in the meantime."

"Thanks." The thought of a hot bath brightened his mood. "Oh, and can you spare some twine, too?"

"Aye," Caira replied, moving through the doorway to the kitchens. Gitta gave a grin and followed.

The older woman returned a minute later with a mug of ale, the grin still lighting her face.

"What's with you?" Brian frowned, taking the drink from her.

Gitta arched her brows and glanced around. "No one's with me." She frowned. "Can ye not see that?" She shook her head and toddled back to the kitchens.

Brian climbed the stairs to the tower room. As he removed his boots, the tub arrived, followed by a stream of servants carrying buckets of water.

He slipped his shirt off just as Gitta came in carrying a bowl of soft soap and a length of cloth for him to dry with. Moving the stool beside the tub, she placed the items on it and turned to the bed, stripping it.

Her arms filled with linens and blankets, she left the room without saying anything.

Must be laundry day, he thought, closing the door. He slid his pocketknife from his belt and took everything from his pockets, placing it all on the stool. Shucking the rest of his clothes, he slid into the hot water. This tub was larger than the first he'd used, but he still couldn't stretch his six-foot-plus body out. At least his knees weren't under his chin, he thought.

Dunking himself under the water, he came up just as Gitta returned.

"Well now, ye canna put a clean body back into

these." She held up his clothes. "I'll just be washing them."

"Don't bother. I'll do it later." He'd been saying that to himself for the last few days, but tonight he would wash them and hope they dried by morning.

" 'Tis no bother. The water is hot, and the last of the linens have been washed." She bundled up his clothes, snatching his socks from the tops of his boots.

"But—"

The door closed behind him.

"Well, what the hell am I supposed to do now? Sit in the damned tub until my clothes are dry?" There wasn't anything in the room besides the thin towel he could use to cover himself.

"Guess I'll be parading through the keep wearing nothing but a towel and a smile," he said to the empty room. He grinned, picturing Caira's reaction. He'd rather see *her* wearing only a towel. His body responded to the thought.

Pushing the picture from his mind, he rubbed his whiskered face, wishing he had a razor. He'd never liked facial hair; damned stuff itched, he thought, eyeing his knife.

Gitta returned a few minutes later. "These are the old laird's. They should fit ye well enough."

"Gitta, I'm not wearing a kilt." He shook his head. "I don't wear skirts."

"Tsk, tsk. Have ye spindly legs, then?" She cackled. "Or is it ye dinna have a talent for pleating it?" She waggled her eyebrows. "I can help ye with it." Her gaze swept his bare chest. " 'Twould be a pleasure." She grinned.

"Maybe for you," he grumbled.

"Well, then, if ye're shy." She laid a leather belt on the bed. Then, taking the length of material from the pile of clothing, she quickly pleated it, leaving a length at one end.

Brian stared at the material, trying to figure out what she expected him to do with it. His confusion must have shown on his face, because she looked from him to her work and said, "Ye just lay yerself down and belt it, then bring the loose end over yer shoulder and pin it." She gave him an odd look. "Ye've never worn a kilt afore?"

Brian shook his head.

"Ye're a strange Scot, ye are."

Brian opened his mouth to tell her he was an *American* Scot, but she left the room before the words were out. Which was a good thing, he thought with a shake of his head.

He felt stupid as he made his way downstairs a while later. Kilts were drafty and itchy. The wool fibers of the kilt managed to penetrate the material of the long shirt he wore. He resisted the urge to scratch his butt, knowing that would only make things worse. Damn Gitta for taking his skivvies!

He touched the edge of his jaw. His knife was a poor substitute for a razor, but at least the cut had stopped bleeding. His beard had itched almost as badly as the kilt. Now, he had to admit, it was nice being clean and in clothes that didn't smell like sulfur or saltpeter.

He glanced down at the hall and met Caira's appreciative gaze. There was another benefit to cleanliness, he suddenly realized.

* * *

Caira looked up as Brian descended the stairs, and she grabbed the table for support as her knees wobbled. In her father's garments, he looked every inch a Highlander—even if he was Irish.

The white shirt emphasized the breadth of his chest; the belted kilt, the narrowness of his waist. The hem of his kilt flipped about his knees, drawing attention to his well-formed calves and the black boots encasing his feet.

She pulled her gaze up and swallowed her gasp at the sight of Brian's face. His beard was gone, leaving his skin an angry red, and small cuts marred his sculpted cheeks.

His blue eyes were a stark contrast to his dark hair and tanned skin. His naturally arched brows accented his forehead, and a lock of hair dipped down on one side. The clean lines of his jaw led to corded tendons in his neck. A sprinkling of dark hair showed at the open neck of his shirt.

Willing her heart to slow its beating, she let her gaze wander over Brian again.

Aye, he made a braw Scotsman.

Chapter Seventeen

Caira looked out her window, watching the early-morning light stretch its fingers out to hold Kilbeinn in its warm hands. Even at this early hour, many of the clan were busy coming and going.

Caira shook out her braid. Running a wooden comb through her long locks, she caught sight of the three-legged dog and his jerky stride as he made for the gate. Absently, she braided her hair, searching for Brian even as the dog bounded back toward the keep.

She tied off her braid with a ribbon and flipped the plaited length over her shoulder just as Brian came into view, the dog beside him. Smiling, she admired his confident carriage and the swing of his kilt. He passed two women at the well, and Caira saw them smile and turn to watch him as he continued to the gate, unaware of the admiring looks they cast his way.

She pushed back the surge of possessiveness that welled up within her. Of late, the feeling had intensified, confusing her. Never had she felt so about a man, not even her husband.

Why now? Why Brian?

It was his kiss, she realized as he disappeared beyond the gates. The memory of their last embrace stayed with her, heating her blood, causing her heart to race. But coupled with the pleasure of it was the feeling she'd had of being safe, protected, and utterly a woman. Those things she'd not experienced since becoming a widow. Or even before.

She shook herself from her thoughts.

As head of the clan, she should know what Brian planned for their defense. He'd been so secretive. So had all the men working with him. As laird of the Mackenzies, she should have been privy to all things concerning the safety and well-being of the clan. Her ignorance was not right, and she meant to correct it.

Turning from the window, she glanced at her old brown tunic hanging on a peg. She didn't feel like wearing it. 'Twas too beautiful a morn for such. Nay, today she would wear her favorite tunic.

From her chest she brought out a red tunic. The color complemented her hair and the black lacings at the side hugged her curves. She pulled it on over her white undertunic and donned her wimple.

She left the keep, following the path Brian had traveled. She had no idea where he was bound, but with a question here and a question there, the villagers were able to give her his direction.

The Mackenzie holdings were located in a valley ringed by rugged mountains. There were only three viable routes to enter that valley. Had she the warriors, Caira would have stationed guards at those entrances; but there were no soldiers, and the village men's responsibilities were to sow and harvest their fields to feed their families and the others within the castle walls.

Caira caught a glimpse of Brian on the path ahead of her as she neared the border of Mackenzie land. The crunch of pebbles beneath her shoes must have alerted him to her presence. He turned from his work, his gaze meeting hers.

"I would learn what you are doing, Brian," she said. She held herself rigid, expecting her request to be ignored.

He smiled. "Sure," he said, then turned back.

She blinked in surprise, but wasted no time stepping up behind him to watch as he stretched a length of twine across the path and tied it off to the base of a small tree. She followed the direction of the twine and saw a cloth bundle on a bed of green leaves.

He stood up. "What we have here is an early warning device." Caira looked from the bundle to Brian and frowned. "See, when someone trips this"—he pointed to the twine—"it will cause a spark from the flint that will ignite the fuse. When the fuse burns into the black powder, it will cause an explosion." He grinned. "It'll scare the hell out of any English and send them running in the other direction."

"Will it work?" Caira cast a doubtful gaze at Brian's mechanism.

"As long as I can keep the powder dry, it will. I've spent the last couple days testing it."

"But how will you keep it dry?"

"I thought about putting it in a clay pot with a lid, but the pot would explode, and then there would be flying debris."

Caira shook her head, not certain she understood

exactly what Brian was saying. But she comprehended the results. "And that would not be good?"

"No, Caira." His gaze filled with concern. "We can't engage the English. First, we don't have the manpower. And second, they would consider any harm we caused them as an act of aggression and use it to justify an attack."

"Aye, though they didna seem to need a reason when they attacked me." She touched her temple. The lump had disappeared, and she knew the bruise to her cheek was not much more than a shadow. She'd dispensed with the uncomfortable bindings around her chest and found her ribs pained her little.

"Still hurt?" he asked. The concern in his voice warmed her as a cooling breeze ruffled the edges of her wimple.

"Nay." He arched a brow, so she smiled. "Truly, Brian—I am well."

"Good." Their gazes met and held. The intensity in his eyes went straight to Caira's heart.

Life wouldn't be the same when he left. She knew that. She blinked back the sudden burn of tears and looked away.

Brian cleared his throat.

Gathering her wayward emotions, she shoved all distressing thoughts from her mind and looked up.

"As I was saying, I had to find a way to keep the powder dry. By placing it beneath the protection of a hardwood tree, making a bed of fresh, green leaves, and covering the powder with more, it should stay dry." He placed several large fresh leaves over the bundle. "If it doesn't stop them, at least we'll know they're coming and from which direction."

He covered the twine with leaves and pine needles. Picking up his supplies from a nearby rock, they walked a ways up the path, where he constructed another of these traps.

"I've placed a series of traps on the path the English use most. But I've been thinking it might be better to warn them with a single explosion first and *then* go for the big guns."

Caira shook her head, thoroughly confused. "But how will this scare the English? And what is an explosion?"

Glancing up from arranging leaves to cover the cloth bundle, he frowned. "Oh, yeah." He stood and turned to her. He was silent a long moment. She waited patiently, knowing that he was a cautious man who weighed his words carefully.

"An explosion is a noisy burst of energy."

"So there will be a fearsome noise?"

Brian nodded and gave her a grin. "Followed by a noxious cloud of soot." He chuckled. "Come on, I want to place another charge on the main path."

He held out his hand to help her over a fallen tree as they cut through the woods. Could he feel her pulse quicken, hear her heart thundering in her chest?

She glanced at his profile but could find no reaction to their contact in his face. Her emotions were in turmoil. She could not label them as love, for she could not honestly say she'd experienced that emotion.

Oh, she'd thought she loved Jamie, but that had been nothing more than a young girl's foolish notions. Her dreams of a warm, loving marriage died after their wedding night when Jamie informed her that their marriage was for political gain. He'd confessed to telling her that he loved her only to make her more co-operative when it came time to consummate their vows.

Brian released her hand and she pushed aside the painful memories.

They came to another path that led to Kilbeinn castle. Unlike the others, this one was wide enough for two horses to travel abreast. It was the easiest way to reach the keep, and as such was the weakest point in the castle's protection.

They rounded a bend in the track, and Caira spotted comfrey growing just off the path ahead of them.

"Ach, 'tis perfect," she said, quickening her pace.

"Caira, the trip wire!" The warning in his voice barely registered before his arm circled her waist and he spun her around. A moment later, her feet left the ground and he held her against the length of his muscular body. Their gazes met, and Caira watched the concern in his eyes change to awareness as the heat from their bodies mingled. Her breasts pushed against his chest as she breathed, inhaling the scent of his skin, pulling it deep within her. Anticipation hummed in her veins as she gazed at his lips, a mere breath away from hers.

Kiss me, she thought, lifting her gaze. She stared into his eyes, seeing the flecks of silver lighting the passion in their depths; felt the beat of his heart against her breast.

He loosened his hold on her, and she slid down his body until her feet touched the ground. He brought his head down, and his lips whispered across hers. With a groan, he matched his mouth to hers and she clutched his shoulders, lest her knees melt along with the rest of her body.

Deepening the kiss, he ignited the fire of passion, infusing her with a need to be closer to him, to meld their bodies into one.

He started to pull away, and Caira cried out, bringing her arms up around his neck, holding him close, dipping her tongue between his lips.

His chest vibrated with his groan, and he swept her up in his arms. A moment later, he sat with his back against the trunk of a huge tree and she was perched across his lap.

His hands skimmed her tunic, lightly grazing her breasts. They seemed more sensitive than ever. Her lips and his performed an age-old dance of passion, kindling the fires, but still it wasn't enough.

The hard length of Brian's masculinity pressed against Caira's bottom. Reluctantly, she pulled her lips from his and shifted to straddle him.

He cupped the weight of her breasts, and through the layers of fabric he teased her nipples to peaks. She wanted, nay, she *needed* to touch him—to feel the heat of his skin beneath her hands. Frantically, she tugged at his shirt, his hand helping her remove the garment.

She stared at the expanse of his chest, from the sculpted muscles to the springy dark hair adorning it. She flattened her hands against his skin, feeling the rapid beat of his heart and the heat of his body. She caressed him, moving her hands over the flat, dark disks that were his nipples, and he jerked against her bottom.

"Caira." He groaned her name. His hands cupped

her cheeks, and he pulled her to him to bless her with a deep, soul-searing kiss.

He tugged at her wimple, pulling the cloth from her head. His hands slid down her braid, snatching the ribbon at the end. Then he tunneled his fingers through it, allowing her hair to sift through his hands. Breaking off the kiss, he opened his eyes and held her gaze.

Nay, she thought, *do not stop.* He must have read her thoughts, because in the next second he was bunching up her skirts and, in the process, his kilt. She raised herself to aid him, her mouth descending on his, her hands caressing the naked flesh of his chest.

She gasped against his lips as his hands slid beneath her tunic. They closed over her breasts, palming the nipples. She lowered her bottom and felt the heat of his rigid arousal push against her most sensitive part. Liquid fire pooled between her thighs, and she moved against him, coaxing the fire, building it into an inferno. His fingers worked the laces of her tunic, and cool air skimmed over her passion-warmed skin as he pulled it off.

His mouth closed over her nipple, and he flicked his tongue over the sensitive tip. She moved against him, a tingling ache centered on her woman's mound as his hardness massaged it. Her breath came in short gasps, and her body tensed as she climbed passion's mountain. With a moan pulled from deep within her, she crested the summit and waves of release washed over her.

But it still wasn't enough. She needed him inside her, filling her. Frantically, she rose up, positioning him, and then slowly took him into her body.

Brian gritted his teeth against the exquisite torture as she did. He entered her passion-swollen sheath, the silky length of her auburn hair falling over her shoulders, teasing him with glimpses of the creamy fullness of her breasts.

She brought her mouth down for his kiss. He caressed the sensuous nub of her pleasure, and she gasped against his lips. Pulling back from the kiss, she locked her gaze with his, moving faster, ecstasy glazing her eyes.

Her muscles began contracting then, and she sensed it stripped him of control. They both rode the tidal wave to release.

Chapter Eighteen

Kilts weren't all bad, Brian thought as he held Caira, willing his heart back to its normal rhythm. Hell, they were a lot more convenient than a pair of jeans. At least, for sex.

He rubbed Caira's back, enjoying the way it tapered to her small waist and the satiny smoothness of her skin. With each breath she drew, her breasts rubbed against his chest, causing the blood to again rush to his groin. How the hell could he be hardening once more? The rest of his body felt boneless.

She stirred in his arms, pulled away from his chest. He saw the wonder shining in her gaze. Male pride bubbled up inside him. *He'd* put that look in her eye. He grinned.

She shifted again. Her brow arched when he moved within her. " 'Twould seem we're not finished yet," she whispered.

He leaned back against the tree, wincing only a bit as the bark cut into his back. "Maybe a bed this time?"

Her gaze clouded as she realized: "Ach, your back is sure to be paining you."

In one quick movement, she stood, grabbing her dress from the ground beside her and slipping it on. A cool breeze rustled the leaves overhead and touched Brian's exposed body, effectively tamping down his rampant desire.

He stood up, the hem of his kilt falling to cover him. Caira turned him around to examine his back. Glancing over his shoulder, he said, "It's nothing. Don't worry about it."

She dusted him off. "Aye, you've only a wee scrape here and there. I'll put some salve on them when we return to the keep."

He pulled his shirt on and watched Caira run her fingers through her hair. Picking up the ribbon he'd taken off, Brian said, "Here, turn around."

He read the surprise in her gaze and smiled. She turned her back to him, and he gathered her silky locks in his hands and quickly braided them.

"How did you acquire such talent as lady's maid?" she teased.

He tied off her hair. "Not much different than splicing line." He gave her bottom a playful swat. "Done."

Touching the back of her hair, she commented, " 'Tis well done." She turned. "But what is this splicing?"

"When you join two lines," he explained. When she frowned in confusion, he added, "When you join two ropes together." He shrugged. "It's a sailor thing."

"Ah." Comprehension brightened her face, and she smiled.

"I'm going to set that other trip wire before we go back." He pointed to an area of the path. "Careful, there's one here."

ra nodded and watched as Brian worked. Her heart swelled with emotion. Was it love? She smoothed her hands down her skirts. Mayhap.

She picked up her wimple and brought her hand to the braid falling down her back. 'Twas the second time he had groomed her hair. Never had she heard of a warrior doing such. She frowned, slipping her wimple on and adjusting it. He was a sailor; he must live on the coast of Ireland, and had learned different traditions there.

She added this bit of information to the rest she'd gleaned from him. He wasn't one to talk about himself, but by watching and listening, she'd discovered much of the man beneath the mask of cool indifference.

He was a strong man with a soft heart. And while he did all that he could to hide it, he would not turn his back on those in need.

Like her clan.

And herself.

Nay, he was not cold like she'd first thought. She smiled. Of that she had intimate knowledge. Remembering the heat of his kisses and the power of his response brought a tingling warmth to her face.

Nay, passion flowed through his veins.

And compassion as well, she realized, thinking of the concern that had filled his gaze when she'd opened her eyes after the attack. Anger had turned his eyes the color of a thundercloud, and determination had tightened his jaw. He'd set about devising a way to protect the clan without incurring the wrath of the English.

How he would do what he claimed, she still didn't quite understand.

He joined her a few minutes later, and they started back for the castle.

"Caira?"

She looked over at him.

"Black powder can be very dangerous. If mishandled it can kill or maim. I don't want anyone handling it but me, okay?"

Caira looked from Brian to the sack of powder in his hand. How could such a small, innocent thing as that be as dangerous as he said?

"Caira, promise you won't touch it."

"But when you leave, who will tend to it?"

"We'll deal with that when the time comes."

He reached out and took her hand. His steps slowed, and he turned to her.

"Just promise me. If need be, I'll train one of the men to handle it."

"Aye. I'll not handle it." She hesitated. "When will you be leaving, then?" She steeled herself for his reply.

He shrugged. "I don't know."

Caira's spirits plummeted.

"Not for a while," he added, and her spirits rose again. The change near made her dizzy and she reached out, grasping his hand.

"What's wrong?" He stopped and frowned down at her.

She smiled at him. "I'm fine." She gave his hand a squeeze.

"We'll need to caution everyone to avoid the areas where the trip wires are."

"Aye."

"And they need to know what to do if they hear an explosion."

Caira glanced at him and frowned. "What should they do?"

"Get to the castle as quickly as possible, especially if they hear a series of explosions. That'll mean the English weren't scared off, and that they are advancing on Mackenzie land."

Later that evening, as the hall began to empty after the meal, Caira started for the stairs only to stop when Malcolm called out to her.

"A word, lass?"

She sighed, her gaze locating Brian, who spoke with one of the village men near the door. How she wished for a few private moments with him. Though what she would say, she didn't know. Still, his presence alone soothed her.

"Caira?" Malcolm touched her arm.

"Aye?" She pulled her gaze from Brian and focused on Malcolm.

"There's a wee problem." He shifted and glanced around nervously.

"Aye?" Dear God, not another problem she had to solve.

"Well, ye see, Skelley left Tripod in our cottage this morn, ye ken?"

"Aye." She fixed the old man with a steady stare, willing him to get to the problem so that she might find a bit of solitude to examine her feelings for Brian.

"Well, the cur took a liking to the net Brian uses for a bed, and, well . . ." He glanced up at her. "Ye see, the dog ate his bed. And he has no place to sleep. Can he not sleep in the tower room?"

A surge of joy shot through her body, but Caira schooled her features into a mask of concern. *Pray God it be so,* she thought. Taking a moment as if to reflect upon the problem, she looked across the hall to Brian. He glanced up and met her gaze with a smile and a nod.

Her cheeks heated, and she looked back to Malcolm.

"Very well. I canna see any harm now."

Malcolm grinned and nodded. "I'll just tell Skelley, eh?" He backed away.

"Aye." It would be comforting to know Brian was so close, she knew as she watched Malcolm approach him.

Brian frowned, then glanced up at her, then back to Malcolm. He nodded and looked at her, a smile tilting the corners of his mouth.

Her heart thudded in her chest, and a fluttering began low in Caira's belly, sending a tingling awareness through her body. How could she wait for tonight?

Three days later, Brian stood beside Caira on the steps of the castle. "We'll be back before sunset," he said. He resisted the urge to kiss her, remembering Malcolm, Callum, and a few of the farmers gathered nearby. "Remind everyone to stay within the bailey while we're hunting."

Caira nodded.

Brian moved a little closer to her, drawing her hand

from the folds of her gown. "Will you be okay?"

She nodded again and squeezed his fingers.

Since setting the explosives, Brian had taken up residence in the tower room in the castle, though he didn't actually sleep there. That first night, he'd tossed on the narrow, lumpy bed, unable to find rest. Finally giving up on sleep, he'd left the room and found Caira descending the stairs from her chamber. She held her hand out to him and, stepping over the sleeping bodies of some of the villagers, he made his way to her. Without a word, they'd returned to her room. They'd made love repeatedly.

Unsure how the clan would take the sleeping arrangement, Brian always made sure he was back in his room before the sun rose, with no one the wiser.

"We're ready, Skelley," Callum called out, jarring Brian from his thoughts.

"Have a care," Caira whispered to him, giving his hand another squeeze before pulling away. "I'll see to the preparations we discussed, in case of a siege. 'Tis something I should have done long ago. I should have known the English canna be trusted."

"Don't beat yourself up over it, Caira. You've done a good job taking care of everyone. You can't do everything at once."

She nodded, and he turned and joined the men.

Hunting wasn't something he would normally do, but he was sharing in the food and it was the right thing to do—especially now, with the English threat so close. The idea of a siege hadn't entered his mind until Caira mentioned it at dinner last night. They would need to lay in large stores of food; hence the hunting party that was organized and set out this morning.

Tripod walked beside him, bumping into his leg once in a while, just to let Brian know he was there. He reached down and patted the dog's head. As they left the inner bailey gate, he stopped. "Tripod, go home." He pointed to the keep. "Go home." The dog looked at the castle, then back at Brian. "Tripod, go home," he tried a last time. He pointed again, and the mutt loped off toward the steps of the hall, detouring to chase Goose.

He sighed, loving the beast. His plan not to get involved was in the toilet now.

He grinned.

That plan had been damned from day one, if he was to be honest with himself. And the strange thing was, he was now happy about it.

He hadn't even thought about returning to his own time since Caira's attack. Hell, in the days since he and Caira had made love in the forest, he'd completely put his other life from his mind.

By now, if time was progressing there as here, his commission in the Navy as well as his career was a thing of the past. They weren't likely to promote a missing sailor. And if he were even to return, he'd either find himself in the brig for being AWOL, or in a mental ward when he tried to explain his absence.

"Let's hope Longshanks doesna learn she's a widow," he heard Callum say ahead of him as they walked.

"Aye," Malcolm responded. " 'Tis a dangerous predicament. He could force her to wed with an Englishman who'd take control of Kilbeinn."

"The lass needs a husband, and the clan needs a laird."

Brian listened harder to the conversation, then called out: "The clan *has* a laird. Caira is doing a fine job. And she doesn't have to marry anyone she doesn't want to."

Both men glanced over their shoulder at him.

"But ye dinna understand—"

"Where I come from," Brian cut Callum off. Then he realized what he'd almost blurted, and clamped his mouth shut.

"Aye?" The men stopped and turned around, blocking the narrow trail.

"Never mind." He nudged Malcolm forward, then stomped down the path, swearing at himself.

But the two old Scots' conversation played over and over in his mind. Was it possible that Caira could be forced into marriage?

Yeah, he thought, remembering *Braveheart*. And if she didn't marry whom the king wanted, he would likely attack Kilbeinn. All the black powder in the world wouldn't save the Mackenzies then.

Worry settled on his shoulders. He shook his head. "Just deal with one problem at a time," he mumbled.

The path narrowed, and the hunting party tramped on single file. Brian stepped over a log, then glanced back at Callum. The man's limp was a little more pronounced.

"You all right?" he asked.

Callum glared back at him in response, and Brian chuckled. Tough old geezer.

"Does Malcolm know where we're going?" he asked Callum as the group progressed.

"Aye. Though he could get lost in a one-room cottage, he can track an animal better than most."

"That so?" Brian raised his eyebrows, then searched for Malcolm up ahead. "Who would have thought it."

Callum chuckled. "Aye, 'tis amazing, eh?"

Around midday, they came upon the stag they'd tracked all morning. One of the farmers brought it down.

As the men gathered around the kill, they slapped the farmer on the back and recounted the event.

Ah, male bonding, Brian thought with a grin. A couple of the hunters went in search of a stout pole, and Malcolm wandered off.

Brian had just tied the forelegs of the stag together when Callum approached, a worried frown on his face.

"Have ye seen Malcolm?" he asked.

The men all looked up from their work and shook their heads.

Brian scanned the area. "Last I saw of him, he was headed that way." He nodded toward the dense forest on his right.

"Bloody fool—went to relieve himself and got lost," Callum grumbled, heading in the direction Malcolm traveled.

"Hold on, Callum. I'll come with you."

"I'll come, too," one of the farmers said.

"This is still Mackenzie land, isn't it?" Brian asked. He walked beside Callum as the Scot picked up his friend's track.

"Aye. Do ye think we'd hunt on another clan's property?" Callum bristled.

Brian shook his head. "No, just wanted to get my bearings."

A few minutes later, the forest came alive. Men dressed in kilts, swords drawn, crashed through the foliage and surrounded their little party.

"Who are ye, then?" The speaker, the smallest of the group, brought the tip of his weapon up to Callum's neck. "What do ye here?"

Anger simmered in Brian's veins. Were the Scots now attacking one another?

He stepped in front of Callum, knocking the hostile Scotsman's sword aside. "Those are questions we should be asking you," he said in Gaelic. "You're on Mackenzie land."

"That's right!" Malcolm swaggered into the fray, stepping between two of the warriors.

"Where the hell have you been?" Brian asked, glaring at the old man.

"Got lost," Callum offered from behind him.

Malcolm stuck his chest out and turned on his friend. "I didna get lost, ye old fool—"

"Enough," the hostile Scot growled. "Are ye the Mackenzie laird?" He looked straight at Brian.

"Not officially, yet," Malcolm piped up. Brian cut him a glare.

What the hell did he mean by "not officially, yet"?

"Wallace will be wanting to speak with ye, then." The hostile Scot's words distracted Brian from Malcolm's statement.

"Wallace?"

"Aye."

"Ach, Skelley, imagine meeting up with yer friend

202

like this." The old fool Malcolm grinned, and excitement sparkled in his eyes.

Holy shit, Brian thought as they were herded through the forest to a small clearing. He was about to meet a well-known historical figure who'd lived seven hundred years before him.

He was separated from the others and taken to a smaller group of men, deep in discussion.

"William," his escort said, and the men parted. A tall, redheaded man stood up. Brian felt the man's measuring gaze travel over him.

"Aye?"

I'll be damned, he doesn't look anything like Mel Gibson, Brian decided, meeting the bigger man's stare. Maybe now Malcolm would believe he didn't know the Scottish rebel.

Wallace wore a brown kilt and sported a full beard that matched his hair. His once-white shirt was stained and streaked with dirt.

It was a hard life in this age, Brian thought. *Harder still if you were on the run.*

" 'Tis the Mackenzie."

Brian opened his mouth to correct the man, but William Wallace stepped closer, and their gazes locked. Brian stood his ground, refusing to be intimidated. He waited for the other man to speak.

"You'll be explaining why the Mackenzies refuse to stand with their countrymen."

Brian didn't like the way Wallace demanded an explanation. "Listen, I'd love to stand around discussing the merits of war, but I've got men waiting for us."

Wallace looked over Brian's shoulder.

"Send one of them back to tell the others their companions will join them later," he said.

Brian glanced back to see one of Wallace's warriors nudge Malcolm. The old Scot glared at him, then pushed the farmer forward.

"*He'll* go."

The farmer looked from Malcolm to Wallace, and then to Brian, his gaze questioning.

"Go ahead," Brian said. "Start back to the keep. We'll catch up with you shortly. Tell the others the same."

The farmer scooted off, glancing behind him only once before he disappeared.

"Now, then . . ." Wallace folded his arms over his chest. "You will explain the Mackenzies' refusal to fight."

Brian arched a brow and held his silence, recalling a conversation with Callum. After a few moments, he said, "The Mackenzies don't refuse to fight, they simply can't. The years of war have taken a toll on the clan."

"Aye, I've heard of the bravery of the Mackenzies in the past. 'Tis why it troubles me that they now treaty with the English."

Brian folded his arms over his chest. "The laird did what he had to, to preserve the lives of his people. The Mackenzies chose to remain neutral. It was the only logical choice."

"Logical, mayhap. Honorable, I think not." He squinted at Brian.

Brian matched the man's stare. "Survival is both logical and honorable."

A gleam entered Wallace's eyes. "Survival? Have the Mackenzies turned cowardly?"

Anger inched up Brian's spine, and he stepped forward, coming nose to nose with the rebel general. "A free Scotland would be nothing without Scotsmen to preserve the land, their way of life. Hell, even the language would die. Freedom is worth the fight, yes. But at some point everything comes down to survival."

"So, you are content to let others fight your battles?"

"What do you want me to do? Send out women and children to fight the English? Is it better to commit suicide than to preserve the remnants of a decimated clan? We're not aiding the English, we're simply not confronting them."

Wallace squinted at Brian's shoulder. " 'Tis an unusual clan badge you wear." He indicated the EOD crab.

Brian tamped down his anger, puzzled by the sudden change of subject.

" 'Tis a surprise to find bolts of lightning in the badge of a clan content to hide in their keep."

Brian clamped his jaws shut. Wallace was really pissing him off.

One of the rebel men spoke up: "Aye, William. 'Tis better suited to you—you strike fast and without warning. *You* should be wearing the badge."

"Aye, John, mayhap." Wallace eyed the silver pin holding the end of Brian's kilt to his shirt, then met Brian's glare.

Silence stretched and tension filled the air. Brian clenched his fists. No one was taking his crab. He waited, his gaze locked with Wallace's.

The Scot nodded and grinned, taking a step back.

Brian let out a breath, and the tightness eased away from his jaw down through his shoulders.

"You truly think the English will honor a neutrality agreement?" Wallace asked with a laugh.

Brian returned the man's grin. "We'll deal with them if they don't."

The rebel leader looked interested. "How will you do that without a fighting force?"

"Oh, there are ways to defend Kilbeinn," Brian answered. And part of him looked forward to seeing them work.

Chapter Nineteen

Caira paced the wall. Nibbling at her lip, she scanned the horizon. It was getting late, the sun beginning its descent, and still the hunting party had not returned.

"They'll be along," Gitta said beside her. "Ye ken Malcolm's sense of direction."

Caira smiled. "Aye. Mayhap he wandered off and canna find his way back." But she didn't believe her own words, and the fear that they'd met with an English patrol pulled the smile from her lips.

"Ye care for Skelley, do ye not?" Gitta asked.

Caira sighed, searching the road leading to the keep. "Aye."

"The clan's made note of it."

Caira ceased her pacing and faced the old woman. " 'Tis hard to miss, Gitta." But she stopped short of asking what was being said about where Brian laid his head at night, unsure if anyone knew.

Gitta smiled and nodded. "He would make a good laird. Have ye thought of that?"

"I've thought of naught else." Though she knew

Brian would return to his home, she couldn't help the hope that sprang in her heart that he would remain at Kilbeinn.

" 'Twould keep ye safe from the clutches of Long-shanks were ye to wed with him."

Caira shook her head. "Aye, but 'tis not the reason to join him to the Mackenzies." She started pacing again, Gitta beside her.

"Well, then, what is the right reason?" Gitta asked. The woman touched Caira's arm, pulling her gaze from the forest beyond the keep.

When Caira didn't respond, Gitta's brows rose and a smile teased her lips.

"Ach, then 'tis love?"

Caira shrugged. "Mayhap."

"Ye're not certain?"

"I've not felt this way before. I canna tell if 'tis my heart speaking or my body responding."

Gitta grinned hugely, her eyes sparkling with delight. "Methinks 'tis both." Her gaze lifted from Caira's. "Look ye there." She pointed over Caira's shoulder to the village.

Following her direction, Caira said, "Thanks be to God." The hunting party returned. She squinted against the shadows. But . . .

"Sweet Mary," she cried out, her heart thudding painfully in her chest. She rushed down the steps and through the inner gate to the outer bailey.

She questioned the first man as he walked through the gate: "Where are the others? Where are Brian, Malcolm, and Callum?" She grabbed the farmer's arm.

"He lied," the man said. Caira read the betrayal on his face, and she didn't understand it.

"What? Who lied?"

"Skelley. He doesna know the Wallace—he isna one of his men."

Caira's heartbeat slowed. "He's been claiming that all along." Frustration lent a sharp edge to her voice. "Where *is* he?"

"Wallace has him."

The breath whooshed from Caira's lungs, and she dug her fingers into the farmer's arm, fighting a wave of dizziness. "Jesus, Mary, and Joseph," she gasped. "What happened?" She thought she'd throttle the farmer did he not get the story out, and quickly.

The man recounted the events of the afternoon.

"Wallace said he'd let them go?"

"Aye, but Skelley told us to start for home."

"You left him there?" Disbelief coated Caira's words.

" 'Twere naught we could do. 'Twas getting late, ye ken, and we had the stag to tend to."

Fear lodged like a stone in her chest. Everyone had heard how vengeful Wallace could be with those who betrayed Scotland. Would he view her father's agreement with the English as a betrayal? And would he exact revenge upon Brian, Malcolm, and Callum?

Tears burned behind her eyes, and the farmer moved off with the others to the butchering shed.

Caira didn't know where to turn, what to do. Would Wallace release the men? Would he release Brian?

"Dear God, what do I do?"

"Caira, lass?"

Surprised, she turned to find Gitta beside her. Choking back the tears threatening to fall, Caira clutched the woman's hand and shook her head.

"Wallace willna harm the men," Gitta said.

"How do you know? You've heard what he did to the Scottish nobles."

"Aye, but those men sided with the English. Wallace willna harm a mon for remaining neutral—especially when he hasna warriors to fight with." Gitta squinted into the distance beyond the gates. " 'Twill be full-dark soon—there is naught ye can do till morn, lass."

"But I canna just leave him out there."

Gitta chuckled. "What do ye propose to do, then?" She wrapped her arm around Caira's shoulder and turned her toward the keep. "Ye havena the tracking skill of a warrior, and even if ye did, ye couldna search for him in the dark." The old woman gave Caira's shoulder a gentle squeeze. " 'Tis a woman's lot to wait and worry about her mon."

Caira opened her mouth, but Gitta held up her hand.

"Dinna be so quick to argue, lass. Think upon it."

Together the two women entered the hall. The hunters were all seated at a table, quaffing ale and recounting their story to the listening clan:

"He lied, I tell ye. I saw William Wallace with me own eyes, and the mon is a great giant with red hair and a full beard to match." The farmer Caira had questioned took a long pull from his cup. "And he didna seem too impressed with Skelley." He shook his head. "Nay, he wasna happy with him even a wee bit." He met the gazes of his listeners. "The mon lied to us. He isna one of Wallace's men."

She couldn't tolerate Brian being labeled a liar—especially when Brian was unable to defend himself. "*He* never said he was with Wallace," she called. Heads turned in her direction. "Those were Malcolm's words, not Brian's."

"What of the stories, eh?" another man shouted. "Those were tales of Wallace he told, spoken like a mon who'd experienced the battles." He glared at the farmer.

"He's a storyteller, is he not? And a very good one, 'twould seem, if every one of you believed his tales." She took a step closer to the table, clenching her fists in the folds of her skirt. "Do you not recall him telling you that he wasna one of the rebels?" She met the farmer's gaze. "I'll have no more of this. Brian didna lie to anyone. I'll thank you to finish your meal and hie yourselves home. 'Tis been a long day and 'twill be another tomorrow—for we go in search of the men at first light."

The men grumbled around her, and the farmer stood up. "Does that mean ye'll be going with us, then, Caira?"

"Aye. As head of the clan, 'tis my duty. You'll be leading us back to where the men were last seen." She raised a challenging brow. "You can do that, can you not?"

"Aye." The man thumped his empty mug down on the table. "Though ye may not like what ye find."

Caira sucked in a breath in shocked dismay. "You willna speak such! Wallace wouldna harm another Scot. Especially an innocent one."

She turned and marched up the stairs, blinking back tears of anger, frustration, and worry. But the moment she closed her chamber door, the sorrow rolled down her cheeks in a steady stream. Lying down on the bed, she bit back a cry of anguish and inhaled Brian's scent from the linens. Her heart was engaged, of that there could be no doubt.

She loved Brian Skelley. It was a new, debilitating emotion: to love someone so completely your life would be unbearable without them. Never had she felt thus about her husband. Nay, she had been a good wife and loyal, but his death, while tragic and sad, had not affected her as did the danger Brian was in now.

Curse her womanhood! She thumped the bolster with her fist. Curse the night! The bolster received another frustrated punch. She hated her inability to go to Brian's aid. She feared his life hung in the balance, and she was unable to do anything but wait for word of his death. Gitta's assurances had not convinced her that Wallace would allow Brian to return unscathed.

She paced her chamber until the embers in the hearth turned to ashes and the lavender shadows of morn streaked the floor. Her eyes were stiff and puffy from crying, and her feet sore from constant use.

She splashed cold water on her face, changed her gown and wimple, and went below. With determination, she strode across the hall to the group of men gathered around a table eating a meal of bread and cheese.

"Finish quickly, we must be off." The men glanced up at her with raised eyebrows, and she frowned. "Did you not understand that I meant to leave at first light?"

They scrambled to their feet, stuffing the last of their food in their mouths and gulping their ale.

"Aye, my lady, we're ready."

Caira nodded and led the way out. The farmer caught up with her.

"Are ye sure ye should be coming with us, Caira? 'Tis a hard track we follow."

Caira nodded.

They walked for a short while, and the farmer spoke again. "Ye dinna have to come with us—we'll find the men."

Caira glared at him. "You call Brian Skelley a liar when he isna one. I wonder if you would put forth the effort to save him if he is in danger."

"My lady!" The man gasped, clearly affronted by her lack of trust. "We go to save Callum and Malcolm as well. I wouldna turn my back on clansmen."

"Aye, but can you say the same about Brian?"

She noted color rise in the farmer's face, and his silence shouted an answer.

The sun was just peeking above the treetops when the search party heard a crashing ahead and muted voices. Moving from the track, Caira and the men melted into the thicket. To one side, they silently waited.

The voices became louder.

"I am not lost, ye fool. 'Tis this way."

"Aye. I ken 'tis the right direction, but can ye tell me why we had to walk the entire forest to get there?"

"Come on, you two, quit fighting. We found it, didn't we?"

Caira sprang from her hiding place to the track, a smile stretched across her lips, her heart thumping gloriously in her chest. "Brian!" She called his name just as the three missing men appeared single file on the path.

Tears blurred her vision, and she blinked them back as she looked Malcolm and Callum over quickly. Then her gaze hungrily traveled to Brian, searching him for signs of injury. She drank in his face, their gazes locking for a long moment. She read the question in his blue eyes, just as Malcolm put voice to it.

"Ach, what are ye doing out here, Caira?" Her old friend planted himself in front of her, and she drew her gaze from Brian.

"When you didna return with the others, we worried something had happened to you."

"Didn't the men tell you?" Brian asked. His deep voice was like a warm balm to her soul.

She met his eyes again. "Aye, that you were being held by William Wallace. I didna know what to make of it."

Brian smiled at her, and her knees wobbled. Grasping a sapling growing beside the path lest she throw herself into his arms as she longed to do, Caira allowed Malcolm and Callum to pass her.

Brian stopped and looked at her intently. "Are you okay?"

She smiled up at him and nodded. "Just relieved to find you well."

"I'm sorry you worried. Wallace didn't really give us an option. We had to stay."

"You need not apologize. We're grateful for your return."

"We?" He arched a brow, a smile playing at the corners of his lips.

Caira glanced down at the hem of her gown. Dared she answer his question honestly? Did he share her feelings, then? And what if he didn't? She bit her lip in uncertainty.

The warmth of his finger beneath her chin surprised her. He tipped her face up, and she met his serious gaze.

"I missed you," he said. His low voice vibrated through her, and a flood of joy followed.

"And I, you."

He held her gaze for a long moment, then took her hand and led the way down the path. They caught up with Callum and Malcolm where Malcolm was arguing with the farmer.

"He didna lie!"

"Oh, then why is it his description of Wallace didna match the mon?"

"Because . . . because he was protecting the mon, ye fool. Longshanks and any number of others are hunting Wallace. Skelley wanted to throw them off the trail, 'tis all."

Brian groaned. "How many times do I have to tell Malcolm?" he muttered. Shaking his head, he added. "Well, at least now it's the truth." He glanced at Caira and smiled. "I *do* know Wallace."

Chapter Twenty

The way Caira's face lit up when she saw Brian warmed the cockles of his heart. Whatever cockles are, he thought with a grin.

Her hand tucked within his warmed more than his heart. The urge to pull her into his arms was hard to resist, but he wasn't one to show affection in front of a bunch of Highlanders. In front of anyone.

But later . . . maybe he could convince her to wash his back. He grinned as he imagined her hands moving over his body.

"So, what was William Wallace like?"

Caira's question pulled him from his lascivious thoughts.

"Impressive." He met her gaze. "Intelligent—but a bit quick to draw his sword, from the things he told me." Brian still had a hard time grasping the thought of having met Wallace.

And how many errors there were in *Braveheart*. Nowhere in the movie was there mention of a younger brother, John. Yet Brian had met him. And in the movie Mel Gibson had portrayed Wallace as a little less bloodthirsty.

But, then, reality didn't necessarily make for a good movie.

Early in their conversation, it had dawned on Brian that his knowledge could affect history. And though Wallace prodded him about how he would protect Kilbeinn without direct confrontation, Brian kept his knowledge of black powder to himself.

Thank God, Malcolm and Callum had been struck dumb. He'd never seen the two so quiet. Hell, they hadn't started arguing until the rebels' camp was far behind them.

"Aye, from the stories I've heard, he doesna seem like one to turn the other cheek. And he canna tolerate Scots who side with the English," Caira said. Her fingers tightened around his hand. " 'Twas that worry which kept me from sleep last eve."

Brian glanced down at her. "Caira, the Mackenzies aren't siding with the English. Wallace knows that." He rubbed his thumb over the top of hers. "You thought he would try to kill us?"

"Aye." Her eyes glistened with unshed tears and Brian swallowed against the emotion rising within him. Until this moment, he'd never had anyone waiting for him when he came home. Nor had anyone ever been so concerned for his welfare.

The men he worked with had been interested in his survival, but that was different than having a woman care so deeply that she'd trek . . . He stopped dead in his tracks. "What the hell are you doing out here, anyway?" The thought of her hiking through the hills searching for him and her friends rattled his nerves.

They could have come upon the English bastards at any time, without warning. Caira had barely recovered from the first attack; she might not survive a second assault.

She pulled from his grasp and propped her hands on her hips. "I couldna sit at home waiting on you. It fair drove me crazy last eve." Her gaze burned into him. "I'm not such a weakling that I canna lead my clan in search of our own. So, dinna think to coddle me like a babe."

Our own.

Damn, but it felt good to be included in the clan.

"Whoa, Caira." Brian put both hands up to ward off more of her tirade. "I'm not saying you're weak." Lord, no, he thought as he looked at the irate woman before him. "But you are a woman, and the English . . . Well, you know what I mean." Putting his fear into words brought to mind the day he'd found Caira in the woods, injured, and his palms became damp.

"Ach, I was so worried over you, I didna think about it. But the English willna come this far onto Mackenzie land. Their horses canna travel the rocky paths here. They would have to travel on foot." She canted her head, her eyebrows rose, and her eyes widened. "And you ken they dinna do that very often."

Brian chuckled. Taking her hand in his again, he made his way back with her to Kilbeinn.

Later that day, the entire Mackenzie clan filled the hall to celebrate the return of Brian, Callum, and Malcolm.

"Skelley, ye'll be telling us of yer meeting with Wallace after the meal, eh?" a villager asked as Brian made his way to his seat.

"Not much to tell, I'm afraid." He had other plans for the evening, and they didn't involve a long story. Not unless he was whispering one in Caira's ear while they made love.

"Ach, now, Skelley—ye ken ye talked with the mon for a verra long time. If ye willna tell them"—Malcolm nodded to the people filling the hall—"then I will."

Brian groaned. No doubt Malcolm would exaggerate the whole episode, and the finished product wouldn't even come close to actual events. Oh well.

He ate heartily from the trencher he shared with Caira, his thigh pressing intimately against hers all the while. He couldn't wait to get her alone. They'd had only a few minutes together before some calamity in the kitchen pulled Caira away.

His gaze met hers and he grinned. It wouldn't be long now, he thought.

As servants cleared the tables, a loud boom echoed from outside, out in the Mackenzie valley. The sound rolled over the castle, and for a split second everyone sat frozen. The women's gazes were wide, the men's mouths dropped open.

Brian reacted first. He was out of his chair and opening the door of the great hall before the others began to move. He raced across the inner bailey and up the steps to the wall. He scanned the area beyond the village but could see no movement. Glancing back over his shoulder he watched the clan stream from the hall.

The taller boys and men split up, some manning the wall of the inner bailey, others the outer wall. All of them hustled up the stairs, grabbing old claymores and bows and arrows. The archers took cover behind the highest part of the wall.

Others helped bring the portcullis down in the outer bailey, then climbed the walls to take up their positions.

Caira had taken the skeletal plan he'd given her and refined it, giving everyone tasks to do. She was one impressive woman. And he was damned grateful for her organizational skills.

Pulling himself from his thoughts, Brian turned back, scanning the village and the woods beyond. If there came a succession of explosions, whoever trespassed would be coming in through the village. But everything remained quiet, and he let out a relieved breath.

He started to grin, but then a series of explosions—three, each forty-five seconds apart—brought everyone to a standstill.

Secretly, he was amazed that the multiple explosions had worked, that the powder had stayed dry and the trip wire and flint had functioned properly. But he'd be damned if he let anyone know about his misgivings.

His grin disappeared as he squinted, trying to see into the distance.

Damn, what he'd give for a pair of binoculars. He stared out beyond the village, waiting for the English approach.

Someone touched his arm, and Brian glanced over to meet Caira's worried gaze. "Look there." She pointed beyond the village.

The thud of hoofbeats turned his attention to a riderless mount galloping toward the keep. Brian looked beyond the horse, expecting to see the English in pursuit, but the lane remained empty except for the animal coming straight for the gate of the outer bailey.

The horse must have tripped the second set of wires.

"Hooyah!" he shouted, his fist raised in the air.

A few yards to his right, Brian saw Callum and Malcolm. "Hooyah!" he shouted again, grinning at the men and punching the air wildly.

"Hooyah!" Malcolm shouted back, mimicking him.

"Do I know my explosives or what?"

Callum gave him a puzzled frown.

Brian grinned at the old man. "Damn, that was fine."

"Oh, aye." Malcolm grinned back. "Hooyah!"

Brian stared at the English horse headed toward them. "Looks like you two have got another pet," he said to the two Scots.

"Aye, that we do." Malcolm's eyes filled with joy. "That we do." And he and Callum left to capture the Sassenach mount and acquaint themselves with it.

"Well, I'd better get down there and set another trip wire," Brian said. Caira's hand on his arm stopped him, and he met her worried gaze.

"Is it safe? Do you think the English soldiers will have left?"

Brian nodded and looked into the bailey. Waving his arm, he shouted, "All clear." The gates opened, men left their positions, and the villagers all headed back to their homes.

He turned back to Caira. "I'll be careful." He gave her hand a pat, leaned over, and kissed her forehead, surprising himself with the need to back up his verbal assurance with a sign of his affection. Glancing down into her eyes, he noted her surprise as well. And then a smile bloomed on her lips, making him glad he'd followed his impulse.

"Ye should take a few men with you," she suggested.

He shook his head. "I'll be fine."

"But—"

Brian put his finger against her lips to stop her objection. "But nothing. The more men that go with me, the more I have to watch to make sure they don't trip any other wires." He ran his finger over her lips, arching his brow. "I'll be back, you can count on it." And then he brought his lips down to hers in a quick kiss.

Gathering up his supplies, he left the castle, leaving Tripod in the care of Malcolm and Callum. The pair were in the stables, getting acquainted with their new pet, but they agreed to watch the dog.

Brian chuckled as he walked the track through the village. The old Scots were going to get an even larger collection of English horses.

The villagers nodded to him or called out greetings as they went about the last of their daily chores.

"I dinna ken how ye made such frightful thunder, but I thank ye!" one man called. He came up to Brian, falling in step beside him. "Do ye think they'll return?"

Brian grinned. "I doubt we drove them out of Scotland, but maybe they'll think twice before entering Mackenzie land again."

He couldn't be certain the English weren't hovering nearby, though, so he left the track, making his way through the woods to the discharged traps.

Replacing the charges, he made it back to the keep just as the sun started to set. Entering the room he shared with Caira, he came to a stop. Flickering candlelight illuminated the chamber, and steam rose from a tub placed before the hearth. Caira stood beside it, wearing only a linen tunic. The light from the fire gave him a tantalizing view of the outline of her body.

"Shall I bathe you?" she asked.

He exhaled, his gaze traveling up her body to her face. She smiled and arched a brow.

"Only if I can return the favor." He waggled his eyebrows. Unpinning his kilt, he advanced on her.

She backed away. "Brian?"

He stalked her and his belt hit the floor.

"Brian?" Her voice rose in pitch.

He grinned, allowing the material of his kilt to slide down his body. He kicked it aside.

She moved between the wall and the bed. As he came closer, she scrambled over the mattress.

He stopped. Holding her gaze, he removed his boots and socks, then followed her with slow measured movements.

She backed away until her legs touched the tub.

He pulled his long shirt over his head, tossing it toward the bed.

"Ach, Brian," Caira said. He felt the heat of her gaze as it traveled over his body.

Moving quickly, he reached her, scooped her up in his arms, and stepped into the tub.

Caira's musical laughter filled the room. "The tub isna big enough for the two of us."

"Oh, yes it is—as long as we don't mind being really close."

"How close?" she whispered.

He sat down in the tub, settling Caira onto his lap,

her back to him. Water sloshed over the sides as he leaned back.

She glanced over her shoulder; and her eyes rounded. "Oh, *this* close?"

He groaned as she wiggled her bottom against him.

Bringing his arms around her, he cupped her breasts through the wet material of her dress. "No. Closer," he said. He grazed her nipples with his fingertips.

She sucked in a breath and wiggled again. Glancing over her shoulder again, she protested, "I canna get closer."

"Oh, yes you can."

He tugged at the material covering her.

She offered him an innocent look, then grinned.

"Ach, you mean . . . ?"

Brian nodded.

She levered herself up and stood, offering him a tempting view of her bottom, the wet material of her clothing clinging to her curves.

She turned and faced him. His gaze roamed her body. The thin damp fabric of her shift, nearly transparent, allowed him a wondrous glimpse of the woman beneath.

Reaching down, Caira gathered its hem and slowly tugged her shift up her long, shapely legs. When the bottom of the dress rose to the tops of her thighs, she stopped.

"You ken the tunic is wet," she said.

Brian nodded. His gaze fixed on her thighs, trying to will the thing up higher.

"And if I pull it over my head, 'twill get my hair wet." She looked at him pointedly. " 'Tis dangerous to sleep with wet hair."

"You won't be sleeping for quite a while."

"Oh?" Her smile was seductive. "What will I be doing, then?"

Brian's body hummed with desire. If she didn't strip that dress off soon, he was going to tear the thing from her shoulders.

She tugged the hem up a little higher.

"Caira," he growled. His hands itched to caress every inch of her—to feel her body slide over his, her breasts to rub against his chest, and her legs to wrap around his waist.

The shift rose a little higher, offering him a glimpse of the dark red hair at the apex of her thighs.

He cupped the backs of her calves, moving his hands up her legs. "Take it off," he rasped.

"What? This?" And she whipped the shift over her head. Reaching over, she scooped soap from a dish beside the tub and began slowly rubbing it over her arms and chest.

Enthralled, Brian watched her hands cup her breasts then slide down her sides and over her hips. Iridescent bubbles captured the light from the candles, and the sweet scent of heather surrounded the tub.

With her hands still soapy, Caira bent down and reached for his chest. He captured her hands and shook his head.

"I've got a better idea." He stood up and pulled her into his arms, covering her lips with his and moving her soapy body against his.

Caira gasped against Brian's mouth as their bodies slid together. This *was* a better idea. His hardness pressed against her belly, and liquid heat pooled between her legs. She moved her soapy hands over his wet back, feeling his muscles flex beneath her touch as she pulled him closer.

He groaned and deepened the kiss, his tongue dipping into her mouth. It teased the sensitive inside of her lips.

Rising up on her toes, Caira captured his arousal between her thighs and moved against him. He cupped her bottom, pulling her closer to him, massaging her along the length of his erection.

Tension built within her and she moved faster, craving more. The sound of her heartbeat thrummed in Caira's ears, her body tingling where it met Brian's. Her legs trembled, and she clutched his arms, crying out against his mouth as she climbed the peak of passion and found release.

He held her close, supporting her when her legs refused. He placed gentle kisses on her face and down her neck as her heart slowed its frantic beating.

Taking the bucket of water from beside the tub, Brian rinsed them off, his body still hard with desire. They stepped from the tub, and Caira took her turn: She dried Brian, lingering over his heated member.

With a groan, he drew her hands away and led her to the bed.

She opened to receive him, knowing the earlier release was but a prelude to the joy to come. He slid into her and all her body's muscles rippled in response.

Raining soft kisses over her face, Brian moved within her. Caira matched him, her hands smoothing down his back to clutch his hips. Her breath caught in her chest as heat built at the core of her womanhood—hotter and faster, and finally they rose together and shared a soul-shattering climax.

Bracing his weight on his forearms, Brian rested his forehead against hers. When his breathing slowed, he rolled to his side.

"Ach, dinna abandon me," Caira said.

He moved closer, tucking her up against him. "I won't leave you," he whispered, holding her closer.

"I dinna think I could stand it again."

"Again?" He rubbed her arm.

"Aye." She sighed, snuggling closer. "I lost my mother, then Jamie and then Da." She threaded her fingers with his, pulling their twined hands to her lips.

He hesitated a moment, wondering if he should delve into her history. But he wanted to know what had shaped her. "What happened to your mother?"

Caira sighed. "She became ill with head pains. I tried feverfew. 'Tis the best cure for such. At least I thought it was, but the pain didna ease. I sat with her day and night for over a week." She sniffled. "The pain stole her mind and she didna know me when she passed."

Brian rubbed his cheek against her hair and gave her a gentle squeeze. "She knew you were there."

"I couldna ease her pain. I should have paid attention when she explained the herbs. Mayhap then she would yet live."

"How old were you?"

"Thirteen."

"And you think a girl of thirteen should have been able to save her mother from an illness her mother probably couldn't have cured?" He kissed her hair.

"Caira, it sounds like the illness was something beyond an herbal cure." Probably brain cancer or something like that, he thought.

"Aye, 'twas. But I should have applied myself to her lessons."

"I think you did. You tend to the clan and Callum and Malcolm's pets."

A wry chuckle floated up to him. "They started bringing them home so that I might practice."

Caira fell silent, then she added, "Da's passing was quick. 'Twas a spasm of the heart." Her chest expanded beneath his arm as she pulled in a deep breath. "There was no time to say good-bye."

Another silence fell, and Brian sensed Caira struggled to broach the subject of her husband. He'd wondered what had happened. No one in the clan held Jamie Munro in respect.

"I never said good-bye to Jamie either."

"It was sudden, too?"

"Aye, but not the way you think." She wiggled against him, scooting her bottom closer. He swallowed a groan as his body reacted to her warm, smooth skin.

"When I was fourteen, Jamie caught my eye. I thought him the most handsome of lads at the gathering of clans. Many of the young girls cast their eyes in his direction, but he lavished attention upon me."

"At least he had good taste," Brian said, hoping to lighten her mood.

She chuckled. "Truly?" She turned her head to gaze at him, her lips tipped up at the corners.

He couldn't resist. He lowered his mouth to hers for a quick kiss. "Yup. So, then what happened?"

"Well, I didna see him again until I was eighteen, but I dreamed of him. He sent messages often over the years, and I thought 'twas love we shared.

"Jamie didna want me saying anything to my father. 'Twas his duty, he said.

"I didna truly know the man.

"Jamie and his da had planned well—his father would side with the Scots and Jamie with the English. That way, no matter which way the war went, they would be assured of keeping their land."

She glanced up at Brian and then looked away, pulling in a deep breath. "You ken, we didna learn of this until after the marriage." She shook her head. "One day, a few months later, the Munro laird sent a missive to Jamie. He wouldna tell me what it said. He simply gathered up his things and left.

" 'Twas but three months later I received word of his death. He'd fought for the English, dying at the hands of the Scots."

"I'm sorry, Caira." He pressed his lips against her temple, inhaling her scent. "You've lost so much."

She yawned and closed her eyes. " 'Tis the way of life."

He pulled the covers over them and in a few minutes, her body relaxed against his and her breathing became deep and regular.

Dinna abandon me.

He understood her feelings of abandonment. Even though he'd never been close to his father, after the man died Brian remembered feeling deserted. The doctors had warned his father about alcohol and liver disease, but he'd chosen to ignore them. He'd chosen drink over life.

And Henry had chosen a bullet over life. That was a betrayal Brian still struggled to understand. Henry had abandoned life and Brian. He'd quit.

With the loss of Henry, Brian had turned to drinking and picking fights with anyone he could. He'd hated Henry, his father, and himself.

It had finally come to a head one night when, staggering-drunk, he'd gone home and his mother had told him he was just like his father. He'd raised his hand to her. He hadn't hit her, but just the thought of it had made him sick.

The next morning he'd went to the Navy recruiter, moved his enlistment date up and vowed to never get drunk again or let anyone get close to him.

One out of two wasn't bad, he thought, closing his eyes.

Brian woke in the middle of the night to the patter of rain. Caira slept beside him, her arm draped across his waist, her knee resting on his thigh.

He lay there, listening to the rain, trying to sort out his feelings—not something he'd done much of in his life. He didn't know where to start.

He slid his hand over Caira's and a now-familiar wave of protectiveness washed over him. The delicateness of her bones contrasted sharply with her strong will.

It was the same each time he looked at her: It didn't matter what she was doing, he wanted to reach out and touch her, to protect her from the hard life she lived.

On more than one occasion, he'd compared her to the women of his time and was amazed at her strength.

She didn't have modern technology to make things easier. She worked alongside the other women, never once complaining.

She was kind, caring, and loyal to the clan, determined to see her people into safer times.

He couldn't imagine finding a woman her equal anywhere, either in his time or hers.

Was it love? he wondered.

The patter of the rain increased, diverting Brian's attention from the object of his affection. In the morning he'd have to check the charges he'd set and probably replace them with dry ones.

Caira shifted, snuggling closer to him, her hand wandering down below his waist. He held his breath, his body jerking to attention. The mere thought of her warm hand encircling him made him crazy. After several long, torturous moments, her breathing again became deep and steady.

Amused disappointment followed Brian into slumber. His arms wrapped around her, and her heather-scented hair lulled him to sleep.

Brian woke early, as usual, and silently left Caira to sleep. He headed out to check the trip wires and the black powder. After handling the charges on the secondary trails, he made his way to the main path into the Mackenzie valley.

Only one of the three charges was dry, so he replaced the two damp ones, setting the charges aside to collect as he left. Stepping over the trip wire, he walked the distance to check the single charge that was the first line of defense.

He reached into the bracken, and his fingers encountered the soggy bag of powder. Releasing the trip wire and flint, he replaced the wet bundle with a dry one, clearing away the damp leaves. He arranged layers of dry leaves over it.

A twig snapped, and Brian looked up from his crouched position on the ground. In the next instant, three men on foot surrounded him, swords drawn. Brian recognized them from the encounter with Malcolm and Callum.

"So, what do we have here, eh? A Mackenzie beyond his borders?"

Brian looked up at a fourth man on horseback, whose cold dark gaze was fixed on him. Even though the man's helm covered his head, his plump, ruddy cheeks and the slash of his mouth were exposed. His belly stretched the material of his tunic, and the unpleasant odor of onions surrounded him like a cloud. Brian recognized the man from his visit to the laird's bedroom.

Brian rose slowly to his full height and arched a brow. "You obviously don't all know your boundaries. While you're not trespassing"—he nodded to the man on the horse—"these three are."

The man gave a negligent shrug. "What are you doing out of your hovel?"

"I'd ask you the same thing."

One of the foot soldiers brought the tip of his sword to Brian's neck. "Ye'll answer Lord Whitcomb," he said. Then he screwed up his face. " 'Tis the one who knows Wallace, my lord. Said he was dead, he did."

"Well, well—is that so?" The leader grinned, leaning his forearm on the pommel of his saddle. "My men report having found the rebel's camp." His grin faded.

"What—" Brian cut himself off before he could ask what the hell they were doing so far into Mackenzie territory. He didn't want to give himself or Wallace away.

"Yes?" The Englishman's brows crashed down into a frown. "You were saying?"

"What makes you think it was Wallace?"

"He's one of them, my lord," the foot soldier said.

"I'm not one of Wallace's men, if that's what you mean," Brian said.

"Mayhap we should investigate your claims a little more closely." Lord Whitcomb nodded to the men around him, and suddenly Brian's arms were in a vise-like grip. He struggled against it. Freeing his right arm, he landed a solid punch to the chin of his closest captor. The man went down with a thud, but another hit Brian in the stomach with the power of a sledgehammer. The air whooshed from Brian's lungs, and then the man planted a stinging blow to his temple.

Brian's knees buckled and the world went black.

Chapter Twenty-one

Caira woke and reached for Brian, but her hand found only cool, empty linen. Rolling over, she buried her nose in Brian's bolster, inhaling his scent. She rubbed her hand over the place where he'd slept, a delicious contentment seeping into her bones.

This morn she felt so different. More than happy, much more than satisfied. She frowned, searching her mind for the right word.

She sat up, her gaze traveling to the open window as the first fingers of morning stretched toward the floor.

Complete. The word popped into her mind.

Aye, she thought; never had she felt so complete.

She smiled and slid from the bed. As she dressed, memories of the night before played in her mind. Never had she so enjoyed a bath. And later, he'd patiently listened to her pour out her memories, offered the safety of his arms, and communicated a gentle understanding. Though on the surface Brian had seemed aloof and quiet, Caira now knew the man beneath the facade.

All one had to do was watch him with Tripod or Callum or Malcolm. He had a care for animals and those older, weaker, or smaller than he. His touch was gentle; he was considerate, and none could argue his intelligence. He was not quick to anger, but decisive when he took action.

And when he took her in his arms, her world righted itself. She felt loved and protected.

Love. That was what filled her heart at sight of him. When he was not by her side, an ember glowed steadily in her soul until he was near again, and then the ember would burst into a bright flame, bringing peace and contentment.

"Ach. Caira lass, are ye all right?" Gitta entered the room and stopped, her gaze intent.

Smiling, Caira turned to the woman. "Aye, I'm fine."

The woman shook her head and approached, her head tipped to the side, her shrewd gaze traveling to the bed and back. She arched her brows. Helping Caira don her tunic and quickly braiding her hair, she said. "Ye're in love." She grinned. " 'Tis a good thing, too."

"Oh?"

"Aye. Ye need a husband. The clan needs a laird." She handed Caira a wimple. "Skelley's strong enough and smart enough to lead our people."

"Gitta, you've said this all before."

"Aye, and it bears repeating."

Caira ignored the woman and donned her wimple. "Is he below?"

"Nay, I've not seen him yet this morn."

Disappointment dampened Caira's mood for a moment. "Mayhap he's gone to Callum's."

"He could be anywhere. Ye ken he isna one for idleness."

Caira sat on the bed and pulled on her hose. "Aye, he isna one to watch others work." Slipping her feet into her shoes, she left her bedchamber, Gitta beside her.

"Are we to change the rushes today, then?" the older woman asked.

"Aye, Gitta. We'll begin after everyone has broken their fast."

As was true most mornings, only a few people were at table to eat the morning meal. Caira scanned the room, noting the absence of Callum and Malcolm. No doubt they were with Brian.

"Because of the rain, the bailey is a muddy pit," Gitta complained as they walked through the hall. "Mayhap we should reconsider cleaning the floor in here. Mud will get tracked through faster than we can clean it up."

Caira smiled. "While we clean, no one will be allowed in the main doors of the keep. By the time we've finished, the ground outside will have dried."

And mayhap, she thought, that was what occupied Brian: the rain and mud. He had explained that his black powder must remain dry or it would be useless. No doubt he was tending to it now, and the old Scots were overseeing it. She smiled, recalling the pride puffing out the chests of both men as they regaled her with their contributions to making the powder.

By early afternoon, the old rushes had been removed from the hall and burned, the floor had been cleaned, and the tables and benches had been scrubbed. The ashes had been cleaned from the two massive fireplaces, and fresh kindling and wood stood at the ready.

Caira, Gitta, and several of the village women sat in the sunshine of the inner bailey, weaving new rushes from reeds the boys had harvested that morning.

Several times Caira's hands would still and she would search the bailey for Brian, wondering where he might be and what kept him occupied for so much of the day. Then she chided herself. There was much to do about the keep and the lands of Kilbeinn, few idle moments.

Yet when everyone gathered for the evening meal and Brian failed to appear, concern furrowed Caira's brow.

Malcolm and Callum came through the door, and she rushed up to them.

"Where is Brian?" she asked. She looked beyond them out the open door.

The men glanced at one another, then at Caira.

"We've not seen him all day."

"He's not been with you?"

Both men shook their heads.

"He's not been here?" Callum asked, his voice deep with concern.

"Nay, I thought he was with you . . . that you were checking on the black powder."

Both men shook their heads.

"Ye ken how he is." Malcolm reached for her hand,

trying to reassure her. "Likes to be off by himself. Mayhap he's just lost track of time."

Caira searched Malcolm's gaze. He smiled and patted her hand. "He's a mon, lass. And sometimes a mon needs time to get his thoughts in order."

Caira blinked. "What thoughts?"

The man grinned and raised his brows. "Ach, now lass, dinna play coy. The entire clan knows the two of ye are in love."

"Aye," Callum chimed in. "And a mon like Skelley might need some time alone to adjust to it. Ye ken?"

Malcolm turned Caira around and escorted her to the table. "Dinna worry o'er him, lass. He'll come around." He gave her shoulder a gentle squeeze and took his seat with Callum.

Caira tasted nothing of the meal, her mind consumed with worry.

Had Brian left as suddenly as he arrived? she wondered. Malcolm's words about love would have consoled her had she heard them uttered from Brian's lips. But had he simply gotten tired of tending to the clan and her, and had he left? Had he vanished to make the long journey back to his home?

She chewed on a piece of bread. Had the English found him? Did he lie hurt or wounded? The bread stuck in her throat. Tears blurred her eyes as she fought back panic that threatened to bring her to her feet and rush out to search for him.

Gitta appeared at her side. "Malcolm is right, ye ken. Men dinna accept their emotions as easily as women."

"But what if something has *happened* to him?"

"He's a mon who can take care of himself. Ye must have faith."

Caira nodded instead of voicing her disagreement. There was naught she could do now; evening was falling, and it would be foolish to try to find Brian in the dark.

That knowledge did little to ease her mind.

As she readied herself for bed, her thoughts kept returning to the evening she'd spent in his arms.

I won't leave you.

She wrapped her arms around her waist. Pray God he wasn't lying hurt somewhere. She couldn't bear it. Tears burned her eyes.

"Nay," she said to the empty room. She would think only of his return, not of the possibilities, for they would drive her mad.

She spent the hours until dawn wrestling with her doubts and her worries.

Brian opened his eyes to darkness. His jaw hurt and his body ached. He lay on his side, dirt coating his lips, stones digging into his cheek.

Slowly and with great care, he pushed himself up to a sitting position, bracing his back against the wall. He pulled in a deep breath, the metallic odor of the room burning his lungs as the smell of rotting meat made him choke.

Where the hell was he?

He stood up, splayed his hands on the stone wall. Feeling his way around the room, he'd gone only a few feet when he stumbled.

"What the hell?" he muttered. Kneeling down, he

traced the lines of a smooth stone ditch. He followed it to the other side of the room, wondering what it was for. He found no answers.

Brian continued to explore the room, discovering a wooden door and nothing else. He had no idea what time it was or how long he'd been here.

Or how he would get out.

He completed one lap around the room. The next pass, he felt the walls more carefully, searching for loose stones or any way to get free.

The heavy thud of footsteps and a sliver of light shining from beneath the door stopped Brian's search. The door swung open, a man holding a torch at the threshold.

"You there. Lord Whitcomb will see you now."

The man stood aside, and another guard came into the room, grabbed Brian's hands, pulled them behind his back, and tied them. Shoved from behind, Brian stumbled out into a narrow hall. Following the guard with the torch, he was led through another door.

He blinked against the late-afternoon sun as he was taken to the main building of—he looked around—a castle. It was similar to Kilbeinn, but with gaps in the outer wall—portions of which lay in ruin. The only undamaged section was the corner where he'd been kept. The inner bailey wall was intact, and several men stood at their posts.

"Get along with you," the guard said, shoving him forward.

They escorted him to the great hall. The smell of rotting food and stale beer wafted out. Once inside, the guards knocked on the door of a small room, then opened it, shoving Brian inside. Both soldiers entered and took up positions on either side of the opening.

"Now, then, shall we get down to business?" Lord Whitcomb asked.

He looked better with his helm on, Brian thought as the Englishman stood up and came around the table to glower at him.

His eyes were the color of mud, his hair thin and greasy-looking. Again, the distinct smell of onions surrounded him, filling the room.

Brian arched a brow.

"You're going to tell me where Wallace is."

"Sorry, can't help you."

Suddenly, the guard behind him jerked Brian's arms up behind his head, forcing him to bend over. A burning pain shot through Brian's shoulders. The Englishman in front of him brought up his knee, catching Brian under the chin. Brian's head snapped back, and he swallowed the groan rolling up his throat.

"I am Lord Whitcomb, representative of his majesty, King Edward. You will give me what I request or suffer the consequences."

Brian shook his head. "Like I said . . ." He spat blood from his mouth. "I can't help you."

The guard holding him straightened, easing the strain on Brian's shoulders. He kept his head down as the blood from his cut lip dripped onto the floor.

"I beg you: Take your time. Consider my request." Whitcomb's silky voice held a wealth of menace, and Brian braced himself for whatever would come next.

Whitcomb grasped his hair, pulling Brian's head up to meet his muddy gaze. "You *will* tell me of Wallace's whereabouts. And be warned, my patience will not last forever. And neither will you."

When Whitcomb let go of his hair, Brian held his head up despite the painful grip of the guard. Blood trickled from the corner of his mouth, but still he glared defiantly at the English.

Lord Whitcomb brought his fist up and made solid contact with Brian's face. He did it again. And again. "You bloody Scots should learn your place."

Finally, the beating stopped. "Take him back to the butchering shed."

Butchering shed? No wonder his cell smelled so bad.

The guards took Brian back. Opening the door to his prison, they shoved him in. He slid across the floor, dirt congealing with the blood from his mouth. Rolling to his side, he spat out a mouthful of mud and gore.

Shit, had the bastard had to knee him in the chin like that? He wiggled his jaw. It wasn't broken, but it sure hurt like hell.

And the next time, he might not be so lucky.

He groaned. He couldn't take much more. Pain ricocheted through his body. Every inch of his face stretched as his wounds swelled.

He didn't doubt the bastard was going to kill him, whether or not he gave him any information. This only prolonged the torture.

He closed his eyes and Caira's face appeared. Did she think he'd just left like Jamie?

God, he didn't want to be lumped into a category with Jamie.

He shifted and moaned when a pebble from the floor imbedded in his cheek.

The next beating would kill him.

"There isn't going to be a next time," he said to

himself. His voice rumbled around the room.

He struggled to his feet, making his way to the wall opposite the door. The first thing he had to do was get his hands untied.

Turning his back, he inched along the wall, searching for a sharp-edged stone he could use to work through the rope around his wrists.

He methodically checked the wall from the level of his hands down to the floor.

He stumbled in the trough for the second time. The image of an animal, its stomach slit, blood and organs falling into the spillway, made his insides churn and bile rise in his throat. He pushed the vision away, focusing on the need to free his hands.

After he had checked two of the walls, his thighs trembled from the constant squatting, but he ignored the burning and kept on.

On the third wall, about two feet from the floor, he found a stone jutting out from the rest. He positioned his hands and started working the rope against it, all the time wishing he'd put his pocketknife on the belt of his kilt.

Or better yet, that he'd been able to locate his pants. Damn, Gitta anyway. When and if he got back to Kilbeinn, the woman would give him his britches or he'd know the reason why.

The sun's rays had yet to pierce the morning sky, but Caira and Gitta waited in the great hall for Callum and Malcolm.

"Ye should break yer fast, lass."

"Gitta, I canna eat anything. He hasna returned, and no one has seen him."

The heavy tread of feet heralded the arrival of the two old Scots.

"I'll track him, dinna fash yerself about that. And I'll find him, too." Malcolm's loud voice filled the hall as he and Callum appeared in the keep.

"I didna say ye couldna track him. I just pointed out that we havena an idea where to begin."

"I've been thinking," Caira called out. The men stopped, the surprise on their faces comical if the situation were not so worrisome.

"Aye?" Malcolm looked at her.

"It rained two nights ago."

"So." Malcolm squinted at her, then sat down as Gitta brought out bread and cheese and a pitcher of ale.

"Mayhap the place to begin is where he set the traps for the English."

"Aye, lass, ye've the right of it. 'Twould be *exactly* what Skelley would do." Callum grinned and joined Malcolm at the table. "We'll have a bit to eat, then head straight out."

"I'm coming with you."

Both men brought their heads up and stared open-mouthed at her.

"Now, Caira—"

"But, lass—"

"I canna sit here waiting and worrying."

"But, Caira—"

"We'll take one of the boys to act as messenger. He can report to ye whatever we find," Callum offered, his brow furrowed with concern.

"Do ye think I canna find Skelley without ye?" Malcolm bellowed, pushing to his feet. "Do ye have so little faith in me?"

"Nay, Malcolm. I ken you're the best tracker in the clan."

"Aye, that I am. I can track a trout in a fast moving river, I can."

Callum rolled his eyes and shook his head. "Malcolm, ye should be the storyteller, not Skelley. Yer imagination is amazing."

" 'Tis not my imagination. I know me own skills. In fact—"

"Enough!" Caira propped her hands on her hips. "If you canna stop arguing, how will you find Brian? 'Tis why I'm coming with you."

"But, Caira. Ye've only just recovered—"

"I *have* recovered. I'll get my cloak while you finish your meal."

As she walked to the stairs, she heard Callum say, "See what ye did? I could have convinced her to stay here, but ye had to go and spout that nonsense about tracking a fish. Who ever heard of such?"

Caira returned, descending the stairs a few minutes later, her cloak draped over her arm.

At the front of the keep the door swung open, and a young boy slid to a stop in front of the stairs. "My lady, come quick," he said. The lad's face was white, and his thin chest heaved.

"What is it, Shamus?" She put her hand on the boy's shoulder.

" 'Tis Mum."

"Has her time come, then?" The woman was heavy with child, but Caira didn't think the babe was due for weeks yet.

The boy bobbed his head and took her arm. "Please, my lady, hurry. She's in awful pain. Dinna let her die."

Caira's stomach lurched and rolled, and she swallowed against the rising panic. Dear God, she could not do it. She could not watch another woman die, and she didna have the skills to keep her alive.

She looked at Malcolm and Callum standing beside the table, torn between her need to search for Brian and Shamus's mother's need of her paltry skills.

"Go, Caira. See to Martha," Callum said. He strode toward her. "Ye can do this. Ye are yer mother's daughter. 'Twill be fine." He whispered to her. "Take Gitta with ye." He turned to the boy. "Shamus, we'll be needing yer help to find Skelley."

The boy's eyes rounded. "But me mum—"

"Caira and Gitta will tend to her. We'll need ye to carry word to Caira when we find anything. Can ye do that?"

The boy turned to Caira. "But what if me mum needs me?"

"She'll be needing you more after the babe is born." Caira's smile felt brittle upon her face, and she prayed her voice didn't betray her concern. "Go along with the men. I'll see to your mother and the babe."

Gitta came from the kitchen, Caira's herb box in one hand and a cloak in the other. Caira resigned herself to doing her best.

Later that morning, Shamus stood before her. "How's me mum, my lady?" He clenched his fists at his side. "Has the babe been born, then?"

Caira stepped outside the cottage, squinting against

the glare of the morning sun. "Nay. Not yet." She met the boy's worried gaze. " 'Tis a long and difficult job to bring a new life into the world. But your mother is a strong woman. She'll do fine." Silently Caira prayed for the babe, worried that it would come too soon and she wouldn't be able to save it. Still, there was naught else she could do. "What have you to report?"

"Malcolm says I'm to tell ye that he found tracks, and that he and Callum will follow them. He said to tell ye there was four men—one of them might be Skelley—and one horse. He thinks 'twas the English."

Cold dread trickled down Caira's spine and anxiety wrapped around her heart.

"Caira?" Gitta called to her from the door. Worry wrinkled the woman's brow.

"Aye?" Caira nodded to her, then turned back to the boy. "Thank you for delivering Malcolm's message. Go now and catch up to them. I would have word of their progress."

With one more worried glance to the door, the boy nodded and trotted off.

Caira entered the cottage and went to Martha's side, smoothing the damp hair from her forehead.

" 'Twill be soon now. You must rest between the pains."

Later, Caira tucked the bundled babe beside her exhausted mother. "She's a tiny lass, but she's healthy."

Martha cuddled her daughter, raising her tear-filled gaze to Caira. "My thanks, my lady, for all ye've done."

Gitta answered the knock at the door.

"Caira, the men have returned," she said a moment

later, fixing Caira with an unreadable gaze.

With a nod to the new mother, Caira left the cottage, dread settling low in her stomach.

The boy stood between Callum and Malcolm, his face drawn with worry. Caira pushed aside her concern for Brian and smiled. "You've a sister to look after now," she said. When a grin split the boy's face she added, " 'Tis a big job to care for two women."

"Aye, my lady, 'tis, but I can do it. And da will be back soon."

The boy's father was one of the men who'd gone to fight the English, leaving behind his kin. No one knew the fate of the Mackenzie warriors who'd joined other clans in the rebellion, and Caira was pleased that the boy remained optimistic. She tousled Shamus's hair, and he entered the cottage.

She looked to the old men. "Where is he?" she asked. Her words were quiet, but her voice vibrated with emotion.

"We dinna ken for sure, but 'tis likely the English have him."

Caira's breath slowly hissed out through her lips. "But why? What would they want with him?"

Callum glared at Malcolm. "I told ye not to go spreading tales about Skelley. No doubt they reached the ears of the English lord."

"What tales?"

"That Skelley is one of Wallace's men."

"Well—"

Callum turned on Malcolm. "Well, nothing! How many times did he tell ye that he wasna? But ye insisted he was, and ye convinced most of the clan."

"Whist." Caira's sharp command silenced the two.

"Now isna the time for this. We have to find out where Brian is and get him back."

"Aye, but how are we to do that? Can't verra well go knocking on the English door, now can we?" The reply gnawed at Caira's patience.

"Malcolm, you're not helping." Frantically, Caira searched through possibilities as she and the men started walking to the castle.

"Where's that mangy dog of his?" Gitta asked. Everyone stopped and turned to her.

"Tripod?"

"Aye." The woman shrugged. "I've not seen him for a while."

"Ach," Callum mumbled, and started for the castle again. "Ye ken how the dog followed him wherever he went." They nodded. "Brian worried Tripod would set off his traps. He usually would lock him in one of the unused sheds when he checked—to keep the dog safe, ye ken. Mayhap we'll find him there. I didna see the dog's tracks anywhere else."

Chapter Twenty-two

"Slop for the swine," a voice called.

Brian squinted against the light from the torch one of his guards held as the other set a wooden bowl and cup on the floor just inside the cell. Both guards peered into the room and laughed at the joke.

Brian heaved a sigh of relief. These were two different guards, and they probably didn't know his hands should be tied.

"Eat up. You'll not be getting more until tomorrow," one said.

The door slammed, and Brian scrambled over to the food. Right now, it didn't matter if the bowl held hated gruel; he was too hungry to care. Wiping his hands on his kilt, he picked up the bowl and dipped two fingers in, scooping out a glob of congealed mess.

"God, I must be hungry. This stuff is almost edible," he mumbled, taking another portion.

He finished off half of the gruel and took a few swallows of foul-tasting water. He'd save some for later, he decided as he placed the bowl and cup in a corner.

He started pacing the room. Three strides brought him to the trough; three beyond that, the wall. It wasn't much exercise, but it was better than sitting on the hard dirt floor. Besides, he could think better while moving.

Somehow, he had to escape, and he had to do it before Malcolm convinced Callum to do something stupid—like try to rescue him. That was if the others even knew where he was. He certainly didn't.

And had anyone found Tripod? The poor dog had been in the shed since yesterday morning. Thankfully, Brian had left a bucket of water for him.

And Caira? His chest tightened at the thought of her and the worry his absence must have caused. And the danger she and the clan were now in.

Damn it, he had to get away. But how? The only way out was the thick wooden door. The hinges were on the outside, and a stout bar held it closed.

Even if he could bring the door down, he'd walk right out into the bailey, where the English guards on the wall would see him trying to escape.

Same problem with overpowering his guards at the door to his cell: He'd eventually have to elude the entire watch. He might be able to do it under cover of darkness, but so far the guards had come only when it was light.

He stepped over the trough and stopped. If it was used to divert the muck from slaughtered animals, there should be an outlet, some place for the stuff to go. He followed it to the wall and bent down, running his hands down to the floor, tucking his fingers around the stones that met the top of the trough. What he wouldn't give for a flashlight, he thought as he felt around each stone.

Moving his hand down to the base of the trough, he touched grainy dirt. He scraped at it with his fingers and grinned into the dark.

"Oh, yeah." If he could dislodge one of the small stones blocking the opening, he could use it to dig at the rest of the debris.

A few minutes later, he was rewarded with a small stone. He had no idea what he would do once he cleared the opening. He certainly couldn't crawl through it, but it might give him some fresh air and light.

And hope.

Hours later, his fingers raw from his labors, Brian took a break and finished off his gruel and water. He ran his fingers around the cup, testing the thickness of the wood.

Laying it on its side in the trough, he brought his booted foot down on it. The third time, the crack of wood made him smile. With renewed determination, Brian attacked the blocked opening using a chunk of wood from the broken cup.

The slide of wood across the door interrupted his work. He dropped his digging tool into the trough and moved away just as the door swung open. Brian blinked against the glare of a single torch, held by a guard.

"Where the hell is your bloody food bowl?" The man moved his torch around, casting light over the floor.

One guard? Hope filled Brian's heart. He could overpower one.

"What's taking ye so bloody long?" another guard shouted as he stomped toward the door, dashing Brian's hopes.

Brian picked up the bowl. "Here." He tossed it at the guard. "How about a blanket next time you drop by?" Maybe the man would come back alone. He'd have a better chance of overpowering one guard than two. At the very least, he might escape the discomfort of the floor.

The guard picked up the bowl. "Piece of cake," he said. And the door slammed shut.

"Piece of cake?" Brian shook his head; he must have heard wrong.

A little later, the opening of the door interrupted him again. Two different guards entered. The one with the torch remained by the door; the other walked to Brian. Grabbing him by the arms, he hauled Brian up and escorted him out.

As they left the building, Brian squinted up, making note of where the sentries were on the inner wall, how many men moved about the area outside of it.

As before, he was taken to Lord Whitcomb. His two guards remained in the room, holding his arms while the Englishman resumed his questioning.

"Where is Wallace?"

Brian remained silent.

"Answer me." The lord stepped closer, and Brian eyed him.

"You won't like the answer," he said.

"Ah, so you do know." Whitcomb sounded pleased.

"No, I don't."

The man's fist came out of nowhere, hitting Brian in the side of his face so hard his ear rang.

"See, I told you that you wouldn't like the answer," Brian said, and laughed.

The guards adjusted their hold on him while Whitcomb vented his frustrations. It felt like the beating went on for hours. One of Brian's eyes was swollen shut, his ears were ringing, and one well-placed fist to his stomach had the gruel he'd eaten earlier erupting from his mouth and spewing all over Whitcomb.

"Bloody bastard!" the lord shrieked. With another blow to the side of his head, Brian sank into unconsciousness.

"Caira, Tripod led us to Brian!"

Caira turned from pacing her chamber to find Callum, Malcolm, and Tripod standing at her open door.

"Where?" Her heart pumped hard in her chest and tears welled in her eyes. "Is he well?"

"The English do have him. There's no question. He's being held in the butchering shed. We werena able to get too close, ye ken, but the shed is part of the outer wall. The window's been filled with stone. The only way in is through the door that can be seen from the inner bailey wall."

"I thought you said you couldna get too close."

"Aye. Well, there was an old woman we gleaned the information from. She seen Brian dragged inside."

"Dragged?"

"Aye. The bloody English have beaten Skelley."

Caira swallowed the scream that tore from her heart. Blinking back her tears, she took a deep breath, her spine straightening with determination. "Then we'd best get him home to heal."

"But, Caira, how are we to do that? The Sassenach are everywhere. How will we get to him?"

"I don't know, but I'll think of something."

"Best think quick. The old woman didna think he could take much more."

Caira began pacing, turning over ideas. "Then we'd best take that into consideration when we go to free him."

"We?" Callum stepped forward.

"Aye. *We.* You dinna think I'll sit at home waiting, do you?"

"But, Caira, 'tis dangerous."

"Aye. And since when was danger meant only for men to bear? Every Scot, be they man or woman, is in danger. I willna sit by while others take the risks."

"Mayhap we could dig beneath the wall," Malcolm offered, stepping up beside Callum.

"Ye fool. 'Twould take too long, and they'd see us."

"Well, have ye a better idea?"

"No, but at least I'm no'—"

"Please," Caira interrupted, closing her eyes and praying for divine intervention. "Leave me. Let me think in peace."

The old Scots grumbled but left.

Caira turned to the door. Tripod stood on the threshold, his head down.

"Ach, Three-legs." The dog looked up at the sound of his old name, his tail moving in a hesitant wag.

Caira put her hand out, and he came to her. Kneeling down, she wrapped her arms around him. "What am I going to do?"

She rubbed his coat, and her fingers came away with black soot on the tips.

"Black powder!" She looked at the dog. "Oh, Tripod, bless you." She smiled. "Let's see what Cook has for you, eh?" Jumping up, she left the room, Tripod at her heels.

The door creaked open and Brian struggled to raise his head. *Not again.* He didn't think his body could withstand another beating.

Light pierced his eyes, sending shafts of pain through his head. He groaned.

"I brought you a couple blankets and some water," a voice said. Footsteps came nearer. "Jesus." The guard brought the torch down lower. "Are you all right?"

Brian turned his head.

"Bloody hell." The voice sounded oddly familiar. "Chief Skelley?"

Brian struggled to sit up, shading his eyes from the glare of the torch. "Shaw?"

"Well, I'll be." Lawrence moved to Brian's side. "Here, let me help you." He worked the end of the torch into the dirt floor and set the water beside it. Placing one of the blankets over Brian's back, Lawrence shifted him so the wall braced him. The Brit took Brian's hand and squeezed it. "Glad to see I didn't blow you to pieces." He shook Brian's hand. "Damn sorry about that."

In the dim light, Brian could read the anguish in Shaw's eyes.

"I thought you were dead, too." Brian looked at the familiar face of the Brit, remembering the regret and the guilt he'd felt. "Damn glad you aren't." He gazed around the room. "What the hell are you doing here, anyway?"

"The English found me. I was in bad shape. Had burns on my face and hands and was unconscious for a couple days. I didn't know what had happened. Thought someone was playing a joke on me." Lawrence shrugged. "They think I'm crazy, so I get the grunt jobs." He placed a blanket over Brian's lap. "Damn, I hope I'm not related to any of these bastards." He handed over a cup of water. "What happened to you?"

"Scots found me. Mackenzies. I tried to get back, but . . ."

"How? Was it the blast that sent us here? That's what I thought, but there's no way to replicate it."

"I tried, but it didn't work." Brian brought the cup up, wincing at its contact with his battered lip. He took a sip.

"You tried? What did you use?" Lawrence sat down in front of him.

"I made black powder."

Lawrence let out a low whistle. "Bloody hell. You mean you made it from scratch?"

"Well, I sure as hell didn't go to the local fireworks stand." Brian shook his head. "Sure would have been easier, though."

"Damn me. And it didn't work, eh?"

"No, but then I didn't have you to help me along, did I?"

"Sorry about that, Chief, blowing us both up. Stupid of me. I should have known better."

"Yeah, we *both* should have."

"I'll get you out of here, just as soon as it's safe."

They traded their experiences of the past in low voices.

"You've been down here awhile. Won't they miss you?" Brian finally asked.

Lawrence shrugged. "Not until they wake up from their drunken stupors and want their slop jars emptied." He shivered. "Bloody foul things."

His torch sputtered and went out, sending the room into blackness.

"Damn," Lawrence muttered. "I'll nip out and see how the guards are doing." Brian heard him making his way to the door. "I'll get us both out of here, Chief. Not to worry."

"Shh," Brian hissed.

Lawrence stopped.

Brian held his breath and heard the sounds of scraping on the other side of the wall.

"What was that?" Lawrence whispered, moving back toward him.

"Tripod?" Brian mumbled through swollen lips. The reality overcame hope. "No, it can't be that crazy mutt—he'd never make it digging with one paw." He sighed. A shiver slithered up his spine. "Must just be rats."

"Caira, are ye sure this will work?"

She shook her head and whispered, "Sure? Nay. But Brian said that if this powder is placed in a confined area and the twine lit, it will burst, causing whatever encloses it to break." She didn't feel wrong about breaking her promise to Brian not to handle the powder; his life was in danger.

Guided by the moon, she, Malcolm, and Callum made their way to the English fort. They used the cover of the underbrush to reach the wall. Locating an area of soft dirt against the butchering shed, they began digging two tunnel-like holes.

Caira stuffed a bundle of powder into each hole.

"Now, you should move off a ways and get down," she whispered. She pulled a flint and striker from a small bag.

"Caira?" Malcolm hissed.

She glared at him and put her finger to her lips. Motioning the others off, she waited until they were settled behind the trunk of a tree.

It took her several strikes to light the first fuse. She dashed to the tree the others were behind, the sizzle of the burning wick loud in the quiet of the night. She waited.

A horrendous boom followed. The acrid smell of the powder blended with the dirt billowing in the air, and Caira wondered what she had done.

Brian had just closed his eyes when a loud concussion shook the walls of his cell. A whoosh of air blew by him, carrying the familiar smell of black powder and dirt.

"What the hell?" he said. Forgetting his aching body, he got to his feet. As the dust cleared, he saw three people outlined in a large hole in the wall. Then one darted off to the left.

"Jesus, Mary, and Joseph, did ye see that?" a voice asked.

"Malcolm?" Brian frowned, trying to make out where his friend was.

"Aye. Do ye need aid in leaving this place?" The man sounded like he was chuckling.

"Lawrence?" Brian called out, glancing around the room. The Brit had been there a minute ago. "Shaw?" He turned in a circle, but the man wasn't to be found.

"Who are ye shouting for?" Malcolm called, his voice a little closer.

I'll be damned. Lawrence was gone.

"Hurry, Skelley! We must leave this place," Callum hissed.

Brian climbed through the hole, his body screaming with pain. The door of his cell burst open just as he stumbled over the last of the rubble.

In the torchlight stood Whitcomb and one of the guards. The disbelieving looks on their faces would have been funny if Brian's body didn't hurt so much.

In a moment of total silence, Brian heard the snap and hiss of a burning fuse. He searched the area, following the sound. Turning, he saw Caira, her gaze locked on the gaping hole in the wall, her face frozen in shock. A bag of black powder dangled from her hand, its lit fuse burning rapidly.

Brian reached her in two strides, snatching the bundle from her frozen fingers and tossing it toward the English.

"Get down!" he shouted. Pulling Caira to the ground, he covered her with his body.

A resounding boom shook the earth, and Brian looked up as the remainder of the butchering shed tumbled down.

When his ears stopped ringing, he asked Caira, "Are you okay?" He could barely make out her face in the dark.

He felt her body move as she nodded.

He glanced at the pile of stones that had once been his prison, still trying to grasp Lawrence Shaw's sudden appearance and disappearance. Had these two blasts sent him back? He'd think about it later. Right now, he and the others had to get away before the English descended.

"Let's go!" he shouted. Though his body screamed in pain, he helped Caira up, and with her hand grasped in his, the pair started running for the cover of the forest. Callum and Malcolm appeared from behind a tree, and the four of them made for Mackenzie land.

A ways into the forest they slowed, listening for the sounds of pursuit. Nothing disturbed the serenity of the night, so they stopped to catch their breath.

Moonlight filtered down through the trees, and Brian turned to Caira. Her eyes were the size of saucers, and she started to tremble.

"Caira," he whispered. Wrapping her in his arms, he kissed her forehead. "Are you all right?" He ran his hands over her shoulders and down her back. Had she been hurt by the blast? Or when he'd knocked her to the ground?

"Aye."

He leaned back to look into her face. "You're sure?"

She nodded. " 'Tis fearful, that black powder of yours."

"What the hell were you thinking? Didn't I tell you not to mess with it?" He ran a hand through his hair. "I've already lost one person I care about. I won't lose you." He grasped her shoulders. "You are never going to touch the powder again. Do you understand? You could have been killed!" The picture of her holding the bundle of powder and the fuse burning toward it played again in his mind. "What the hell were you doing holding it?"

She gazed up at him, her face pale in the moonlight. "After the first one broke the wall, I saw the sparks ignite the second twine. I ran to get it. 'Twould have killed you if I hadna moved it. But, then, when I looked up and saw you climbing over the fallen stones, I . . ." She sniffed. "I was that relieved—and shocked at the devastation." And then she cried: great racking sobs that tore through her.

"Shh. It's okay. You did fine." He pulled her close and rubbed her back, let her cry it out.

One of the two other men cleared his throat, and Brian and Caira moved apart.

"Best be getting back to the keep."

As the village came into view, Callum and Malcolm left Brian and Caira to go to their cottage. Caira hadn't spoken, and Brian's jaw hurt too much to question how rashly she'd acted. Thank God she hadn't been hurt in the explosions, just scared half out of her mind. They would talk more once they got home.

Home. It wasn't the first time he'd referred to Kilbeinn that way. He glanced at Caira. *She's one hell of a woman,* he thought. One he wanted to hang on to.

He looked up and saw the moonlight casting a silver glow over the keep.

No, this wasn't an easy life. But if it were easy, anybody could do it. Thinking of his friend, he grinned. Then he grimaced in pain.

His gaze traveled back to Caira and warmth seeped into his heart, radiating outward, the aches and pains of his body soothed by it. Yup, he realized; I love her.

* * *

Caira held herself together through sheer force of will. Never had she been so frightened. Never had she seen such power and destruction as the black powder had wrought.

She refused to think of what could have happened to Brian had the other bundle of powder not been moved. She clutched his hand. She would not think of life without him.

As they entered the hall, Gitta greeted them with a rushlight in her hand.

"Well, I canna say the English have improved yer looks, Skelley."

Caira turned, and gasped when she saw him. "Jesus, Mary, and Joseph," she said. There wasn't a spot on his face that wasn't bruised. One eye was swollen and black; his lower lip was split and his chin was red and abraded. "Your poor face."

"Careful, your compliments will go to my head," he warned.

"Gitta—"

The woman cut her off: "Aye, I'll get yer box and rouse someone to bring up water."

Caira and Brian climbed the stairs to her chamber.

"Sit there on the bed." She went to the hearth and, using twigs, lit several candles.

Gitta knocked and then entered, carrying Caira's herb box. Several servants followed, buckets of hot water in their hands. They emptied them in the linen-lined tub off to the side of the fireplace.

"Would ye like something to drink?" Gitta asked Brian as she handed the box to Caira.

263

"No, thanks. Right now I just want to get cleaned up and sleep for a few days."

The older woman nodded and left.

Caira helped Brian off with his clothes and gasped again at the bruises marring his chest and stomach.

"Ach, Brian." Tears blurred her vision.

"It looks worse than it really is, Caira." He stepped into the tub. "I'll heal." He sank down into the water.

Gently, she bathed him, then poured cool water over his body to rinse the soap. As he dried, she opened her herb box, pulling out the various salves she needed.

He settled in the bed, the linens covering his lower body, and closed his eyes.

With great care, Caira applied salve to his wounds. But no matter how gentle she was, he tensed when she touched his jaw or the cut near his swollen eye.

"Ach, Brian, I dinna mean to cause you more pain."

He took her hand and opened his eyes. "You're not hurting me. In fact, I hardly feel any pain at all now."

She knew he lied, but smiled anyway. Sliding her hand from his, she applied salve to the split in his lower lip.

"Do you think Lord Whitcomb survived?"

"I'd be surprised if he did. The rest of the building fell on him!"

"Good."

"Bloodthirsty little thing, aren't you?"

"Nay, but there is much to be said for justice."

When Brian at last slept, Caira took off her clothes and washed in the cooled bathwater. She then slid into bed, taking up as little room as she could, careful not to disturb Skelley.

She fell asleep in the midst of a prayer thanking God for Brian's safe return—and for the love she felt for him.

Chapter Twenty-three

"I would have you make a good, nourishing broth and fresh bread for Brian to break his fast with when he awakens."

"A broth, my lady? A mon like him needs meat and vegetables." Cook frowned at Caira.

"You are right in that, but 'twill do no good if he canna chew."

"What's this? Did the bloody Sassenach knock out all his teeth?"

"Nay." Caira put up a hand. "But his jaw is sore. Mayhap in a day or so 'twill not pain him so much."

"Aye, my lady. I'll see to it."

Caira started to leave, but Cook stopped her by asking, "Would it be possible, my lady, to see that mutt from my kitchen? He's been warming the floor there." He pointed to Tripod, who raised his head and looked pitifully at Caira. "He's been moaning and whining until you came in."

Caira nodded. "Come along, Tripod. Shall we check on your master?"

The dog jumped up and stretched, his hind end rising as his front end went down. He gave a shake and his tail started wagging.

Caira smiled and held the door for the dog, who ran past her and straight for the stairs.

"Dinna go racing up those stairs!" she called. Tripod slid to a stop in front of them.

"You'll not be disturbing him now, ye ken?" Caira added.

The dog whined, but waited for Caira to pass him, then followed up to the next floor. Trotting to the door to the room where Brian slept, Tripod sat down and stared at Caira. She opened the door, and the dog went to the bed, his nose lifted in the air, his tail wagging.

Brian shifted in his sleep, and his arm flopped over the side of the bed. Tripod's tail moved so fast, the dog could barely keep its feet.

Caira chuckled as the dog nudged Brian's hand. "Whist," she called. She frowned, and advanced to the bedside to gently place Brian's arm back beneath the covers—but his hand curled about hers as she lifted it.

"There you are," he said.

She gazed into his beautiful blue eyes and lifted a brow. "Aye. And so, too, is your beast."

The dog whined and then barked.

" 'Twas Tripod who followed your scent to the English keep," Caira told him.

"I knew he was a good dog." Brian tugged on her hand. "Come, sit down."

"Only for a moment. Then I'll check on your food." She sat on the edge of the bed. "How do you feel this morn?"

"Stiff. Sore. But I feel better than I did last night."
She plucked at the coverlet. "Brian?"

"Yeah?"

"What did you mean when you said you'd not lose another?"

His gaze shifted away from her, and she feared he wouldn't answer.

"Henry."

Caira blinked. "Henry?"

"My best friend." His gaze came back to her and she caught her breath at the pain and sadness turning his eyes to a stormy gray. "He killed himself."

Caira gasped.

"I found him." His voice cracked. "I was just a kid . . . He was just a kid." Brian shook his head. "He was my lifeline when my world was spiraling out of control. My one true friend, and he just ended it when things got tough."

She took his hand. " 'Tis sorry I am for your loss."

"It was years ago."

"Aye, but you suffer still."

He gave her a slight shrug. "I just never got close to people after that."

She nodded and slid from the bed. "I'll see to your food now."

He stopped her before she left. "Caira?" She turned and faced him, and he frowned. "We need to talk."

"Later, when you've rested." She was suddenly full of nervousness. What would he say?

"I'm rested now."

"Nay. First you need food, then more rest," she commanded. "Later we'll talk."

She escaped then, closing the door, her stomach

knotted with anxiety. Would he leave now? What would she do if he did? Despite how she wanted to protect herself, she'd fallen in love with Brian. Worse, she feared he did not return her feelings.

"Well, there. Ye dinna look much better this morn." Gitta came in, a tray in her hand. Brian looked at her.

"At least I've got an excuse," he teased, trying to cover up his disappointment that it wasn't Caira bringing the meal.

She glanced up from the tray and frowned. Brian grinned, careful not to resplit his wounded lip.

"Ach, now, is that any way to talk to the woman with yer food?" She chuckled as she set the tray on the table.

"Where's Caira?"

"Tsk, tsk. Ye're not the only one in the keep, ye ken?"

Brian winced as he sat up. Gitta glanced at him and frowned. "Whate'er did ye say to that English bastard to make him beat ye like this." Her gaze fastened on the bruises on his chest and stomach.

"He asked to meet you." Brian shrugged. "I said no."

"Well, ye should have brought him to me door. Then 'twould be him who looks so bad this morn."

Brian laughed. The crusty old bird had plenty of spunk; he'd give her that.

She placed the food tray on his lap, then stood back and folded her hands across her chest. "Now, then, what did he really want?"

Brian looked down at the food: chunks of bread beside a bowl of broth. Dipping the spoon into the bowl, he brought the broth to his lips and carefully tasted it.

The damned spoon was too big for him to get into his sore mouth, and he made a slurping sound as he ate.

He glanced up to meet the steady gaze of Gitta. "Well?" she prodded.

He tore the bread into small pieces and dropped each into his bowl. "He wanted to know where Wallace was."

"I take it ye didna tell them what they wanted to know."

Brian snorted. "You could say that," he agreed.

"Good." The woman went to the door.

"Gitta?" he called. She turned. "Where the hell are my clothes?" She nodded to the trunk at the end of the bed.

"Ye'll find yer strange belongings there. So, too, is yer kilt and tunic." She opened the door, then glanced over her shoulder. "If I say so meself, ye look better in good Scottish cloth." With that, she closed the door.

Brian finished his food and moved the tray aside. He sat for a moment, thinking about Lawrence. The man had vanished so quickly and thoroughly, he was almost certain of what had happened. Difficult to believe, but hell, he had proof . . . twice now.

Why had Lawrence gone back and not him? Not that Brian minded. He'd come to some decisions over the last few days, and one of them was to remain here with Caira and her clan. That is, if she was agreeable.

With food in his stomach, he felt better, stronger.

He got out of bed, swallowing a groan as his body protested. He used the garderobe, then went to the trunk and flipped it open. There, on the bottom, were his neatly folded cammies. Beside his clothes was material that made up a kilt and a long white shirt. His

EOD crab had been placed on top of the stack.

He glanced between the two sets of clothing. No way did he feel up to trying to pleat the material of the kilt. Groaning, he pulled out his cammies.

He managed to get dressed. After doing so, he made his way down to the hall in search of Caira.

Malcolm and Callum sat at a table, a pitcher of ale in front of them. Malcolm looked up.

"Ach, Skelley, ye look a fright."

"Thanks, Malcolm, I hadn't noticed."

"Come share a cup of ale with us." Callum raised his mug and grinned.

Brian shook his head. "Thanks, but I'm looking for Caira. Have you seen her?"

"Aye." Callum's grin disappeared. "She's tending a new mother down with a fever."

"Aye. She'll be busy awhile." Malcolm held up an empty cup. "Ye willna see her till the evening meal."

Brian sat down, taking the mug. "There's something I wanted to talk to you two about. Might just as well do it now."

"Oh?" Callum took a sip of his drink.

Brian nodded. Looking from Callum to Malcolm, he explained, "It's about last night."

"Aye." Malcolm grinned. "Never in my life did I see such." He chuckled.

"Yeah, exactly. I don't think it's a good idea to spread that story around."

"But, Brian, yer invention is akin to magic."

"Exactly. And I wouldn't want to be burned at the stake for it, either."

Callum nodded, elbowing his friend. He seemed to understand. "Ye've the right of it. Ye ken, ye'll have to keep yer big mouth silent?" he said to Malcolm.

"My big mouth?" Malcolm bristled. "Ye've the mouth—"

"Hey!" Brian interrupted the old men. "It doesn't matter. What's important is that the English never know that you and Caira freed me. No doubt they'll be coming down here with questions."

"Ach, I didna think of that."

"I don't want you three involved. I'll take care of whatever fallout there is."

"Fall-out?" Malcolm turned to his friend. "Ye ken what he's talking aboot?" He turned back to Brian. "There are times, Skelley, 'tis like ye're not speaking our tongue."

"Problems. There could be problems from my escape. That's what I meant."

"What will ye do?" Callum's brows furrowed. "The bastards had no reason to take ye prisoner in the first place."

"Exactly. But I'll handle that. I just want you to keep Caira's use of that black powder to yourselves. It would be safer for everyone."

"Aye." Both men nodded.

"Mayhap *later* I can tell the story?" Malcolm asked, hope brightening his gaze.

Brian shrugged. "Yeah, maybe later. Much later."

Caira tended Martha through the night. She feared her paltry skills were no match for the fever raging in the woman, but she would do her best.

She'd given the babe into the care of another mother with milk enough to feed the poor mite.

272

As the lavender hues of morn lit the sky, Martha's fever rose.

"Will me mum die?" Shamus whispered to Caira as she coaxed him to eat a bowl of porridge she'd prepared.

"I pray not, but if 'tis God's will, there is naught one can do." She would not lie to the lad. Best to prepare him, she thought sadly.

"Not me mum."

The boy began to cry, and Caira pulled him into her arms, praying God would show mercy and spare Martha. But childbed fever was often fatal, and Caira's hope had dwindled as the hours passed and she applied cool cloths to the woman's face.

She sat on a stool beside her patient's bed, and exhaustion weighed her body until she slid into an exhausted sleep.

She awoke when her shoulder was prodded.

"My lady?" Shamus stood at her side, the door to the cottage open, the late-morning light flooding the room.

"Caira?" Brian's voice pulled her to her feet, and in the next instant, he was inside the cottage and holding her in his arms. "Is there anything I can do?"

She shook her head, taking deep breaths, fighting back her tears. Dear God, how she needed this man's strength. But . . .

He rubbed her back. "Where's the baby?"

"She's being cared for by another mother."

"How's the mother?"

"I've done all I can. 'Tis up to God now."

She tightened her arms around him, longing to

purge herself of the fear and doubt clogging her throat. She wanted to explain her terror, but Shamus watched, from the shadows, so in the end she let go of Brian and returned to the woman in the bed. Placing a hand upon Martha's dry, hot brow, she frowned.

"If only the fever would break." She dipped a rag in a bowl of water and placed it on the woman's forehead. Her hand shook. *Please God, dinna take Martha.*

Looking up, she noticed Brian wore his old strange clothing. "You look better in a kilt," she offered, hoping to hide her unhappiness. "How do you feel?"

Looking down at his pants, he grinned. "So, you like my legs, do you?"

She nodded.

"I'm feeling a lot better than yesterday. Thanks to you," he added. He scanned the room, a look of surprise on his face when Shamus stepped out of the shadows.

The boy glanced at Caira.

" 'Tis Shamus," she said to Brian. She turned to the boy. "Shamus, have you heard of Brian Skelley?"

"Aye, my lady." The youngster's eyes widened, and he took another step forward. "Ye're the one whose clan weavers fell into the whisky barrel afore they started their work."

Brian's laugh filled the room. "Yeah—it kind of looks that way, doesn't it?" Again, he glanced at Caira. "Why don't you fetch some fresh water?" he asked the boy.

Caira agreed: "Aye, 'twould be good to have some nice cool water for your mother."

Shamus hastened out the door, snatching up the water bucket on his way. He seemed glad to have something to do.

"My thanks, Brian. The boy is very worried that his mother willna make it."

"Will she?"

Caira swallowed against the lump rising in her throat. She shrugged. "I havena the skill of my mother. I didna apply myself to learning the healing arts from her." A tear traced a warm path down her cheek. "And when she became sick, I couldna save her." She sniffed. "I am no healer."

Brian wrapped his arms around her. "Shh, Caira." He rubbed her back and kissed her temple. "You're too hard on yourself. You did everything possible. No one could have saved your mother." He nodded to Martha. "Why don't you cover her with a damp sheet to cool her body?"

Caira nodded, gathering her composure, and moved out of his arms. "Aye, 'twould help, I think."

She found extra linen and dampened it with the last of the water in her bowl. Draping it over Martha, she pressed it against the woman's fevered body.

Each time the heat from Martha sucked the coolness from the cloth, Caira ladled more cool water over it. Brian kept Shamus gathering wood and working around the cottage.

By midafternoon, Caira's efforts were rewarded. Martha's skin was dotted with moisture and wasn't as hot.

Caira warmed a pot of soup prepared by one of the villagers and fed Shamus, Brian, and herself. She checked on her patient while Brian and Shamus cleaned up.

Martha opened her eyes as Caira touched her brow. "The babe?" she asked in a weak voice.

Caira smiled. "She's well. I've sent her to a wet nurse."

Tears welled in Martha's eyes, and she took Caira's hand. "My thanks, healer."

Caira squeezed the woman's hand, unable to speak for the emotion clogging her throat.

"Shamus?" Martha asked, looking into Caira's gaze. She cleared her throat and blinked. "He's here."

"Mum?" The boy approached, his eyes bright with tears. "Ye're not going to die?"

"Nay, lad. 'Twas just a wee fever, ye ken?"

Caira moved away, giving Martha time to assuage her son's fears.

A few minutes later, she'd gathered up her herbs and packed her box. She stood at the end of the bed, feeling proud that the woman would live. And grateful to God for having answered her prayer.

"You'll be weak for a while," she told the woman. "Dinna be too quick to rise. One of the others will come to help you."

"Thank you, my lady. Yer mother would be proud of ye and yer good work."

Caira nodded, swallowing back her tears. Then, with Brian beside her carrying her box, she left the cottage.

Her legs trembled with fatigue. It was an effort just to keep her eyes open as she walked, and she stumbled halfway back to the keep.

As if he'd been awaiting the opportunity, Brian swept her up into his arms. As Caira buried her face in his neck and allowed her emotions to overcome her, he said, "You *are* a healer, Caira." His deep voice washed over her, and his words soothed her battered soul.

If only he would stay and soothe her always.

Caira slept the dreamless sleep of the exhausted, waking late the next morning.

"Ye're not going to sleep another entire day away, are ye?" Gitta asked entering the bedchamber. "Yer mon has been below, pacing like a caged animal."

Caira rose, washed, and dressed. Gitta chattered about the happenings in the castle during her absence.

"And ye ken, Malcolm willna say a word about what happened the other night."

"Truly? Is he feeling unwell, then?"

Gitta chuckled. "Could be. But I think 'twas Skelley who told him to hold his wayward tongue."

"But why?"

The woman shrugged. "Who's to ken a mon's mind."

She went downstairs, and Brian greeted her on the last step. His smile brightened her world, and the touch of his hand spread warmth through her body.

"Did you get enough rest?" he asked.

"Aye." She smiled back. "And now I'm famished."

She sat down and a servant brought food, setting it before her.

"We'll talk after you've eaten," he said.

Caira took a sip of ale and looked into Brian's eyes, but she could find no hint as to what was to come. Had he changed his mind? Her appetite fled, and anxiety filled her stomach. Did he wish to tell her he was leaving? Was he joining with Wallace? Possibilities spun in a dizzying circle in her mind.

"I should check on Martha." She didn't want to hear the words that would break her heart. She pushed to her feet. " 'Twill take but a moment."

It didn't take Caira long to walk to Martha's cottage, and she found the woman weak but doing well. Now she would face Brian, she thought; she was laird of the Mackenzies and, as such, she should stand and face all difficulties. She stiffened her spine, resolutely tamping down her fear.

Brian had watched Caira go, silently welcoming the extra time to gather his thoughts and refine his plan.

He climbed the stairs and entered the bedroom. Opening the trunk, he pulled out the kilt and tunic. He stripped down to his skivvies, pulled on the white shirt, and stretched the wool kilt the length of the bed. He stared at it in annoyance.

He had to do this.

And he did! After several attempts, he finally had the material pleated and belted around his waist. Using his crab, he pinned the excess length to the shoulder of his tunic.

"You wear it well."

Brian turned at the sound of Caira's voice.

"Damn thing's a pain to get right," he said, feeling foolish.

She came over, and her hands trembled as she adjusted a few of the pleats. He touched her hand. "How is Martha?"

Caira smiled, and a strange look came into her eye. "Much better."

"Good." He folded his fingers around her hand and pulled her toward the bed. "Come and sit down. There's something I need to say to you."

Caira perched on the edge of the mattress, her worried gaze meeting his. He sat beside her and took a deep breath. He'd never said the words before, and he wasn't certain he'd do it right.

"Caira?"

"Aye?"

He took another deep breath, his heart beating a little faster, his palms beginning to sweat.

"I've never met a woman like you before. You work so hard and care so deeply for your people. And they love and admire you for your loyalty." He squeezed her hand. "And so do I."

"You admire my loyalty?" She frowned.

"Damn it," he mumbled. He wasn't doing this right. He cleared his throat and straightened his shoulders. "Yes, I do—but more importantly, I love you."

Her eyes filled with tears, and Brian watched in surprised dismay as they traced twin paths down her cheeks. Shit. Shouldn't he have said it that way? Hell, how else could he have said it?

A sob tore from Caira's throat, and she flung herself into Brian's arms. "Ach, Brian. I love you, too!" Never had she thought to love a man as she did this one. This was her heart's desire come true.

She smiled.

The door burst open. Caira and Brian turned to find

Gitta standing on the threshold, panic etched in every line of her face.

"Ye must come downstairs. 'Tis the English lord."

Fear rippled through Caira, wiping out her joy.

"You must stay here, Brian. Dinna let him see you."

"But, how did he get here without tripping the booby traps?"

"Ach, Brian. While you recovered, it rained. The powder must have gotten wet."

"Caira, ye must come. *Now.*" Gitta hustled from the room.

"No, Caira. I'll handle this."

"Aye, I know you can—but think of the English reaction to you." She smoothed her hands over her gown. "I canna believe he lives. 'Twas nothing but a pile of rubble, and he was beneath it. Surely he could not have survived." She rushed to the door and stopped. "Promise you'll stay here?"

"Caira?" Gitta's anxious voice echoed down the hall.

With one last glance at Brian, Caira left the room and descended the stairs.

As she stepped outside the hall, her gaze scanned the crowded inner bailey. The entire village surrounded the English soldiers and their leader.

Gitta hadn't invited the man inside, and he awaited Caira at the foot of the steps to the keep.

"Are you Caira Mackenzie?" the man asked. She descended the stairs, halting halfway down to meet the Englishman's cool gaze.

"Aye." Relief washed over Caira at sight of the stranger.

"I would meet with the Mackenzie laird."

Panic clawed her throat. Brian had said that she couldn't hide the truth forever. It would seem the time had come.

She straightened her shoulders, unwilling to give up the secret. "And what do you want with him?"

"I do not discuss the Crown's business with a mere woman. Now, show me to the laird."

"*There* is the laird," Malcolm shouted, pointing over Caira's shoulder. She turned and saw Brian framed in the massive door of the keep.

He stood, his legs braced apart, his arms folded over his chest. Despite his poor battered face, or mayhap because of it, he appeared a force to be dealt with.

Caira glanced back to the Englishman. The man's eyes rounded at the sight of Brian.

"You are the Mackenzie laird?"

"Aye, he is," Malcolm answered.

The Englishman looked from the old Scot to Brian. Brian nodded.

"I am Lord Hillsboro, the new commander of the English garrison at Garethmuir. I would speak with you."

"I'm listening."

Pride bubbled through Caira at Brian's strength. He would not bow to the English.

"I would rather speak in private."

Brian arched a brow. "If it has to do with my people, then we'll discuss it before them."

Hillsboro glanced around him. A menacing crowd of Mackenzies closed in. The Englishman swallowed.

"Very well." He cleared his throat, climbing up a step toward Brian. "I'm searching for an escaped prisoner who might know of the death of Lord Whitcomb and his guard. I was told a Mackenzie villager trespassed on English soil."

"I am that prisoner."

"You?" Hillsboro paled. "But—"

"I was taken from Mackenzie land, not English—by Whitcomb."

The Englishman seemed shocked. "But surely there is a mistake."

"Yes, and the English made it." Brian moved from the door to stand at the edge of the top step. One brow inched higher as he glared at the man. "You broke the pact made by your king."

Hillsboro swallowed and glanced over his shoulder. "You there, were you not present when the Mackenzie was captured?"

One of the soldiers moved his mount forward. "Aye, my lord."

"And where was the man found?" He nodded toward Brian.

"Ah, my lord . . . Well, you see . . . The boundaries are difficult—"

"Was he on Mackenzie land?" Hillsboro shouted. His face reddened.

The soldier ducked his head. "Aye, my lord."

Hillsboro turned back to Brian. "The borders of your land must be clearly marked, or I cannot ensure the safety of your people."

"*I'll* ensure their safety." Brian raised his chin. "It would be a good idea if *you* learned *your* borders." The men glared at each other for a long, silent moment.

The English lord looked away first, and a thrill of

victory washed over Caira. Truly, it would be wonderful if Brian were laird.

"I would have your account of what happened to the butchering shed at Garethmuir."

Brian shrugged. "What can I tell you? The walls collapsed. I escaped."

"The walls simply collapsed?" Hillsboro narrowed his gaze. "Some of the soldiers said they heard a loud noise—like thunder."

" 'Twas God—avenging your treatment of the Scots!" Malcolm shouted. A rumble of agreement rose from the gathered crowd.

Hillsboro shifted, wiping sweat from his temple. "One of our English servants is missing, also."

"Probably ran off." Brian's gaze swept over him. "Can't say I blame him." He descended a step. "I don't expect to see you on Mackenzie land again."

Hillsboro straightened, shooting a glance up to Brian. He fell silent a moment, and Caira glanced from Brian back to the Englishman.

"I was told the Mackenzie laird was of mature years. Are you his son?"

"No." Brian propped his fists on his waist.

"Well, if you're not his son, then who are you?"

"Caira Mackenzie's husband."

Caira stifled her gasp with her hand. Her gaze bounced from Brian to the pleased grins of Callum and Malcolm, then to the nodding villagers in the bailey.

Does he know what he says?

Would an Irishman know of handfasting?

Her heart thudded in her chest. Dared she hope? Did this mean he would not be making the long journey back to his home?

She tamped down the joy blossoming in her heart. He was doing what was needed to ensure both his safety and that of the clan. That might be all.

Hillsboro's voice intruded on her thoughts. "Very well." He nodded. "There is still the issue of the neutrality agreement the old laird made with the king."

"We'll abide by it if you will."

Caira watched Brian descend the steps to stand beside her.

Hillsboro nodded. "Very well, then. I expect you to keep to your borders and honor the agreement."

Brian arched a brow and nodded as well.

Hillsboro mounted his horse and led his men out of the bailey.

Caira looked up at Brian, her heart pumping erratically in her chest. "Do you ken what you just did?"

"Saved our butts?"

She ignored his response. "Before witnesses, you proclaimed yourself my husband."

"Yeah, well?"

"And do I proclaim you my husband, we will be wed."

"Just like that? No fancy wedding and all that stuff?"

"Aye."

"Cool." He grinned. "So, if I were to say, 'I take Caira Mackenzie as my wife.' And you said . . . ?"

"That I take you for my husband—"

"We'd be married?"

"Aye."

"Well, hello, Mrs. Skelley!" His grin widened.

" 'Tis what you want?" Tears misted her eyes. "You willna be returning to your home?"

284

He put his arm around her, pulling her close. "I *am* home." And he kissed her: a quick, firm touch of his lips.

The bailey erupted in cheers, and heat warmed Caira's cheeks as she turned from Brian to see the happy faces of her clan.

They reentered the keep, and those in the bailey followed. Gitta stood at the foot of the stairs, tears rolling down her weathered cheeks. "Ach, lass, 'tis a wonderful day. Aye, 'tis." And she bustled off to the kitchens.

Malcolm and Callum came up to them. "Welcome to clan Mackenzie." Malcolm grinned, glancing at Callum. " 'Tis why we've been pushing ye two together."

Caira and Brian looked at the two old men, then at one another and smiled.

"Aye. We ken ye'd be the right mon for our Caira and the clan." Callum slapped Brian on the back and beamed at Caira.

" 'Tis time to celebrate!" Malcolm called. The keep filled with cheers. The two old Scots escorted Caira and Brian to the dais, and ale was brought out.

"To the new laird of the Mackenzies and Caira!" Callum called. Cups were raised, and amid shouts of approval Caira and Brian drank to the toast.

Brian stood and, turning to Caira, lifted his cup. "To Caira, my wife," he said. He bent down and kissed her, and she could see that she was the love of his life—past, present, and future.

Epilogue

"I'm sure 'twill work," Malcolm said. He followed Callum through the woods, their new invention cradled in his arms. "The black powder willna get wet in this." He frowned. "I canna believe Skelley expected cloth and a few leaves to keep the powder dry." He shook his head.

"Aye," Callum agreed. "Ours is sturdier as well." He looked at the iron pipe Malcolm carried, admiring the neat wax seals on the ends. "What is that ye painted on it?"

Malcolm screwed his face up. " 'Tis Skelley's name, *seanachaidh*." He shifted the pipe. "And here, I painted his clan badge, ye ken?"

"Dinna shake it, ye fool! Skelley said to have a care when handling the powder."

"I know what I'm about."

"Ach, ye do?" Callum rolled his eyes then turned his attention back to the painting. He canted his head, looking at the markings. "Ah. Ye did a fine job of the lightning bolts."

"Aye, well, this one is just a test. I'll practice and do better on the others."

Callum shifted the sack containing the powder-encrusted twine. "If our idea works, 'twill relieve Brian of the tiresome job of replacing the damp packages whene'er it rains."

" 'Twill work," Malcolm said with confidence. "But 'tis a good idea to test it afore we present it to him. Did ye bring the flint?"

"Aye, 'tis in the sack with the fuse."

They reached the spot where they'd found Skelley what seemed like a lifetime ago. It was as though Skelley had always been a part of the Mackenzies. Never had Callum seen Caira so content or calm. There was again much laughter in the keep.

Martha's husband had returned, vowing to stay with her, Shamus, and their new daughter. He'd brought with him a wounded man from another clan. Caira had nursed his injuries, and the clan watched and chuckled as Widow Turner applied herself to capturing that man's attention.

There would be another handfasting soon, Callum felt certain.

"Well—are ye going to stand there looking at the ground, Callum, or are ye going to ready the fuse?"

Malcolm's gruff words penetrated Callum's thoughts, and he jerked to attention. "Ach, ye old Scot, dinna get a thistle up yer kilt." That was Callum's favorite of Skelley's sayings. He grinned as he took out the fuse and stretched a length of it out in the indentation in the ground.

Malcolm grunted, placing the iron pipe across it.

"Are ye sure 'tis all the way it should be?" Callum

asked, eyeing the placement of the thing.

Malcolm cast him a withering glare. "Are ye the expert now?"

"Nay, but neither are you."

"Will ye just light the fuse?"

Callum knelt down and struck the flint a few times to get it lit. Then he and Malcolm scrambled behind the nearby boulder.

They waited. The sizzle of the fuse ended, but nothing happened. Callum met Malcolm's crestfallen gaze.

They left the cover of the boulder and stood over the iron pipe. "The bloody thing didna work," Malcolm complained, his fists on his waist.

Callum stared at it. "Wait." He met Malcolm's gaze. "Ye ken Skelley's wee packages had the fuse going *into* them?"

Malcolm brightened. "Aye. Ye're right." He grabbed a twig from the ground and hunkered down by the pipe.

"Careful ye dinna shake the pipe," Callum said, backing up and eyeing Malcolm warily.

"How big do ye think the hole should be?"

"Not big." Callum took another length of twine from the bag and joined him. "The twine isna so thick."

Malcolm made a small hole in the wax seal, then stuffed the end of the fuse into it.

Again, Callum used the flint to light it, and they took their places behind the boulder.

The sizzling stopped, but nothing followed.

Callum and Malcolm looked at one another in confusion, then climbed from behind the rock.

"It doesna work." Malcolm stood there, glaring

down at the pipe. "I was so sure 'twould."

"Mayhap if we ask for Brian's help?"

"Nay." Malcolm turned on Callum. "I dinna want him to know we failed."

"Aye, nor do I." He walked around the iron pipe. "Mayhap 'tis the wax." He pointed to the end where they'd put the fuse. "The heat melted the wax and put the fuse out." There was a slight indentation where the melted wax had resealed the hole.

"Mayhap we should think on this a bit more."

" 'Twill take a wee bit more experimenting to get this right." Callum started to pick up the pipe.

"What are ye doing?"

"Dinna ye want to take it back with us?"

"And chance that Skelley will see it?" Malcolm shook his head. "The bloody thing doesna work. We'll just leave it here."

"But what if someone finds it?"

"Like who? A bloody Englishman?" Malcolm grinned. "If we've any luck at all, he'll give the thing a shake and . . ."

Callum met his friend's gaze.

"Hooyah!" they both shouted.

DEE DAVIS
WILD HIGHLAND ROSE

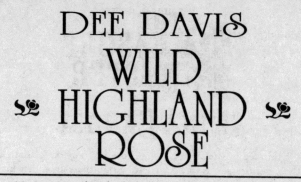

Marjory Macpherson feels rebirth at hand. Ewen—the enemy son she'd been forced to marry—is dead, killed by a rockslide. Marjory rejoices. She can shed her thorns . . . at least, until her husband's father returns.

When Marjory goes to retrieve Ewen's body, she finds instead a living, breathing man, covered in blood, talking strangely but very much alive.

Though he wears her husband's face and kilt, Marjory recognizes salvation. Whether this is a kinder Ewen or another who, as he claims, has been transplanted from the future, the man she finds is a strange new beginning, the root of something beautiful to come.

- -

THE PLEASURE MASTER

⚜ NINA BANGS ⚜

Stranded by the side of a New York highway on Christmas Eve, hairdresser Kathy Bartlett wishes herself somewhere warm and peaceful with a subservient male at her side. She finds herself transported all right, but to Scotland in 1542 with the last man she would have chosen.

With the face of a dark god or a fallen angel, and the reputation of being able to seduce any woman, Ian Ross is the kind of sexual expert Kathy avoids like the plague. So when she learns that the men in his family are competing to prove their prowess, she sprays hair mousse on his brothers' "love guns" and swears she will never succumb to the explosive attraction she feels for Ian. But as the competition heats up, neither Kathy nor Ian reckon the most powerful aphrodisiac of all: love.

___52445-7 $5.50 US/$6.50 CAN

NINA BANGS
FROM BOARDWALK WITH LOVE

The world's richest man, Owen Sitall, is a flop at a certain game, but now he's built an enormous board so he can win on his own. His island is a playground for the rich. But he doesn't know that L.O.V.E.R.—the League of Violent Economic Revolutionaries—has come to play in his hotels . . . and the plans to bankrupt him have already passed Go.

Camryn, novice agent #36-DD of B.L.I.S.S.—the international organization that fights crime anywhere from St. Croix to St. James Place—finds her assignment clear: Protect the fanatical Sitall from financial ruin. But being a spy doesn't just mean free parking. Before this is over, she'll be rolling the dice with her heart.

The Very Virile Viking
SANDRA HILL

Magnus Ericsson is a simple man. He loves the smell of fresh-turned dirt after springtime plowing. He loves the heft of a good sword in his fighting arm. But, Holy Thor, what he does not relish is the bothersome brood of children he's been saddled with. Or the mysterious happenstance that strands him and his longship full of maddening offspring in a strange new land—the kingdom of *Holly Wood*. Here is a place where the blazing sun seems to bake his already befuddled brain, where the folks think he is an act-whore (whatever that is), and the woman of his dreams fails to accept that he is her soul mate . . . a man of exceptional talents, not to mention a very virile Viking.

DOMINION
MELANIE JACKSON

When the Great One gifts Domitien with love, it is not simply for a lifetime. Yet in his first incarnation, his wife and unborn child are murdered, and Dom swears never again to feel such pain. When Death comes, he goes willingly. The Creator sends him back to Earth, to learn love in another body. Yet life after life, Dom refuses. Whatever body she wears, he vows to have his true love back. He will explain why her dreams are haunted by glimpses of his face, aching remembrances of his lips. He will protect her from the enemy he failed to destroy so many years before. And he will chase her through the ages to do so. This time, their love will rule.

Dorchester Publishing Co., Inc.
P.O. Box 6640
Wayne, PA 19087-8640

_52512-7
$5.99 US/$7.99 CAN